D0036572

TACOMA STORIES

Richard Wiley

Bellevue Literary Press
New York

First published in the United States in 2019
by Bellevue Literary Press, New York

For information, contact:
Bellevue Literary Press
90 Broad Street
Suite 2100
New York, NY 10004
www.blpress.org

Earlier versions of the following stories appeared in these publications: "Your Life Should Have Meaning on the Day You Die" and "The Dangerous Gift of Beauty" in *Arches Magazine,* "Home Delivery" in *Prime Number Magazine,* "Let's Meet Saturday and Have a Picnic" in *The American Scholar,* "The Dancing Cobra" in *Snakes: An Anthology of Serpent Tales,* "eHarmony Date @ Chez Panisse" in *The Los Angeles Review,* "The Strange Detective" in *Narrative Magazine.*

Library of Congress Cataloging-in-Publication Data
Names: Wiley, Richard, author.
Title: Tacoma stories / Richard Wiley.
Description: First edition. | New York : Bellevue Literary Press, 2019.
Identifiers: LCCN 2018005026 (print) | LCCN 2018007335 (ebook) |
    ISBN 9781942658559 (ebook) | ISBN 9781942658542 (softcover) |
    ISBN 9781942658559 (ebook)
Classification: LCC PS3573.I433 (ebook) | LCC PS3573.I433 A6 2019 (print) |
    DDC 813/.54--dc23
LC record available at https://lccn.loc.gov/2018005026

Bellevue Literary Press would like to thank all its generous
donors—individuals and foundations—for their support.

 This publication is made possible by the New York
State Council on the Arts with the support of Governor
Andrew M. Cuomo and the New York State Legislature.

  This project is supported in part by an award
from the National Endowment for the Arts.

Book design and composition by Mulberry Tree Press, Inc.
Manufactured in the United States of America.
First Edition

1   3   5   7   9   8   6   4   2

paperback ISBN: 978-1-942658-54-2

ebook ISBN: 978-1-942658-55-9

For Lucas Isak Albert

The world breaks every one and afterward
many are strong at the broken places.

—Ernest Hemingway, *A Farewell to Arms*

CONTENTS

TACOMA STORIES

Your Life Should Have Meaning
on the Day You Die

[1968]

Pat's Tavern, up on Twenty-first Street, not far from the old LaPore's Market, had been the best college drinking establishment in Tacoma, Washington, a decade earlier, but by 1968, when I worked there, it had started its coast into oblivion, with Vivian Flanagan running it and finding people like me to tend bar. Vivian's husband, Pat, had managed the tavern during its heyday, hiring *College* of Puget Sound athletes and tough guys like himself, but not long after the college became a university, Pat's lost its cool and even on weekends wasn't full. Still, a schooner of beer cost a quarter and I and my fellow bartender, Mary, often gave it away to friends on a two-for-one basis, so for those lucky few a schooner cost twelve and a half cents. Mary, a knockout, had curtains of hair falling down around her shoulders, while I kept a copy of *Siddhartha* in the pocket of an old army jacket, in the hope that it might help with my guise as a writer. It was Saint Patrick's Day, and Pat himself sat in the corner booth with two other Irishmen, pointing out the photos on the walls.

"That's Harold Bergh above you, Fatty," Pat said. "He still comes in. Played semipro football after college."

Fatty was actually thin, with the face of James Cagney.

"Harold Bergh," he said. "H-a-r-o-l-d B-e-r-g . . . h!"

Earlier, they'd been playing Irish Spelling Bee, a drinking game, and Fatty was too drunk to know that the game was over.

"Stop fookin' spelling everything," said Paddy, the third man in the booth.

"Harold Bergh was in last night," I said, bringing them the pitcher Pat had ordered. Pat himself didn't drink. Vivian told me that he had once, terrifically, but quit because drink brought the fighting man out in him.

"Did you give Harold Bergh the news about your grandmother?" Fatty asked, and all three men howled. A few weeks earlier, I'd used the excuse of my grandmother's death to get the weekend off to go to Westport, Washington. My dad came in when I was gone, and when Vivian consoled him over our loss, he said, "Thanks, I guess, but she's been dead since 1960." Vivian fired me the following Monday but hired me back later on.

"Actually, I asked, 'Aren't *you* Harold Bergh? H-a-r-o-l-d B-e-r-g-h?'"

Though it wasn't very funny, that sent Pat and Paddy into another round of drunken laughter, though Pat, of course, was sober.

"Look behind you, Richie," he said. "Vivian will fire you again if you don't start pouring beer."

"For Christ's bloody sake, is his name really Richie, Pat?" asked Paddy. "No wonder your tavern's gone downhill!"

VIVIAN WAS SHORT AND SOUR and disliked nearly everyone who came into Pat's. Sari and Hani, two students from Saudi Arabia, were at the top of the list of those she disliked, but they were regulars, sitting and drinking like some Muslims do when they get to America, and she didn't want to lose their business. Still, she couldn't keep her mouth shut and whispered, "Look at them, Richie, bold as you like, and on Saint Patrick's Day, too."

Vivian kept a milk shake container full of Mogen David wine by the cash register and sipped from it often, in order to still her outrage.

Sari and Hani were in a booth with Lars, the guy who'd gone to Westport with me; Immy, Lars's girlfriend; Jonathan, recently graduated from Yale; and Becky Welles, the daughter of Orson Welles and Rita Hayworth. Becky looked more like her dad than her mother, had a knowing manner, and enjoyed coming to Pat's because we liked her for who she was, and not for her famous parents.

At the bar sat Ralph, an English teacher in his fifties; Lindy, a woman whose ex was doing time at McNeil Island Federal Penitentiary—a far more exotic presence for us than Becky Welles; a divorced guy named Andy, who was a lawyer; and Earl, a shaggy-headed philosophy professor. So we were Pat, Fatty, Paddy, Vivian, Sari, Hani, Lars and Immy, Jonathan from Yale, Becky Welles, Ralph the English teacher, Lindy the convict's ex, Andy, Earl, and Mary and I. Sixteen characters in search of a play on Saint Patrick's Day, 1968. I haven't mentioned it yet, but I had dyed my hair green for the occasion. I have to mention it now, however, in light of what Lindy said next, which was, "You look good with green hair, Richie."

I'd known Lindy as a kid, and now she came to Pat's most nights, often taking men home with her. She enjoyed saying "McNeil Island Federal Penitentiary" in a low and husky voice to those she wanted to take home. I thanked her for the green hair comment, then hurried off with beer for Sari, Hani, Lars and Immy, Jonathan from Yale, and Becky Welles.

"I'd like two hamburgers when you get a minute, please," said Hani. "In fact, bring two burgers each for everyone at the table, my treat."

Hani was fatter than Fatty and had more money than everyone.

"Cooking's out tonight," I told him, "what with Saint Patrick's Day and all."

The beer I'd brought them was as green as my hair. Jonathan said he'd go get burgers at the Frisco Freeze if Hani gave him the money up front, so Hani pulled out a twenty. As Jonathan headed for the door, I worked my way back past Earl, who said, "I know you've read Kerouac's *On the Road*, Richie, but have you *reread* it?"

When Mary heard that, she came over fast, though people were demanding beer. "I reread the damned thing and it doesn't hold up!" she said. "Rereading makes it ordinary, Earl, just about like you are."

Mary and Earl had had a fling a couple of months earlier, but Earl had told her he was moving on. She glared at him like Gertrude Stein probably glared at Ernest Hemingway, never mind that Mary's beauty far surpassed Gertrude's and that Earl's insufferability more than equaled Ernest's.

Even before Earl dumped her, Mary didn't do much work

at Pat's, and Vivian never did anything but drink Mogen David and growl at the customers, so I was busy for the next hour, with both taps running and green beer flowing and with Andy saying that he'd like to write me a will. He offered the same thing to Lindy. At least as often as Lindy took a man home with her, Andy offered someone a free will, so it, along with Earl extolling the virtues of rereading, had been staples at Pat's that entire spring.

Irish music came from a record player Pat had brought in for the occasion, and Paddy kept trying to make everyone stop talking while they listened to it.

"Shut fookin' up" was how he put it.

"Do you mind if Jonathan works for a while?" I asked Vivian. "We need to get some schooners washed, or we won't have any clean ones in about ten minutes."

I'd forgotten that Jonathan was out buying burgers for everyone in Hani's booth, but Vivian didn't know who Jonathan was anyway, and when she said she'd pay him ten bucks at night's end, I asked Ralph, the English teacher, if he would pretend to be Jonathan until Jonathan got back. But Ralph hated Earl and wouldn't wash schooners if Earl was going to drink out of one of them. So Becky got out of her booth, walked behind the bar, and tied an apron around her overalls.

"Never mind rereading," said Earl when he saw her. "How about *rewatching*? Everyone's rewatched *Citizen Kane*, but it's my belief that rewatching *The Third Man* pays more benefits. I've got two words that explain it, Rebecca, *Joseph* and *Cotten*."

"J-o-s-e-p-h C-o-t-t-o-n!" shouted Fatty. "He was an Irishman!"

"I'm afraid it's spelled with an *e* not an *o*, Fatty," said Becky. "I met Joseph Cotten. He used to come to our house, but he wasn't Irish. He was a working-class guy from Virginia, and had a great big crush on my mom."

Becky was washing schooners fast, running them in soapy water, then plunging them into the rinsing tub and placing them on the drying rack. Orson Welles had come to Tacoma once to visit her and she'd brought him into Pat's. But I'd missed meeting him, since that was the weekend of my grandmother's ersatz death and my trip down to Westport with Lars.

"Well, he's what makes *The Third Man*, however you spell his name," said Earl.

"What makes *The Third Man* is the story and screenplay, both by the great Graham Greene," Ralph said. "And Becky's dad didn't direct it, so why be such a sycophant, Earl? Always the Mr. Know-It-All."

"He did too direct it! *Citizen Kane, The Third Man,* and *The Magnificent Ambersons!*" Earl stood half off his stool, then sat back down.

"You're right on two of them, Earl, but Carol Reed directed *The Third Man*," said Becky.

"Wouldn't you know it, a woman!" Paddy said. "Women direct the entire world."

"Carol Reed was Donna Reed's sister," said Fatty. "And if anyone says Donna Reed wasn't Irish, I'll knock their teeth out!"

"Sorry to tell you Carol Reed was a man," Ralph said.

Both drunk Irishmen doffed invisible hats in honor of Carol Reed's Irishness, or Donna Reed's, at least, while Pat asked Mary to bring them more beer.

"Thanks for helping," I told Becky. "And thanks for the story about *The Third Man*. I'm still sorry I missed your dad."

"It was you I brought him in to meet, Richie," she said. "I'm sorry you missed him, too."

Vivian *had* been here on the afternoon Becky brought her father in. When my dad came in and Vivian gave him her condolences, Orson Welles did, too.

"Orson Welles in Pat's own tavern," said Vivian now. "Can you believe it, Pat? We're the watering hole for famous men. I should have taken Orson's picture. Maybe when the two Omars get famous, we'll put their photos on our wall."

The two Omars—Sari and Hani—raised their glasses. She'd been calling them the two Omars since *Dr. Zhivago* came out. For a while Hani corrected her, but Sari had understood both the joke and the insult from the beginning. Now, however, drink brewed up the fiery side of Andy, who swiveled on his stool to point at the men in the corner. "How would you like it if people started calling you the three Conans?" he asked, though this time it had been Vivian, not them, who'd issued the insult.

"He's talking to you, Pat," said Paddy. "Perhaps he thinks you need a will."

The door kept opening and closing, people coming in and going out. Jonathan came back quickly with his sackful of burgers. When Hani got up to help him pass them out, Lars and Immy got up, too, to dance in the one clear space, intent that their love be known to everyone.

"Why I didn't take Orson Welles's picture, I'll never know," said Vivian, while Pat stood to dance his way over to Lars and Immy. He led them back to their booth, since dancing wasn't allowed, then got plates from behind the bar, took the bag of burgers from Jonathan, and laid them out, only one burger per plate, instead of the two that Hani had ordered.

He gave the burgers to Sari and Hani and Lars and Immy and Jonathan, who now sat at the bar. He got five more plates for the five remaining burgers and delivered them to Earl, Lindy, Ralph, and the two Irishmen in the corner. Vivian, Becky, Andy, Mary and I, and Pat, himself, got no burgers at all.

"Cook up a mound of fries, Richie," Pat said. "The burgers are on Omar, but the fries are from Viv and me, with a happy Saint Patty's Day to all."

Pat truly believed that Hani's name was Omar, and Hani tipped an invisible hat at him. Ten burgers delivered then, and five men tipping invisible hats, and the story's not nearly at its end.

I GOT THE FRIES FROM THE FREEZER. The various tensions in the bar—between Earl and Mary, between Earl and Ralph, between Vivian and the two Omars—seemed to dissipate by general consensus, since Saint Patrick's Day was for exhibitions of good cheer. As I cooked, sweating green sweat out of my hair, I heard Becky tell Jonathan that Vivian had offered to pay him ten dollars for washing the schooners. I also saw that all the schooners were clean and that Becky had taken off her apron. But instead of going to sit with the others in the booth, she took a stool next to Earl, available because no one else wanted to sit by him. Jonathan put the apron on, hoping to get the money without having done the work, while Mary made eyes at Andy, since Andy had offered to write her a will and also since Earl was watching them in the mirror.

"I think I'll stay in Tacoma after I graduate," said Becky. "There's nothing for me in L.A. anymore, and there's something about this place. It's comfortable, it's beautiful, and it leaves me alone."

She was talking to me, though I was facing the french fry basket. Andy was on her left, with Lindy on the other side of Andy. Becky would graduate in June.

"There's something special about every place, Becky, not just Tacoma," Earl said. "If you're in a place, you end up thinking there's something special about it. And there's *really* something special about great books, if anyone ever bothered to reread them."

I could feel warmth coming toward me from two directions, from the crazily cooking french fries and from Becky.

"But what is it about Tacoma *in particular* that makes Becky want to stay here?" asked Lindy. "All I ever wanted to do was get out."

Becky had just said what it was, of course, but Lindy was asking Earl, and by so doing, showing an interest in him. Andy, who hoped she'd show an interest in *him*, was ready with what he considered to be a better answer than Earl's. "Becky's not in probate in Tacoma," he said. "Orson's not the judge and Rita's not the jury."

I thought that was a great answer, but Paddy said, "A person can't be in probate. What law school did ya go to, ya twit?"

"He went to the Will Law School," said Fatty. "When he looks at Lindy, he thinks, I will if you will. But she won't have anything to do with him!"

He roared and fell into Pat, while Pat pressed the tips of his fingers together like a spider doing push-ups on a mirror. He did that often, sometimes before a lecture, sometimes before a fight. This time he said, "Drunkenness will get you nowhere, Andy. Take it from me, the sooner you get over her the better."

No one noticed Pat's midsentence shift from his own past drunkenness to Andy's continued heartache over his wife, save Becky, who put an arm on Andy's shoulder and kissed him on the ear.

"She was a really lousy wife," Andy said. "As bad a wife as Lindy's ex was a husband, though somehow she managed to stay out of jail."

"I was asking why *Earl* thinks Becky is drawn to Tacoma," Lindy said. "I'm still here because Fred's incarcerated, bad husband or not. Fred fucking Kelso. Did any of you know that Fred and I have twins?"

Earl's ears perked up, clearly in the hope that she would say "McNeil Island Federal Penitentiary" to him. He tried to answer her question.

"Tacoma sets Becky free," he said.

It wasn't very enlightening, but Lindy wasn't very enlightened.

By the time the french fries were done, all the burgers had been eaten, so Mary collected the plates, wiped bits of meat and crumbs off of them, then loaded them up with fries. Vivian, meanwhile, retreated to the storeroom to refill her Mogen David milk shake container.

When Ralph came out of the men's room, which no one had noticed him go into, he sat with the two Omars, who were alone in their booth by then. Ralph hadn't finished *his* burger, but Mary'd thought he had and threw what was left of it away. So to make up for it, she gave him extra fries and sat in the booth with him.

"Becky's mother was known as 'The Love Goddess' back in the forties," said Earl. His eyes were still on Mary in the mirror. He wanted her back when he was drunk, gone when he was sober. *I* wanted a beer, and would have poured myself one if Pat hadn't been watching me, his Irish music turned down. Pat had rheumy eyes, a wife in the storeroom, most of his life behind him.

Lindy stood, took a look at Earl, then pulled Andy off his stool and went out into the remnants of the evening with him. Earl sat there nodding. No Lindy for him tonight, and no Mary, either, probably.

"Maybe it's Pat's itself that makes you want to stay in Tacoma, Becky," said Mary. "No one can argue that it isn't a refuge for us. It's all for one and one for all at Pat's."

"No one can argue with that," said Becky, "but I've just now been wondering if a town can actually replace a person in someone's life. Do you think a town can act as a hedge against the unabated loneliness of the human heart, whether mine or anyone else's?"

Those were the days when a person could say "the unabated loneliness of the human heart" aloud in a bar.

Everyone understood that Becky was asking Mary except Hani, who stood out of his booth. "You are talking about Mecca, dearest Becky!" he said. "Mecca, Medina, and Jerusalem! Listen to what I am telling you! Your life should have meaning on the day you die! It is place you must put your trust in, Becky; love of place is life's key!"

There were tears in his voice, though none in his eyes. Tears were in Pat's eyes, though, as he stood to pay Jonathan the ten dollars Vivian had promised him.

Mary said she would stay and close the bar. It was something she often offered after I did most of the work. Lars and Immy left; Sari and Hani pretended they were going to their apartment, though in fact were off in pursuit of the sorts of women who would no longer be available to them when they returned to Saudi Arabia. Earl stayed on his stool until Pat asked him to help carry Paddy and Fatty out to his car. That left Becky, Jonathan, Mary, and me, with Ralph in the booth and Vivian in the storeroom.

Whose story was this, then? Looking back, I am sure that each thought it was their own. . . . Mary thought it was hers, Earl and Andy, Lars and Immy . . . Ralph, Jonathan . . . whomever you choose likely thought it was theirs, whether principals in the tale I've just told or passersby.

Initially, I thought it was Becky's story, told by someone who knew her well but briefly, and remembered Hani's adage when reading her obituary.

> *Rebecca Welles Manning, 59, passed away peacefully October 17, 2004, at home in Tacoma, WA. Rebecca is survived by her loving husband, Guy; son Marc; stepchildren Kristine, Michael, Brandi; sisters Yasmin, Christopher, Beatrice; eight grandchildren; and many other family and longtime friends.*

Sixteen people, the very number of those who gathered at Pat's on that cold Saint Patrick's night. Sixteen lives branched out back then, and in the stories to follow.

Or maybe this was Tacoma's story after all. Maybe Becky understood better than most that place is the secret to not feeling terrorized by everything.

A Goat's Breath Carol

[1958]

Down in the Churchills' basement stood a pinball machine that neighborhood kids were allowed to use if they didn't bother Mrs. Churchill or her daughters, Linda and Winifred—called "Lindy" and "Winnie"—who stayed upstairs. Mr. Churchill was Mexican, a Seventh Day Adventist, and rarely at home. This was back when basement doors were left unlocked and other people's houses were welcoming.

Perry White, a kid who lived with his mother in a three-room hovel in the nearby woods—the Churchills had bayfront property—once asked Mr. Churchill what it meant to be a Seventh Day Adventist, but Perry had only been able to understand from his answer that they believed Saturday was Sunday. Perry went to Jason Lee Junior High School with Lindy and Winnie. Every day the school bus stopped by the side of the road between their two houses, between the rich and poor parts of Brown's Point. Winnie and Perry were seventh graders, while Lindy was in the ninth.

One morning while they waited for their bus, Lindy called Perry "Chief," which was what Clark Kent called the other Perry White, from the *Superman* show on television. A few days earlier, down in her basement, Lindy had asked Perry to pull down his pants and show her his weenie, and when he refused . . . that was also when she started calling him "Chief." Perry hated Lindy but had loved Winnie since first grade. Now, however, on the morning in question, since he not only hated Lindy but was afraid of her, he looked at the sister he loved and sang a snide and whiny song—"Old Winnie Churchill waiting for a bus, All puffed up like an old bullfrog. 'long came Hitler and stuck her with a wire, She went poof like an old flat tire!"—causing Winnie to burst into tears.

Perry was immediately sorry. He'd learned the song from his dad not long before his dad took off. His dad had learned it during World War II, where he was shot in the head, but not by a bullet, as Perry's mother liked to say. Mussolini was in his dad's version of the song, but Perry changed it around.

Perry tried to apologize to Winnie by pulling her hair and otherwise making a nuisance of himself on the bus. During wood shop and in PE, he thought about what he'd done, and came up with the following rule to live by: You shouldn't wrong the ones you love, but only those who wrong you first.

The Seventh Day Adventist church stood across the street from their junior high school. Some days Lindy and Winnie didn't take the bus home but caught a ride with their father, who could be found at the church most afternoons. Perry's dad had once joked that Mr. Churchill looked like Pancho Villa, making Perry think of Pancho from *The Cisco Kid,* whom he and Winnie had seen one time on a field trip to the B&I superstore in south Tacoma. So after school he kept his eyes on the church until, sure enough, he saw Mr. Churchill. Pancho Villa had bullets crisscrossing his chest, but Mr. Churchill only wore a regular business suit.

When Mr. Churchill saw him and called, "Perry, do you

want a ride?" Perry called back, "Sure, Mr. Churchill, but where are Lindy and Winnie?"

"Lindy's upset," Mr. Churchill said. "You should have shown her your weenie when she asked you to! You kids have been friends for years."

Since the day his dad ran away, over a year ago now, Perry had formed the habit of putting words in other people's mouths, as a way of calming himself. This time, however, he went too far, and laughed as he walked across the street.

"What's so funny, Perry?" Mr. Churchill asked.

Iglesia Enferma was Churchill in Spanish, his dad had told him once, when they were down on the beach throwing rocks, but when Perry said, "There's Mr. Iglesia Enferma out fishing," his dad got mad and cuffed him.

"I saw you all eating salmon yesterday," Perry said now. "Was it one you caught?"

Nothing worked better for changing the subject with adults than asking about something they liked.

"Got three silvers at the mouth of the Puyallup," Mr. Churchill said, but then he asked, "Do you know what today is, Perry? It's an auspicious day for the Adventists."

"Monday?" said Perry, since that was the day it was.

"Not the day, the date. It's the one-hundred-and-thirty-first birthday of Ellen G. White, the spiritual leader of the Adventists, and an old-time relative of yours, I think."

Mr. Churchill slapped him on the back. Perry could see Lindy in the front seat and Winnie in the backseat of Mr. Churchill's car. "My grandmother's name is Ellen White," he said. "But she's as Presbyterian as a goat."

That was a bad thing to say, not because it insulted his grandmother, but because Mrs. Churchill actually kept a goat, named Bountiful. Her hobby was painting abstract pictures of him wearing various hats. She told Perry once that abstract goat paintings were the future of modern art.

Just as he reached for the door of Mr. Churchill's car, Winnie pushed down the button that locked it, but when Mr. Churchill glared at her, she pulled it up again, and Perry got in.

"Perry's a Seventh Day Adventist, too; he just doesn't know it yet," Mr. Churchill told his daughters. "I think you should ask your grandmother to tell you the truth, Perry. It's a bigger sin to deny your heritage than to call a pretty girl like Winnie *Winston Churchill*."

At first that sounded like something Perry made people say in his head, but Mr. Churchill actually said it. He could feel Winnie watching him and wished he could call Mr. Churchill Mr. Iglesia Enferma, but all he could do was stare at his shoes for the thirty-minute ride back home.

IT WAS A SMALL THING, MAYBE, but it festered in Perry. The girl he hated had asked to see his weenie, so he'd insulted the girl he loved. In his room that night, he waited until his mother fell asleep in front of the TV, then poured out the beer she'd been drinking, took the half a sandwich she'd been eating with him, and went outside. The sky was clear, the clouds had parted to lay a silver path across the trees, so he loped off through the woods on a shortcut to the houses on the bluff above the beach. He hoped Winnie's light would be on—if it was, he'd throw a pebble at her window and apologize when she opened it—and failing that, he would sneak into their basement and sit under their pinball machine to wait for her until morning. When he got to Winnie's house, however, who should he find in her backyard but Bountiful the goat, tethered to the birdbath. It was Winnie's job to put Bountiful in the garage each night, but tonight she had forgotten him. Perry would do it for her, he decided, and thus make up for putting her name in his father's World War II song.

Perry imagined that he was Pancho Villa as he approached the goat. He whispered, "Howdy, Bounty," while he untied the tether, but Bountiful ran around the birdbath, as if Perry had come to cook and eat him, not to put him to bed.

"Hey, ya nut, it's only me," Perry said, but Mr. and Mrs. Churchill's bedroom window was right above him and he was afraid if he said anything more, he would wake them up.

Maybe goats were different during the day than at night, but Bountiful's fear made him run, not toward the garage, but around the side of the house to the stairs that led to the beach and the bay.

"No, ya dummy, this way!" hissed Perry, but Bountiful was going so fast by then that he could barely hold on to the tether. They ran to the top of the bank, where Bountiful tore off down toward the beach. Mrs. Churchill took him down there during the summer to paint him amid the driftwood, so he easily maneuvered the stairs, leaving Perry to tumble after him. At the last turn, in fact, if Perry hadn't let go of the tether, he'd have crashed into Mr. Churchill's boat.

It was dark on the beach, the tide so high that water climbed halfway up the Churchills' bulkhead. Mr. Churchill had a tackle shed down there, too, which was never locked. Perry had the idea to put Bountiful in it, then go home and let the whole thing be a mystery. But he had to catch him first, and he couldn't even see him in the dark. So he opened the shed and flicked on its light.

The shed smelled of fish but was clean, like it had been when Perry used to hide in there from his dad. Mr. Churchill's fishing poles were lined along the wall and there was an icebox with bags of herring in it. Perry thought of using the herring to lure Bountiful into the shed, until he remembered the half-eaten sandwich he'd taken from his mother and pulled it out. And when he looked up again, Bountiful was staring at him from the door.

"Here, Bounty! Here, boy!"

He broke off part of the sandwich and tossed it onto the floor. The goat was not a dog and didn't wag his tail, but he did come in to eat the sandwich, his tether stretching out behind him.

"Want more?" asked Perry. If he could pet Bounty like he sometimes did when Mrs. Churchill painted him, he might still be able to walk him up the stairs and put him in the garage.

Bountiful had just taken another step toward him when Perry dived for the tether and the goat ran back outside, catching the tether's end under the tackle shed's door. "Ha," said Perry, "got you now!" but when he reached down to try to free the tether Bountiful ran again, this time straight off the bulkhead, like he thought he'd be able to run along the beach and get away. Perry tried with all his might to jerk the tether loose, but it went taut quickly, making the kind of low *thonggg-ing* sound that only a hanging goat could make. Perry grabbed two knives from a drawer, leapt out of the shed and down into the bay himself, where he reached above him and tried to cut the tether. Bountiful's front legs were against his chest as he tried to climb back up to the bulkhead, so Perry dropped one knife while sawing on the tether with the other and also trying to hold Bountiful up.

"Help me, Jesus!" he yelled, but it was late on a Monday in November and he was alone like he always was, and up to his waist in the freezing water of Puget Sound. Soon he dropped his second knife so he could hoist Bountiful up until the tether went slack. But each time he got him partway over the top of the bulkhead, his strength gave way and Bountiful crashed back down, until he finally said *"Maa-aa!"* in a terrible little voice, and slumped into silence.

It was the worst thing that had happened to Perry since his dad left, but he let the goat go and dragged himself out of the bay and crawled back into the tackle shed and closed the drawer that the knives had come from, water dripping from him like it was blood. He turned off the lights and went out to stare at the goat, who was hanging like the mail sack in a Western movie, waiting for a train to come by. The cold and the pain from the wounds Bountiful's hooves made on him had stayed away till then, but soon he started shivering. And after that the hoof cuts began hurting, like those two lost knives had flown back out of the bay and started stabbing him in the chest.

"Oh Jesus," he said again, but Jesus was as silent as He always was.

"PERRY, IT'S LATE," called his mother.

Perry'd been getting himself up for school since third grade, but this morning he stayed in the bathroom until long after he should have been heading to the bus.

"I know, I'm coming," he said. He'd been up since dawn, back down to the beach to look for the knives, and now he was rubbing his goat-hoof wounds with a concoction he'd made from his mother's Noxzema plus some crème de menthe from her booze shelf. The concoction stung like fury and seemed to make the wounds form an *m* and three *a*'s across his chest. At the beach, he'd found one of the knives, but the tide had taken the other. He hadn't looked at Bountiful, who still hung like that mail sack.

Perry went out and slurped some breakfast cereal and left. It was only a five-minute walk to the bus stop, but since the day Lindy asked to see his weenie he'd held back until he saw that the bus was almost there. Yesterday was the first day he hadn't done that, and now he was a murderer with a goat's silent scream tattooed on his chest.

He'd almost reached the bus stop, could hear kids laughing, when Mrs. Churchill's own scream came up from their house. All the kids froze except for Lindy and Winnie, who dropped their schoolbooks and ran back home to find out what was wrong. At first, Perry ran, too, to catch the bus, but when he saw their schoolbooks, he picked them up. And then he followed them home.

Bountiful's funeral was set for late that afternoon, so Perry waited for it, hiding with the schoolbooks in their garage, while his wounds began to swell and fester under his shirt. The garage was a two-story thing with a window in the upstairs part, where Mrs. Churchill kept her goat paintings. Mr. Churchill didn't go to work that day, and came into the garage twice for shovels, each time muttering curses in Spanish.

Oh, Cisco. Oh, Pancho! thought Perry.

It took Mr. Churchill hours to dig the grave, which, Perry

heard from his hiding place, had to be three feet deep. Six feet for humans but three feet for animals because animals didn't have souls—that was what Lindy told her father while he dug. Mrs. Churchill and Winnie stayed inside until 4:00 p.m., then came out dressed in black, while Mr. Churchill and Lindy hurried in to change their clothes. Bountiful was in the corner of their yard in a wheelbarrow, brought up from the beach with the help of the next-door neighbor. Earlier, when all four Churchills were in the house, Perry had sneaked into the yard and lifted the tarp they'd covered him with, found Bountiful's face, and knelt down in the grass to tell him it was an accident. He started to say, "Heck, Bounty, my whole life has been an accident," but that was too much of what he really felt, even to tell a dead goat.

Mrs. Churchill was tall and thin like Olive Oyl, only with a prettier face than Olive Oyl's. She was taller than Mr. Churchill, and taller than both her girls. Mr. Churchill went to get Bountiful, while Lindy and Winnie leaned against their mother. Mr. Churchill said, "Oof" and *"mierda"* while he hefted the wheelbarrow, but when he got to the grave and pulled the tarp off Bountiful, he didn't say anything more. Winnie and her mother both held Bibles, while Lindy and her father did not. All of them stood like a cowboy's family on Boot Hill, with a late wind blowing and Mrs. Churchill and Winnie praying and Mr. Churchill and Lindy casting their eyes toward the clouds. Things were going according to Mr. Churchill's plan, Perry figured, until Mrs. Churchill said, "I don't want you dumping him in there, Carlos; I want him lowered down."

Carlos was Mr. Churchill's first name. Carlos Iglesia Enferma in Spanish.

How am I supposed to do that? said Mr. Churchill's look, though his lips stayed pursed, like they were sewn.

Perry stared at the goat painting next to him in the upstairs part of their garage. It was one in a series Mrs. Churchill had done last summer called "Goat's Breath Paintings." In each of them a cartoon balloon came from Bountiful's mouth, and in the one Perry looked at now, Bountiful was saying, "I am the goat of Christmas yet to come."

Mr. Churchill came into the garage for ropes, but if he was going to lower Bountiful down, he'd need help, so when he went back outside, Perry sneaked out a side door, ran down the street, then came back toward the Churchills' house like he happened to be passing with the books Lindy and Winnie had dropped. He walked into their yard and said, "Hello, everyone. I found these in the street."

All the Churchills looked at him, two faces composed, two faces not. When Perry looked at Lindy and Mr. Churchill, his chest wounds hurt, but when he looked at Mrs. Churchill and Winnie, he said what he'd thought about saying when he was hiding in their garage. "Bounty was a good goat, and a great subject for paintings." He wanted to say more. He wanted to say that Bounty was a better goat than his grandmother was a Presbyterian, but the little he *had* said brought a smile to Mrs. Churchill's face.

Mr. Churchill smiled, too. "Perry, would you give me a hand?" he asked.

"Sure," said Perry.

In death, Bountiful seemed twice the size that he had in life, with the bay water bulking him up. Three feet deep for animals, since animals didn't have souls. When Mr. Churchill shifted his eyes to the floor of the grave a few times and Perry got the hint and jumped down into it, he felt and then *heard* his goat-hoof wounds say . . . *maa-aa*. Mrs. Churchill seemed to hear it, too, and stepped closer to the goat in the wheelbarrow, to search his glassy eyes. She loved him as much as she loved her husband; that was her secret shame.

When Mr. Churchill saw the change come over his wife, he believed it was a signal to start the burial. When he lifted the wheelbarrow handles, it felt like it had last summer when he'd tried to pour a concrete patio by himself. He nearly said *mierda* again, but managed to say, "Are you ready down there, Perry?" instead.

Perry knew he had to do this right, that he had to be strong, though his body was weak. "Yessir," he said. "Ready as I'll ever be."

A tipped wheelbarrow is hard to control if it's loaded with wet cement, though wet cement can be released in dabs and splashes, while a dead goat clings to it by locks of hair twisted on spikes of the previous cement, now grown hard. Bountiful was hanging on above him, Perry briefly thought, for dear life, and that made him smile, releasing in Winnie enough of a sense of well-being for her to smile back.

"You can do it, Perry," she said.

Mr. Churchill pulled the wheelbarrow handles farther up. Bountiful's head was nearest Perry, his eyes still open, his mouth twisted sideways, with some seaweed stuck in it. His body seemed as big as the blimps that rode the summer airwaves, like the blimp of a sky shark Perry had seen one time.

"He's stuck," said Lindy. "I think his weenie's holding on to the wheelbarrow."

Perry thought of his habit of putting words into other people's mouths as a curse. This time, however, he glared up at

Lindy like she'd actually said it. What she had said was, "Tip the wheelbarrow up, Dad," making Mr. Churchill hoist its handles even more, until they were near his armpits.

Yet Bountiful still hung on, his angle so radical now that he reminded Perry of the bombs his father used to drop on the German villages during the war. His father had told him that if a bomb got stuck, he, as bombardier, had had to climb down into the airplane's belly and release it with his own two hands. He'd told that story lot of times, and now Bountiful was the bomb about to be released and Perry was the German village.

Mr. Churchill shifted his grip, so instead of pulling the wheelbarrow handles to his armpits he was pushing them up from underneath, like they were barbells. For a while it seemed that no matter what Mr. Churchill did Bountiful was going to stay there, but then he swung out like a bale of hay from a barn and dropped, covering the distance to Perry and his outstretched hands in no time.

"Oh, Carlos!" Perry heard Mrs. Churchill say as he took Bountiful's head against his chest and wrapped his arms around his shoulders.

He'd jumped toward the descending goat, meeting him in the air, so when they plowed into the muddy grave, they were twisted together like strands of taffy, like the lines on the barber pole in front of the shop where Perry and his dad used to get their hair cut. It felt to Perry like he was being pounded into the earth, like he hadn't softened Bountiful's fall, but had propelled him into his final resting place even less gently than if they'd simply thrown him in. He said, "Oof," like Mr. Churchill had, but his voice was muffled by a mouthful of goat hair.

To Mrs. Churchill and Winnie, however, it seemed as though Perry had caught Bountiful and executed a heroic pirouette, like Nijinsky when they saw him on TV that time.

Mr. Churchill and Lindy watched, too, but they saw only two muddy creatures in a hole.

PERRY WENT HOME TO AN EMPTY HOUSE—his mother was up at the Cliff House Tavern—ate some soup, took a nap, then got up and walked back to the Churchills' house. He intended to go into their basement, play a little pinball, and hope that Winnie might come down. But for the first time ever, the Churchills' basement was locked. When he'd left their house earlier, Winnie had been nice to him, but Lindy had been her same old self. He thought about slipping into their garage to look at the "Goat's Breath Paintings" again, but walked back down to the beach instead. He had changed clothes at his house, putting on one of his father's old jackets, so he wasn't as cold as he had been the night before. His wounds still hurt, but he'd put a new concoction on them, this time made of his mother's Noxzema and a few crushed aspirin. It seemed to be working. His wounds were no longer red, at least, but a shining and satiny white.

In the tackle shed, Perry took two of Mr. Churchill's fishing rods, his tackle box, and a dozen packages of herring. The tide was halfway up the bulkhead again. When he shoved Mr. Churchill's boat into the bay, he was careful to keep a tighter grip on its painter than he had on Bountiful's tether. At home he'd made himself a sandwich out of peanut butter and jelly and baloney. It said *Bologna* on the package, but he didn't like to say it that way.

Mr. Churchill didn't use flashers when he fished, only herring and sinkers painted red, so Perry figured he would have to wait till daylight to catch himself a salmon. At first he thought he would row across the bay, under the Narrows Bridge, and past Fox Island to the Nisqually mudflats, where he and his dad had gone one time to run among the wrecks of stranded old ships. But since he didn't want to find himself in mud again, in the end he decided to row toward Seattle. He knew from last year's geography class, when he and Winnie had made a plaster-of-paris model of them, that if he was lucky, he'd be able to find the San Juan Islands. He looked at a configuration of stars that formed an interesting pattern in the sky. For a second he thought he saw a goat up there, and then he decided it was a shark, and then a goat with a shark's rear end.

He could hear the sound of the water coming off his oars. He wouldn't start Mr. Churchill's five-horse Johnson until he was far enough out to see the lights of Brown's Point. He remembered that painting from the garage where the goat was saying, "I am the goat of Christmas yet to come," and when he looked at the constellation again he somehow understood that it would guide him, that it was a real constellation with a name that other people knew but he did not. He stood up in Mr. Churchill's boat, raised his hands, and shouted, "What's yer name?" trying so hard to project his voice that he rocked the boat badly and had to sit back down.

And then the thought came to him that names can't be learned by shouting, and that he would try to go ashore tomorrow, find a library, and look his constellation up. And once he knew its name, he would never forget it, any more than he would forget that Winnie's name wasn't Winston Churchill and that his name wasn't Chief but Perry White.

His dad, Bob White, had been a bombardier during the war.

A bobwhite was also a bird, a kind of ground quail.

Home Delivery

[1977]

LARS LARSON WASN'T A JUNIOR because of a *K* that he used
in lieu of a middle name. On the sign above the entrance
to his company, there was no *K*; it simply read, LARS LARSON
MOTORS. On documents, however, on his mortgage and his
driver's license, Lars K Larson was in evidence, to avoid confusion with his father. It was a completely legitimate *K*, but
with no meaning other than itself.

One Monday morning in March, Lars stood atop a ladder, cleaning debris from the rain gutters of his house. The
milkman hadn't arrived yet, so Lars was drinking black coffee out of one of his Lars Larson Motors bottom-heavy travel
mugs. The mug sat near him on the slanted roof, whose rough
gray shingles kept it from falling off. Lars didn't like his coffee
black, but on Monday mornings he often drank it that way,
since he usually ran out of milk before the milkman came.
This is 1970s America we're talking about, but contrary to
popular belief, milkmen still made deliveries, and Lars was
of the opinion that such traditions ought to be supported. So,
black coffee or not, he never bought milk at the store.

From the top of his ladder, Lars could hear cars and
trucks passing on the pavement below him, and as he

scooped the muck from his rain gutter into a bucket he'd attached to his ladder, he tried to discern without looking whether one or another of them was the milk truck. He had an insulated box on his porch, meant to keep milk cold for the hours when neither he nor his wife, Immy, were home, but Immy had left him three months earlier, so now it was only Lars that the milk sometimes waited for, and only Lars who waited for the milk.

Lars stepped down to move his ladder every few minutes, and as he was doing so now, and also emptying his bucket into a larger plastic garbage bag, the milk truck pulled up. And when he turned to greet the driver, he got a shock greater than he would have had his Lars Larson Motors bottom-heavy travel mug slid off the roof and landed on his head. The driver was his father, the other Lars Larson, the one without the *K*.

"Dad," said Lars, "what the heck! Did you change your route?"

"Says here you're down to two half gallons a week," said his father. "Didn't know you could drink that much, Lars, since Immy left."

He'd parked his truck behind a Volvo with dealer plates.

"Dad, does Mom know you're doing this?" Lars asked. "She doesn't like you meddling, and neither do I."

The appeal of home delivery had lodged itself in Lars's imagination because that's what his father had done for as long as he could remember: delivered milk. Even now his father wore the white pants and long-sleeved shirt with a blue necktie that Lars had always loved. Lars didn't live far from his parents, but he'd stopped going to visit, hadn't been there, in fact, since the day he went to tell them Immy was moving out.

"You want a cup of coffee, Dad?" he asked.

His father got out of the truck with the two half gallons of milk. "Coffee? I don't think so. I've got my schedule. Unless you could maybe splash a little coffee for me into one of those travel mugs."

Immy had taken most of the travel mugs, all but the one that still sat peeking at them from the roof. Lars looked up at it, but his father thought the look meant something else. "It hasn't stopped raining all week," he said. "Your mother thinks we should move to Arizona after I retire."

For some reason, that made Lars climb back up his ladder to get the travel mug. "Come in, Dad," he said. "There's coffee in the kitchen. You can spare a minute."

The front door of Lars's house led to a living room that was dusty and silent and orderly, but when they got to the kitchen, Lars began apologizing. Dishes were piled in the sink, leftover food littered the counters, and an absolute torrent of unread mail was dumped all over the floor. Lars had been out cleaning the gutters for the same reason he wore a shirt and tie to work every day: to keep his external house in order, though he was a crumbling wreck inside.

"I don't know, Dad," he said. "It sure doesn't get any easier. All I ever wanted was a regular life."

He washed out the Lars Larson Motors bottom-heavy travel mug for his father and grabbed the last remaining clean cup—a dainty little tea-service thing with roses on it—for himself, filled both with coffee, and handed the mug to his dad.

"Listen, Son, you're in a rut," his father said. "When Immy was here, you were in a rut, and now that she's gone, you're in a deeper one. Look at this place. I'm here to tell you, you can wallow in self-pity if you want to, but Immy's getting on with her life."

Lars took a drink from his rose-covered cup.

"You spoke to Immy?" he said.

"Spoke to her, saw her, even had her over for dinner. She's a new woman, Lars, like the girl you brought home to us a decade ago, while you've done nothing but stay the same."

It occurred to Lars that his father had changed his route solely for the purpose of delivering this awful message.

"Did she ask about me? Did she go to your house by herself, or what?"

"She didn't and she did," said his father. He poured some milk into the travel mug. "Okay, Lars, you want to talk, we'll talk," he said, "but I can't ignore my route any longer, so we'll have to do it in the truck. I'll even let you run the deliveries in, like you did when you were a child."

Lars hadn't said he wanted to talk, but he followed his father back outside. As a child, what he'd liked best about going on his father's route with him was that the seats in a milk truck were high up off the ground, with a windshield perpendicular to the street. It was like being inside a TV.

Once they had their seat belts buckled, his father pulled into traffic, but almost immediately slowed again. "Mr. and Mrs. Nix are next," he said. "Second floor of the Biltmore Apartments."

When Lars turned to look into the back of the truck, he saw the Nixes' order moving toward him on a conveyor belt. Directly in front of their order, against the empty mesh, he saw his own name, Lars K Larson, printed in his father's neat hand. His father'd never liked that *K*, but he'd written it down.

"Apartment two twelve," said his father. "My notes tell me to knock and wait. Don't leave the order on the floor. Neither of the Nixes can bend anymore."

Lars got out of the truck and ran under the apartment building's awning. Not only was there no buzzer but the door was propped open by the same junk mail that littered his kitchen at home. As he bounded up the stairs, he worried that the Nixes might be wary of him, since he was still wearing his gutter-cleaning clothes. But their door was open, with both of them waiting for him. Mrs. Nix's head had fallen down on her chest.

"Half gallon of whole milk and two pints of strawberry yogurt," said Lars.

"Sounds good to me," said Mr. Nix. "Where do I sign?"

Mrs. Nix laughed. "'Where do I sign?'" she said, "Oh, Don, you kill me."

Mr. Nix had a smile on his face that Lars would never have. The Nixes were well into their nineties. It made Lars pause to think that he and Immy would never reach that age. Not together anyway.

Lars went back to the truck, where his father sat drinking coffee. Lars's dainty rose-patterned cup was on the seat where he'd left it. Its coffee was already cold, but steam still came from the bottom-heavy travel mug.

"One thing this job has taught me is that you have to be prepared to give people what they want," said his father. "Take these folks coming next, the Wilcoxes. My notes say that three weeks out of three now, Mrs. Wilcox changed her order when the truck arrived. Johnny, the regular driver, takes milk, she wants orange juice. He takes juice, she wants some other damned thing. Yet she's down for two half gallons of nonfat, just like you are, Lars."

Lars looked at his father. Was he saying that he hadn't given Immy what she wanted? He reached around and brought the Wilcox order onto his lap, where he could feel the bottoms of the milk cartons, cold against his thighs. They drove along that way for a couple of minutes before arriving at the Wilcox house. It was nicer than Lars's and on a quieter street. Lars was startled to remember that he and Immy had looked at this house, had actually thought about buying it. Immy had *adored* the kitchen, he remembered, and had irritated Lars by saying so in front of the real estate agent. It was because of this house, in fact, that she'd claimed to hate the kitchen at their place.

Through the beveled glass beside the front door, Lars saw someone walking down a hallway, and that gave him the idea that he wanted to see the kitchen again, in light of the wreckage of his marriage. So instead of knocking, he hurried around the side yard to the back of the house. The kitchen had a Dutch door, the top half of which was open, though it was raining and chilly.

"Hello?" Lars called "Anyone home?"

He held up the two half gallons of nonfat milk.

A head appeared at the breakfast nook window to his left, and then Mr. Wilcox came to the door. He said, "What are you doing back here?"

"Milkman," said Lars. "Knocked out front. Guess you didn't hear me."

Why he had to lie about it, he didn't know.

"Winnie!" called Mr. Wilcox.

"Two half gallons of nonfat milk," said Lars. "That's what you ordered and that's what you goddamn get."

Mr. Wilcox looked at him blankly, and Mrs. Wilcox came into the kitchen wearing a robe.

"Listen," said Lars, "once a long time ago my wife and I nearly bought this place. She adored the kitchen."

He spoke only to Mrs. Wilcox. "My father's the real milkman," he said, "I'm just helping him out."

"The kitchen's what sold me on it, too," said Mrs. Wilcox. "It's got such great light."

She unlatched the bottom of the Dutch door, swinging it open to meet its top. She asked, "Is your father okay?"

"He's fine," said Lars. "He's waiting in his truck, probably having a conniption fit that I'm taking so long."

It was the first time he had ever said "conniption fit" in his life.

Though there were fewer windows here than in Lars's kitchen at home, the whole room was bathed in the kind of light that Lars had always associated with happiness, with birds and whistling and such. It was a great kitchen! How could he have missed it before? The counters were made of granite with little flecks of gold, and the pale yellow walls seemed to dance like the shimmering skirts on hula girls. Even the Mr. Coffee, ordinary by anyone's standards, perked out the last throes of a new pot of coffee like a chorus of happy frogs.

"You don't want to sell this place, do you?" asked Lars.

"As a matter of fact, we do," said Mr. Wilcox. "I'm only home this morning because we're expecting our Realtor. Moving to Portland next month."

"Speak for yourself, John Alden," Mrs. Wilcox said.

"Cancel the Realtor," Lars heard himself say. "I'll buy the house."

Lars Larson Motors was not the business he'd thought he'd have when he was young, but it had made him a lot of money. "How much are you asking? We could split the difference, maybe, of whatever your real estate agent would charge."

"Seven percent, if you can believe it," said Mr. Wilcox. "And the price is eighty-seven thousand five hundred, so that would be . . ."

"A savings of six thousand one hundred and twenty-five dollars," said Lars. "Three thousand sixty-two dollars and fifty cents each."

He was used to doing calculations in his head.

"Are you serious?" asked Mr. Wilcox, as Mrs. Wilcox went over to stop the Mr. Coffee in the middle of its climax.

"As serious as a cancer patient," said Lars.

Mr. Wilcox took his Realtor's card from beneath a refrigerator magnet. "No contingencies, no nothing, just a straight-out purchase, right?" he said. "Because if I call her and cancel this appointment, it won't be easy to call her back."

"Eighty-seven thousand five hundred dollars," said Lars. "Twenty percent down is seventeen thousand five hundred bucks, in a cashier's check as soon as I can get to the bank."

His prowess with percentages impressed Mr. Wilcox.

"Winnie can show you the rest of the place while I go down to the stationer's for a real estate contract?" he said.

"I'd better go tell my dad," said Lars.

When they all walked through the house, heading toward the front door, however, things went downhill fast. There was evidence of water damage on the living room ceiling, plus a hairline crack in the picture window that looked out to the street where the milk truck was parked.

"We really do live in the kitchen," Mrs. Wilcox said.

Outside, the rain had increased, but Lars's father paced on the parking strip, looking at his watch.

"What's wrong?" he asked when he saw them all come out.

"Sorry to keep you waiting, Dad," said Lars, "but I'm buying this place."

"I'm going to the stationer's for the forms," said Mr. Wilcox.

Three of them were smiling, and four of them were getting wet.

"You'll have to do the rest of your route alone, Dad," said Lars.

Behind the milk truck sat a Volvo 240 from 1974, the first year the model came out. Lars knew it because he had two of them for sale on his lot. He'd gotten one from a guy moving down to a Volkswagen, the other from a woman moving up to a Jag. Volkswagens and Jaguars were what Lars sold, "Master Craftsmanship for Any Pocketbook" his slogan.

"Well, you better get on with it if your mind's made up," his father said. He was upset with this evidence of Lars's lifelong impulsiveness, and upset with himself because of his own lifelong reluctance to tell Lars what he thought.

Mr. Wilcox unlocked the Volvo and Lars's father stepped back into his truck. Lars reached in and took his Lars Larson Motors bottom-heavy travel mug, leaving the china cup.

"Don't do this for Immy, Lars," said his father. "She's a lost cause."

He put his truck in gear and headed up the road.

"Who's Immy?" asked Mrs. Wilcox.

The wind was whipping them with rain, so Lars didn't answer until they got back to the house. They would have run, but Mrs. Wilcox was wearing slippers and actually slipped on some leaves, taking Lars's arm.

"Oh, the chill of these Tacoma mornings," she said. "I won't miss them very much, I don't suppose."

Lars thought that the weather in Portland wasn't much different from the weather in Tacoma, but he kept it to himself. He'd seen a movie once in which a housewife in a robe seduced a man who knocked on her door asking directions.

"Immy's my wife," he said. "Or she was, I guess. Our marriage ended three months ago."

In the movie, the housewife took out some maps and leaned against the stranger as he looked them over. Mrs. Wilcox was staring at Lars so steadily that he feared she might have read his mind.

"Want to see the bedrooms?" he thought he heard her ask.

"What?"

"Do you want to see the bedrooms? And there's a den upstairs, too."

"Could I get more coffee first?"

Lars held up his mug.

In the movie, the stranger swept the maps off the table, pushing the woman down on it so firmly that the table's legs broke. Lars followed Mrs. Wilcox into the kitchen. Her robe was conservative, utterly circumspect.

"How long have you and Mr. Wilcox been married?" he asked. "I mean, is this your first house, or what?"

Once in the kitchen, she sighed and turned to face him. "Nate's the one who's moving to Portland," she said. "Just like you and Immy, we're breaking up."

"I didn't mean to pry," said Lars.

But in a great kitchen like this one, prying seemed the order of things. In here, prying looked exactly like caring and kindness.

"I don't know why I didn't point this out to Mr. Wilcox," Lars said, "but the stationer's isn't open yet. And as far as I know, he still hasn't called your Realtor."

"Nate knows what he's doing," said Mrs. Wilcox. "And what are you saying? You don't want the house now?"

Except for the rain against the windows, the kitchen grew quiet, and was darker than it had been earlier. It shamed Lars deeply that all he could think of was that horrid movie.

"Of course I want it," he said. "Do you think I'd go back on my word? You can't sell very many cars if your word doesn't stand for something."

Mrs. Wilcox poured coffee into his Lars Larson Motors bottom-heavy travel mug. "There's work to do in the living room, and I should tell you there's been talk of a new roof," she said. "We even had an estimate, seven thousand dollars."

"In the automobile business, we have what's called a 'lemon' law," said Lars, but he smiled when he said it.

"There should be a lemon law for marriage," said Mrs. Wilcox.

They were sitting at the kitchen table by then, but the sudden lack of light made it hard for Lars to see her face. "I don't mind about the roof," he said. "I'm handy, can do a lot of the work myself."

He smiled again to let her know he meant it. When she returned his smile, Lars got the urge to take her hand, which was lying on the table. He looked out the window at some water falling over the lip of the rain gutter. Eighteen thousand dollars. He decided he would ask if he could come clean the gutters before the deal was closed, maybe even start tearing the old roof off.

"If Nate thinks he'll be happy in Portland, Oregon . . ." said Mrs. Wilcox, but just then the phone rang and she reached around behind her to pluck it from the wall. "This better be an emergency," she said, before she even said hello. Lars put his hand where hers had been. He felt a bit of warmth on the tabletop.

"I know that, Lindy. Who doesn't know a thing like that?" she said. "What do you take me for, Nate's doormat?"

She looked at Lars. *My sister*, she mouthed.

Lars thought of the comment his father had made before he drove away, and imagined himself saying, "What do you take me for, Dad, Immy's doormat?"

Mrs. Wilcox shifted the phone to her right hand, and when she turned to sit properly again saw Lars's hand where hers had formerly been, his fingers drumming the tabletop. She rested her left hand on his. Lars continued looking at the water pouring over the rain gutter. He let out a rueful laugh. People were nuts when it came to houses, constantly trying to turn them into homes.

"Yes, Lindy, I will," said Mrs. Wilcox, "but now I've got company and Nate's not here, so I have to go."

Lars did it then. He moved his free hand over and placed it on top of hers, which was still on top of his. He waited for her to pull her hand away, leaving him holding hands with himself. He felt her start to do it, but then, quite miraculously, her hand stayed where it was. The rain gutters would need replacing, too, if someone didn't tend to them. Her hand felt familiar. It made him realize that she and Immy were about the same size, but also that human warmth, of this most basic kind, at least, was universal.

When Lars finally looked across the table at her, she was watching him. "You work and work," she said. "A nice kitchen, a beautiful yard . . ."

She put her other hand on top of his in a way that reminded him of summer pickup baseball games. They sat that way for a while, talking a little but really just waiting for Mr. Wilcox. When the rain let up, they stood and went out into the backyard to look at the roof and the gutters. And when Lars saw a ladder lying in the grass, he lifted it and propped it against the wall of the breakfast nook where it just reached the roof.

"One quick look," he said. "Do you have a trowel and bucket? While I'm up there, I might dig a bit of that stuff out."

Water was still spilling over the gutters, and as he climbed, careful of his footing, Mrs. Wilcox went back into the house. Lars had his Lars Larson Motors bottom-heavy travel mug with him, so he set it on the roof and pushed a hand down into the gutter to see how bad the damage was, his fingers slowly sinking into the muck. Then he stepped back down to wait for Mrs. Wilcox in the yard. When he looked off toward Puget Sound, he saw an even darker sky than the one overhead. More rain was coming, another real storm. March is a whole lot crueler than April, he thought.

When Mrs. Wilcox came back outside, she was carrying two buckets, two trowels, plus a plastic garbage bag. And she had changed into work clothes similar to Lars's. "Tag-team gutter cleaning," she said.

Lars let himself go a little then. He remembered that the Wilcoxes had the same standing order he did, for two half gallons of nonfat milk. He also remembered that they didn't have an insulated box on their porch and decided he would bring them his while the house was in escrow, for when neither Winnie nor Nate Wilcox was at home. He would call it a gift to seal the bargain, say that milk had brought them together and they shouldn't let it spoil.

He looked at Mrs. Wilcox and then at the roof again, where his Lars Larson Motors bottom-heavy travel mug peeked down at him. The slanted rough gray shingles kept it from falling off.

"Let's get to work," he said.

The Man Who Looks at the Floor

[2010]

I TEND TO WALK FAST, so I want the outside lane of the indoor track I use at my YMCA to be free for passing, if it isn't used by runners. The clearly posted track rules do say "Slower athletes use the inside lanes," after all. Athletes, they call us, but 90 percent of us walk, changing directions daily.

I try to vary the times I go to the Y in order not to keep meeting the same people, basically because I'm inclined to form a negative opinion of them without any evidence other than track behavior—it is something I've done all my life. And I also tend to give them nicknames. Here's a list of those I have currently: "The Two Chatting Women," who stretch across all three track lanes, so I have to make a big deal out of passing them; "The Lying Bully," who clips those walking in the running lane and then pretends it was an accident; "The Tea Party Shrew," who walks in the running lane like she owns it, saying, "I'm a citizen of this country, too!"; and "The Guy Who Looks Like One of the Actors from *Soap,*" who moseys along at the farthest edges of the running lane like he's creating a *new* lane outside of it. I also dislike people who bring their cell phones onto the track, as well as those who try to strike up conversations with me. By now you may be saying, "I don't have enough jerks around me already that I have to listen to this guy?" but let me tell you, an indoor track is a microcosm of life.

Now, the title of this story is "The Man Who Looks at the Floor," which is what I call this one fellow. He's about my age and something is wrong in his neck, causing him to aim his face *squarely* down while he wheels around the track. And when I say "squarely," I mean that if the floor were a mirror, he'd see himself in it straight on.

On Saturdays, I usually go to the Y an hour before closing, and one recent Saturday, I saw the man who looks at the floor coasting along on the opposite side of the track, staring down like an eagle looking for a lost contact lens. I did a bit of torso twisting in order to avoid him, but when the man walked by, he said, "Good luck, Jonathan" to me in a clear and sarcastic voice. It was the first time I'd ever heard him speak, and it caused me great suspicion, since Goodluck Jonathan, against all odds—and you may know this—happens to be the name of the president of Nigeria. *I* know it because before my retirement I was a U.S. Foreign Service officer, with my last posting to Nigeria.

The next time he came around the track, he didn't say anything. He could have simply been wishing me luck, of course, since my name *is* Jonathan, but I was sure he was giving me a message.

"Good God, Jonathan, you need to find a hobby," said Millicent, my wife, when I told her about the encounter during our stroll that evening.

"I do have a hobby," I said. "It is getting into shape after all those years of sitting behind embassy desks."

"Oh, those embassies," said Millicent. "If I never have to go to another cocktail party . . ."

Millicent hadn't grown up in Tacoma, Washington, the town we live in now, but in England, where they still name children Millicent. We met in London during my first posting, and we go to England yearly to see our only daughter, Millicent Junior, a psychiatrist.

"Maybe it's a stretch," I said. "But he said it *very* sarcastically."

"Stretch, my ass, you're starting again! You're Jonathan Fleming, not *Ian* Fleming, Jonathan. If you keep this up, I'm telling Milly the next time she calls. This man who looks at the floor is *not* giving you a message! But read my lips, because *I* am giving you one. *You're starting again!*"

We took our usual stroll, with Millicent's dog, Fathead, down to a spot that has wonderful views of Puget Sound, with ships and sailboats on it.

"Do you think Milly gets tired of talking to us?" Millicent asked. "I mean, she does have her own life now."

"I don't think so," I said. "When has Milly been reticent about saying what she's tired of?"

Millicent squeezed my hand while Fathead twisted his leash around his neck, like he'd hang himself if he had to listen to any more of our banter.

When members get to the Y, we leave our cards in this little wooden box at the front desk. It's an absolutely ancient system, but perfect for snooping, especially for an old spook like me. Yes, I was the spy at the various embassies I was posted to, though always officially attached to the economics section. In Nigeria, my job was to report on corruption among Goodluck Jonathan's cronies, prior to his ascent to the presidency. I'd worked hard at it, courted certain members of his party (the ruling PDF), and reported that by Nigerian standards they were relatively clean. Perhaps with retirement looming, I hadn't worked hard enough, however, because my report was eviscerated. I even received a cable from Langley telling me to rewrite the damned thing, and this time not to give them a pass. How humiliating that was! I can remember complaining to Millicent and Milly, who was visiting from England at the time. Milly was going to the Marine Ball with one of our embassy guards that night, in fact, so we were standing in our living room, Millicent, Milly, the young marine, and I, having a preball cocktail.

"I give someone a clean bill of health and they want dirt," I had said, and Millicent shushed me. "Loose lips sink ships," she told the marine. My real job at the embassy was an open secret, but what a breach! I really was tiring of the CIA.

Anyway, back to the man who looks at the floor. Late the following Saturday, I saw him again and doubled back to the front desk. The kid who works there was chatting up a couple of girls, so while pretending to read a flyer about the Y's next squash tournament, I flipped the wooden card box open, rifling through it until I saw a photograph of the top of the head of the man who looks at the floor, in the upper left-hand corner of one of the cards. His name was Jules Rules, of all things, and he lived at 817 North M Street, not very far from Millicent and me. I thought I might say something like "Good luck, Jules" to him when I passed him on the track, but it's harder than you might think to speak to a man with such a radical physical impairment, so in the end I didn't say anything. Before our evening stroll that night, however, I told Millicent that I wanted to walk up into Tacoma's middle-alphabet streets, J, K, L, and M. We lived on G Street ourselves, and below us, toward the bay, were A, C, D, and E, our usual haunts. B Street was missing; don't ask me why.

"I thought our purpose was to look at the bay," she said.

My purpose had been to get Millicent looking at the *boats* on the bay, in preparation for suggesting that we buy one.

"That's true," I said, "but let's walk up the hill tonight."

I'd grown up in Tacoma, and my grandmother lived on K Street, so perhaps Millicent thought I wanted to walk by her house, which had gone to the dogs. But let her think what she wanted; 817 North M was my goal. Jules Rules wouldn't be fooling me much longer!

"You know, Milly called last evening when you were out. I can't believe I forgot to tell you," Millicent said.

"What's up with Milly?" I asked. "I hope she didn't cancel her visit."

"*Au contraire,* she moved it up to next week," said Millicent, "*and* she's bringing someone with her."

This she forgot to tell me? It was so unlike Millicent to forget anything regarding Milly that I suspected she'd neither forgotten nor told me everything. Maybe Milly was married, maybe even pregnant. Milly had never been a girl with measured pleasures. Once she brought seven puppies home from a garage sale.

At the corner where we usually turned toward the bay, we walked up past Yakima Avenue, then headed toward the middle of the alphabet. "Look at the way those oak tree roots are breaking up the sidewalk," said Millicent. "Nature and human nature both break everything up if you give them enough time. Don't you think so, Jonathan?"

"Nature and human nature both break everything up" was my second warning that something was wrong.

Our strolls weren't meant to help get us in shape but as a time for us to talk about the regular busyness of our days, even though we were retired. Retirement meant volunteer tutoring for Millicent, and local government watchdogging for me. She wanted Tacoma's children well educated, and I wanted my hometown's continued revitalization.

Millicent dallied beside me, pointing out places where other tree roots had buckled the sidewalk.

"Is Milly bringing a guy?" I asked. "If so, what are we going to do about the sleeping arrangements?"

We had worked our way up to Eighth and J, past the house of a girl I had liked in high school. Beautiful girl, a Mary Tyler Moore look-alike.

"His name is Philip," said Millicent. "I hope it isn't Philip Pirrip. And we'll ignore the sleeping arrangements, Jonathan. She's thirty-one years old."

Philip Pirrip, ha! I loved it when Millicent got literary.

Once we got to L Street, we headed down to Ninth, then cut up to M and doubled back. Jules Rules's house was one away from the corner on our left. Someone had put a ladder against his roof, as if repairs were going on.

"That's where he lives," I said. "I got his address at the Y."

"That's where who lives?" Millicent asked before rolling her eyes and saying, "He wasn't talking about the president of Nigeria, Jonathan!"

"Maybe not, but you know what happened the week

before we left that place. Once fooled, twice . . . Twice what is it, Millicent?"

But she wouldn't tell me. We were still on the corner when Jules Rules's front door opened and the man himself came out, dressed in overalls and staring furiously at his lawn.

"At least he isn't faking it," I said. "*Or* he's very well trained."

"He's not going to climb that ladder, is he?" asked Millicent. "Look, there's a paint bucket in his flower bed."

"I don't know what he's going to do, but let's watch him do it," I said.

It was easier to spy on someone who couldn't look up than on anyone I had ever spied on in my life. On the track, Jules sometimes violated the borders of the lanes, which was fine, considering his condition, but for him to try to climb that ladder really did seem foolish. He might break his already-broken neck.

"One of us should steady that ladder for him," Millicent said.

I couldn't steady it for him, even Jules Rules would catch me then, but it did give me an idea. "You do it, Mills," I said. "Go get to know him. Be my mole."

Millicent kicked at the broken sidewalk, but she also shot across the street and into Jules's flower bed before he was half-way up the ladder. "Howdy, partner," she said. "How about I hold this for you? Don't want you getting bucked off."

Millicent is English, as I've said, but good at accents—a natural spy herself.

"Thanks," said Jules. "It does get a little shaky. You live around these parts?"

These parts? Good Christ.

"Yep," said Millicent. "How about you? Lived here long? Ever lived in any other country?"

That was *not* the way a mole should act! You don't come right out and ask something. You hang around, *glean* the information, like you don't care much about it either way.

"I *have* lived abroad, but I grew up here," said Jules.

Okay, so once in a while the direct approach pays off.

"I've lived abroad, too," said Millicent.

She'd slipped out of her cowboy accent and was British again, but Jules didn't seem to notice. He'd climbed up as far as his rain gutters.

"What are you up to?" she asked. "Do you need this paint up there with you?"

I sprinted to a nearby oak tree, my back against its trunk on the side they couldn't see.

"It's turpentine," said Jules. "I was spray-painting my house last week when I accidentally sprayed a bit of the roof, and it's driving me crazy. I thought I'd try to turpentine it off."

Sure enough, a few of the roof's shingles right above where his ladder was had a mist of grayish color on them, fanning out in the pattern that a paint sprayer might make. Oh, he was good! Deep, deep cover, if you ask me!

"You spray-painted your house?" asked Millicent. "How in the world did you manage that, with mirrors or something?"

In all the times I'd seen him at the Y, I had never heard anyone ask Jules what made him look down, yet Millicent asked it right away. Milly was like that, too. No bones about anything with the women in my family.

"I've got Bean's facedown syndrome," Jules said.

Millicent picked up the turpentine can and stepped onto the ladder.

"It's a rare condition, not life-threatening, but terminal as far as having things look up again," he said.

He was a fast-talking con man, that's what he was, with Millicent standing there on his ladder with him. I edged my way around the oak tree, back still flat against it.

"Things will look up again!" said Millicent. "Your face might not, but things? Have some faith, Ju—"

He had climbed onto the roof and hooked his heels on the rain gutter, head between his knees. Millicent put the turpentine can on the spray-painted shingles and scooted up next to him. She gave me a look that said, Get the hell out of here, Jonathan.

"Just what?" asked Jules. "You were about to say 'just,' but stopped."

"Just get on with your life," she said. "Stiff upper lip and all of that."

To get one's wife on the roof of the house of the man you suspect of spying on you . . . not bad for someone as completely retired as I.

MILLY AND PHILIP ARRIVED A FEW DAYS LATER, so for a time I had to put my Jules Rules obsession on hold. We rented a boat and cruised up to the top of Puget Sound, fishing and eating and talking. Milly was different this time, in love with Philip Pirrip, who had rowed at Oxford, finished medical school at Cambridge, and was now a cardiologist, his offices next to Milly's in London. He was thrilled with the boat adventure and rowed our dinghy each night after we anchored while Milly snorkeled around him like a little wet duck.

Over drinks one night, Millicent and I listened to Milly and Philip's plans: a short engagement, marriage at Philip's parents' house. We were anchored off Point No Point, sunburned on the deck, and when Millicent went inside to use the loo, as she called it, I asked Philip, "Have you ever heard of something called Bean's facedown syndrome?"

"What's that?" he said. He was flipping burgers on the boat's tiny grill.

"Bean's facedown syndrome."

I'd looked for the condition online but hadn't found it. Milly, who'd been sitting nearby with Fathead, said, "Bean's facedown syndrome is an interesting condition, Dad. Utterly psychosomatic, and usually connected with feelings of shame over something that happened in childhood."

"What?" said Millicent, who had just come back on deck.

"Bean was the doctor who first observed it," said Milly.

Millicent and I told Milly and Philip the whole story, from that first snide "Good luck, Jonathan," right up to Millicent sitting on the man's roof.

"He invited your mom to dinner," I told Milly. "I think she would have accepted, but we had you coming, and then this boat trip."

"Poor guy," said Philip. "Probably the first time that an attractive woman has taken an interest in him."

"Easiest thing in the world to fake, though," said Milly. "Why doesn't Mom accept the invitation now and the rest of us can ring that oak tree, Dad. Wouldn't that be fun?"

"I'm not so sure it would be easy to fake," said Philip. "Think what havoc it would play on one's back and neck."

Milly served the burgers while Millicent fed Fathead. To

my surprise, she didn't scold me for bringing the whole thing up. "I'll do it as soon as we get back," she said.

PHILIP'S FAMILY NAME WASN'T PIRRIP, of course, but Hertweck. I usually said Hartwick, and each time I did so, Milly got this condescending expression on her face. But ask yourself, isn't Philip Hartwick a whole lot easier to remember than Philip Hertweck?

Over the next two weeks, Milly and Philip got passes to the Y, and Millicent went back to Jules Rules's house, where she not only accepted his dinner invitation but helped him rip out some ugly paneling on either side of his fireplace, reexposing two small windows and filling his living room with light. She got so involved with it that a couple of times she even canceled her tutoring obligations. She seemed to have forgotten that the whole thing was a ruse, that she was there to discover the truth, while Philip and Milly took turns shadowing Jules on the track, in search of evidence that he *was* faking Bean's facedown syndrome.

"There are no photos in his house," said Millicent, "but he was married once, and he did have children. Every time I bring it up, however, he changes the subject."

She was sorry now, I think, to have wasted so much time helping Jules Rules, since Milly and Philip's holiday was drawing to a close. And Milly seemed sorry also. "We should forget this silliness," she said, but we couldn't forget it, since we were in two camps regarding everything. Philip and Millicent believed Jules Rules was genuine, while Milly and I grew progressively more suspicious, me because his "Good luck,

Jonathan" wisecracking *had escalated,* and Milly because if he actually did have Bean's facedown syndrome, she wanted to study him.

"Most of my patients are dull," she said. "I mean, how many times can a girl get off prescribing antidepressants?"

"Not very many," I said, though I didn't like her saying "get off" in front of her mother. Or in front of me, either, if it came right down to it.

"Well, we have to stop this no matter what," Millicent said. "Jules is falling in love with me, Jonathan!"

"How does he know what you look like?" I asked. "Did you lie on his floor and look up at him?"

Philip laughed, but Millicent said she'd stop going up there right now if she didn't have her dinner date with him the very next night.

"Honestly, Jonathan, you're such a boor," she said. "He's a lonely man, and a funny one, too, though no one gives him much of a chance to show it."

"Right," said Milly. "So much of humor resides in facial expressions."

"I'll have you know I asked him a bit more about his medical condition," Millicent said, "and now he's calling it 'isolated neck exterior myopathy,' INEM for short."

"But INEM *is* Bean's facedown syndrome," said Philip. "Otherwise, there'd be a specific neuromuscular diagnosis, amyotrophic lateral sclerosis, God forbid, or Parkinson's disease. . . ." He paused, then added, "I've been doing a little research. Haven't had to think of these things since I did my head rotation."

Now I laughed, but Milly didn't.

"Do you even care that his wife left him over this thing?"

asked Millicent. "Or that he's conquered his devils, painted his house, and has a bunch of other projects lined up? I sincerely wish that you would conquer *your* devils, Jonathan."

Later that evening, I apologized to Millicent and asked her to cancel her dinner, but she wouldn't do it. "You always act like this, Jonathan," she said. "You get some harebrained idea—a man tells you 'good luck,' and you think he's an Agency plant—and then you drag me into it. Only *then* do you realize your paranoia and try to drag me back out of it again. Well, this time I'm seeing it through. He's making his special Nigerian hot pepper soup."

"*What?*"

I leapt out of my chair like he had just poured the soup in my lap. I asked Milly and Philip to go to the Y without me, so Millicent and I could talk.

"I didn't tell you because I knew it would make you crazier than ever," she said. "But Jules was a geologist before he retired, had a couple of contracts with Schlumberger in Nigeria. The last one at about the time you got into your trouble."

"Ha!" I shouted.

"Even if he did somehow recognize you, it was only a joke, a tease to make his exercise time go by."

"Did you come right out and ask him?" I asked. "I want to know right now!"

After my report on Goodluck Jonathan's cronies was dismissed by the Agency, I got my picture in a few of the Nigerian dailies for something I tried to pull off regarding proving the truth of my report.

"I didn't have to ask him," Millicent said. "He just started talking. What was I supposed to do, tell him *not* to tell me about his life?"

"Is that when he said he was in love with you?"

"That's enough!" said Millicent. "Really, Jonathan. I didn't believe it back in Nigeria, but now I think I agree with Porky. You need help."

"Porky" was our nickname for the U.S. ambassador, who'd had to bail me out. I once accused Millicent of naming Fathead Fathead because she wanted to have a reminder of Porky in our house. It's a long and twisted story, that of Millicent's various crushes.

"Just tell me what you know," I said. "Then call this sucker up and cancel on him."

I'd gotten thrown in jail in Nigeria because I had tried to blackmail Goodluck Jonathan. Not directly but through channels. I wanted to prove he *wasn't* corrupt, in order to defend my report, so I kept very good records on the blackmail. Thus, I was able to clear myself of any real wrongdoing, at least as far as the U.S. government was concerned. The blackmail had to do with evidence we had concerning true corruption on the Nigerian World Cup soccer team. I had asked for a meeting with Goodluck Jonathan as my price for keeping it quiet, and when I arrived for the meeting, I was arrested for meddling in internal politics. Goodluck suspended the soccer team from international competition and ordered me deported. Langley was so angry that they nearly docked a portion of my pension, until Porky intervened.

Millicent didn't respond to my second demand that she cancel her dinner, but went out to our backyard with Fathead. I knew better than to follow her—forcing the issue never worked with Millicent—so I grabbed my gym bag and headed out the door. If Milly was still at the Y, I'd ask her advice, and if Jules was there, I'd stick my head beneath his gaze and demand that he uninvite my wife. A geologist! What perfection! The only job where Bean's facedown syndrome was an advantage!

The kid at the front desk had his hands folded over the check-in box, so I couldn't discover who was there without going onto the track. I usually arrived dressed for exercise, but this time I stepped into the locker room to slip out of my jeans and street shoes. No one was in the locker room proper, but two pairs of shoes lay on the floor. I could hear water running in the shower, and also began to hear voices. A tiled parapet separated the changing room from the showers. The two pairs of shoes were inanimate *before* the voices came to me but snapped to attention now, like shoes are wont to do in cartoons: a pair of white Adidas that I had seen traversing the deck of the boat we'd rented, and—you guessed it—the gray New Balances that Jules Rules always wore. Jules Rules, who loved my wife, was in the shower with Philip Pirrip, who loved my daughter! I was in my track suit with my street clothes in my bag, ready to run if I heard the shower stop. But even a fervent antieavesdropper would have trouble in a situation like this, don't you think, not pressing an ear against the parapet?

"Coronary thrombosis is an ischemic heart disease and can lead to myocardial infarction," Phillip was saying. "Sometimes the terms are used synonymously, but thrombosis specifically means that a thrombus occupies more than seventy-five percent of the lumen of an artery. So it's a warning of pending infarction but not the infarction itself. A thrombus, of course, is a blood clot."

"Nice to have that cleared up," Jules Rules said.

I imagined him staring at the shower floor, water streaming off his penis.

"I like discussing heart disease, but I think I come across as rather a boor with my future in-laws," said Phillip. "They don't mind hearing psychobabble all day long, but when the conversation turns to real medicine, their eyes glaze over."

Psychobabble? Was that what he thought of Milly's profession?

"And you?" asked Philip. "What do you do?"

Ah! Maybe he was complaining about his future in-laws to make Jules Rules incriminate himself. My own potential myocardial infarction eased up.

"As you can see, this problem with my neck has kept me from doing much of anything recently, but I *was* a dentist. All that constant bending and looking into people's mouths helped give me this wretched condition."

A dentist! I nearly leapt around the parapet.

"Ah, a fellow medical man," said Philip. "Sorry to go on about thrombosis. Did your doctors not give you hope in their prognosis?"

Right then I heard the showers go off, so I sprinted out of the locker room and down the padded hallway toward the track without having heard Jules's answer. What if he was a dentist? What proof did I have that Jules wasn't truthful and Millicent lying, calling him a geologist in order to say that he'd been to Nigeria and therefore keep on going to his house?

At first, I didn't think anyone was on the track, but then I saw Milly, running along with an ease I'd always envied. Had I not been quite so flummoxed, I might have waited for her to come around, but no, I had to take off sprinting in order to catch her. Milly heard me galumphing up behind her and stiffened, until I asked, "How do you tell a dentist from a geologist?"

"One puts metal in your mouth and the other takes it out of the ground? You don't have better things to do with your retirement years than make up silly riddles, Dad?"

"*Retirement* isn't the word for it. You know very well I was forced out."

She slowed to a walk, as pretty as Millicent had been on the day I met her in London.

"You put your years in," she said.

"I don't think your mother sees it that way. I've been a disappointment to her, Mills. I was the spy in the family, but she spies something rotten in me now."

I knew Milly wouldn't say "That's not true" simply as a platitude, so I waited. We were alone on the track, drifting from lane to lane.

"Now listen to me, Dad," she finally said. "Do you remember how Mom was when we were on that boat? Happy and busy, getting to know Philip and sitting beside me on the deck while the sun went down?"

"Of course I remember; it was only last week. What are you saying, we should always be taking boat trips?"

It was terrible, but images of water flowing off of Jules Rules's penis *would not* leave me alone. I imagined him standing on those paint stains he'd made on his roof, peeing off of it onto my head.

"It isn't boat trips; it's the idea of breaking the tedium," Milly said. "I think what Mom would like to do is go back to school. Finish what she started."

"Tedium?" I said. "Did your mother use that word?"

"Now, now," said Milly. "I'm not telling tales on Mom."

When I met Millicent, she was a budding social anthropologist at the London School of Economics, who attended a concert by the American folksinger, Malvina Reynolds, which I attended, too, in order to scope out the dissidents. We sang "Little Boxes Made of Ticky-Tacky" until the pub we'd wandered into after the concert closed. And now, all these decades later, what was our house made of that she would want to date a man who could look only down?

"She can go back to school if she wants to," I said. "The University of Washington is downtown, and there's the University of Puget Sound."

"That's what I told her," said Milly.

We had come to a couple of benches, had sat on one of them, when Philip appeared, hair all blow-dried by one of those abominable hand-dryer things.

"Philip . . ." said Milly, as in "Philip, don't say anything," but Philip's one true connection to me was that he read Milly's signals as badly as I did Millicent's.

"I've got to have my bicuspids fixed," he said. "I knew there was something wrong and he's just verified it."

"Having mastication trouble, eh?" I said, while Milly called him obtuse.

One night while anchored off Point No Point on the boat, we'd had a lighthearted argument about whether or not cardiologists were the most distant of doctors. *Obtuse* didn't exactly mean *distant*, but Philip looked at Milly as if remembering that argument.

"Philip's an idiot, Dad," she said, "but if you want to know why Mom made up this geologist thing, I suggest you go home and ask her."

Oh God, she really had made it up.

"What time is it?" I said. "She's got her dinner date."

Milly looked at her wrist, though she didn't wear a watch.

She put an arm around my shoulder. "It's a freckle past a hair," she said. "Chin up, Dad."

In fact, it was a freckle past six-thirty, and Millicent's date was set for seven. We could speed home, getting there before she left, but Philip suggested we stop for dinner ourselves, and that I talk to Millicent *after* her date. He held one of Milly's arms as we left the gym while Milly's other arm took mine, which I didn't consider to be a very good omen.

Jules Rules, I couldn't help thinking, must have rushed home after his shower.

We decided to eat at the Harbor Lights, down on Tacoma's Old Town waterfront. We'd putted past the Harbor Lights at the end of our boat trip the week before, to watch the diners, so I thought we ought to look at any boats that might come by tonight, as if we were looking at ourselves. Philip said the meal was on him, in thanks for the hospitality afforded him by Millicent and me during his visit, though Millicent was just then sitting down to eat with someone else. In my old spy world, people were always pretending to be what they weren't: geologists, bankers, businessmen, economists . . . But not doctors or dentists, since good advice on bicuspid maladjustments was a lot more difficult to fake.

We ordered vodka martinis and Milly selected an expensive bottle of wine.

"This all started so idiotically," I said. "But now it seems as serious as a myocardial infarction."

"Let's hope not," said Philip. "But there's no doubt at

all that he's a dentist. He had some terribly vivid pyorrhea descriptions when we were getting dressed."

If Millicent had been with us, she'd have ordered salmon, so that's what I ordered, while Milly asked for lingcod and Philip ordered steak. A couple of boats came by, moon faces staring in at us. When our martinis arrived, one of the moon faces gave us the thumbs-up.

"The trouble is that over the years a lot of things have started out idiotically, Dad," said Milly. "You're a regular Larry David when it comes to absurd situations. But with you, far too often, the comedy is missing. And Mom did say on the boat that she's tired of it, that she thinks she might like to try living alone for a while."

She cast a hand toward the dying sunlight, tipping the rippling waves. The glass my heart was made of broke like it had been stepped on by a passing Jewish groom. "She did, Milly?" I asked. "Your mom said that?"

"Milly, when we get married, what do you say we try to make a happy life?" said Philip.

Milly took a sip of her martini. In the spy world, we sometimes played good cop/bad cop with informants, and I got the idea that Milly and Philip might be playing those roles now, with me.

"But if she wants to live alone, what's she doing at Jules Rules's house? What kind of living alone is that?"

"Shh, Dad," said Milly. "We're in a restaurant."

I hadn't realized I'd been shouting until she said that.

My martini was gone, so when our waiter brought us bread, I ordered another.

"For what it's worth, I think this is a test," said Philip. "By that I mean she has no real interest in the man but wants to see what it's like to eat and talk with someone else. I'd guess she's more interested in taking her own pulse when she's out and about than in whomever she's out and about with."

Milly reached over and took Philip's hand. "That's smart, Philip Pirrip," she said, and Philip smiled.

I had thought "Philip Pirrip" was strictly between Millicent and me.

My second martini came with the bottle of wine, our food right behind it. My salmon sat on the small cedar plank it had been cooked on. Millicent liked to call the current trends in food presentation "cuiscenery." Whom would she say *cuiscenery* to if she lived by herself?

"Okay, I admit to a small imbalance," I said. "But tell me truly, Milly, is this all meant to scare me, or is it serious?"

Milly had a mouthful of lingcod, while a hunk of Philip's steak inched its way toward his face on the tines of his fork. The fork stopped in midair, while Milly's lingcod slid down her throat like it had found a secret passage back to Puget Sound. That a dead cod could rise again, that was about as hopeful as I felt.

"It isn't only your current craziness; it's years and years of it. Of course it's serious, Dad. That's what we've been trying to tell you!"

"Think of it as a plaque buildup," said Philip.

"You two should put your wedding off until Millicent and I get squared away," I said, but Milly didn't hear me.

"Why does everything have to be so difficult?" she asked. "Why couldn't you have tried to look at things like a normal person?"

I noted Milly's past-perfect tense.

My second martini had a couple of extra olives in it, which

I transferred to Milly's glass. It wasn't Milly who liked olives, though, but Millicent. "Should I go over there now?" I asked, "barge in and claim my wife?"

"He lives in a house, not a cave," said Milly. "And 007 you aren't."

"Maybe not," said Philip, "but he did have two vodka martinis."

Two vodka martinis and half a bottle of wine, since Philip didn't drink.

MILLY WANTED ME TO LEAVE MY CAR at Harbor Lights, but I promised I'd drive straight home and they could follow. Philip wasn't used to American driving, though, so it was easy for me to lose them, wending my way up the Thirtieth Street hill, then dodging into a side street, back toward our house, and up the alphabet streets to Jules Rules's place, which had lights on in its dining room, and Millicent's ancient Volvo out in front. It wasn't much of a house for a dentist to live in. Maybe Bean's facedown syndrome had caused such havoc in his life that he'd had to give up dentistry early. Maybe he'd moved from a better place in order to pay his medical bills.

I parked across the street, then sprinted over to hide behind a rhododendron, in order to get my bearings. Thirty years of marriage, with six brief moments when something got hold of me to make me crazy. Six moments! Or eight, at the most. And some of them were funny, like the time I challenged the Russian spies to a hot dog–eating contest, and they showed up wearing Lenin masks. That wasn't funny? I beg your pardon! If you take the humor out of spying, all you have left are reams and reams of unreadable reports.

But was this what I had been reduced to, climbing up a ladder to peer in someone's window in search of my wife? It was true I hadn't climbed the ladder yet, but an unclimbed ladder is the inanimate manifestation of an unexamined life, so three rungs up I went, until my eyes were level with his dining room table, his gauzy curtain like the cataracts that Milly suggested covered my eyes. "Oh, Millicent, do you remember the little boxes made of ticky-tacky?" I cried.

Millicent was facing me, Jules in the chair nearest the window, so all I got to see of him was his back. It looked exactly as if Millicent were eating dinner with a headless man. I leaned in closer, to try to get her attention, my nose against the glass. While I sang the beginning of the ticky-tacky song, Millicent's face flattened out, not as if she heard it coming from me, but as if she heard it coming from within herself. She pushed her chair back and stood. I had promised her a ticky-tacky-free life on the evening we met. "Oh, you can't eat hot dogs through a Lenin mask, even of the slyest agent that's too much to ask . . ." were the lyrics we used to sing to Milly.

Millicent walked across the room, picked up her sweater from the couch, and turned to face Jules Rules, who had stood, too, the top of his head out toward her. She could have drawn a smiling face upon it.

"Good luck, Jules," I wanted Millicent to say. What I didn't want her to say was, "Good-bye, Jonathan."

It wouldn't be good for me to be there when she came outside, so I sprinted back to my car, the vodka martinis and the half bottle of wine sloshing around inside of me to the tune of "Oh, You Can't Eat Hot Dogs Through a Lenin Mask." I changed the words as I drove away from Jules's house, headlights still off, like a spy in an old Aston Martin. "Oh, you can't eat hot dogs . . . Oh, you can't . . . Oh, you can't leave me, Millicent. What would I do without you? What would I do with the rest of my life?"

But it didn't work; it didn't sound good that way. I wasn't the songwriter in the family; I was the spy, and six times the troublemaker. Or eight, at most. I saw Jules Rules on his porch in my rearview mirror, looking down at his doormat as if Millicent's departure would ruin him, too.

A police car came out of a side street, so I turned on my lights, but it was too late. The policeman growled his siren at me and pulled me over. I looked down at my crotch, ready to explain that I'd just had an attack of a long-troubling, terribly debilitating condition, which had accosted me just as I reached for my light switch. Bean's facedown syndrome.

If he bought it, I'd say, "Please, Officer, can you take me to the hospital?" From there, I'd call Millicent, ready with the medical evidence necessary to prove that, for all these many years of our married life together, the man who had really looked at the floor was me.

The Day of the Reckoning of Names

[1960]

I T ALL STARTED ON THE AFTERNOON of my grandmother's funeral. There are these caves down the beach from our house, tucked in among the trees and poison oak, and when Dad and I got home from the funeral and Dad decided to go for a run, I changed into these ridiculous Hawaiian swimming trunks I've got and went down to the caves. The tide was high, giving me only about six feet of beach to walk on, and the bay was still churning from a storm we'd had that morning. When I got there, I climbed the bank and sat at the entrance to the nearest cave in order to decide what to do with a three-ring binder that I'd shoved down the front of my swim trunks just before I left the house. It had my grandma's diary in it, her memoir, I guess you'd called it, which no one else knew about, and which, for some damned reason, she gave to me the day before she died.

Here are the facts about my grandmother. Her name was Flora Magnolia Marigold Lilly, with Lilly being our last name. She was born in 1867 and died right now, in 1960, at the ripe old age of ninety-three. "Ripe old age" is how her minister put it in his pathetic eulogy. What got me was that he came out of retirement to say it, at the ripe old age of about one hundred and fifty himself.

The binder had belonged to my dad when he was in high school and was covered with scribbles that mostly said "Loretta sucks hind tit!"

I had just started thinking about what to do with the binder when down on the beach, hopping from boulder to boulder, came this kid I know named Perry White, with rocks in his hands and a slingshot in his pocket. He was a lousy sort of kid most of the time, but the most amazing shot with a rock in all of Brown's Point, in all of Tacoma, probably. So I had a choice to make before I could decide about the binder, because Perry knew the caves as well as I did and might be coming here to smoke and look at dirty pictures. The choice was this: Should I call to him or stay quiet and hope he'd go away? It was important because if he saw me and I hadn't called him, he might start slinging rocks.

Perry stopped below me to shoot a couple of the very rocks I was worried about at this metal buoy out in the bay. *Ping! Ping!* said the buoy. Two rocks, two hits, like always.

"*Heeeeyyy, Perry!*" I hissed, or not exactly hissed, but brayed, in what I thought of as a good imitation of a goat's voice. Our next-door neighbors used to have a goat in their backyard. Perry was in love with one of their daughters.

"What the hell?" he said, and I said, "Up here" in my regular voice.

"Richie?"

"Yeah. Just got back from my grandma's funeral."

"My condolences," said Perry.

I was surprised he knew the word but kept my mouth shut. He was wearing jeans and a striped T-shirt, his uniform for as long as I could remember. He ran up the bank and fell down beside me.

"How old was she," he asked, "hunnert, hunnert'n one?"

"Ninety-three. We buried her next to her husband, who's been dead since 1945 himself."

"Nineteen forty-five . . ." Perry said it like it was the Jurassic Age, though it was the year we both were born in.

"Wanta know how he got killed?" I asked. "He was a preacher, my grandpa, with the actual name of Tiger Lilly."

I opened the binder so I could read about him, but all Perry did was stare at "Loretta sucks hind tit!" And then he told me in this belligerent way to go ahead and read it. He was changeable like that, cheerful one minute, grouchy the next. I found the spot and read: "'One summer when a local girl was caught drinking with some lumberjacks, Tiger decided to give a sermon about cupid and use his prowess as an archer to drive the point home. So he got out his bow and we walked down to an open space behind the lighthouse.'"

"I didn't know the lighthouse was that old," said Perry, but I could see that he was talking to himself.

"'I'd made some rolls and Tiger was juggling them, roving around and saying that the odds of a girl finding love in a lumberjack bar were about as great as something or other. He was searching for the proper analogy when I said, "About as great as you hitting one of those rolls in midair. I'll throw it up and you shoot. You'll miss, of course, and that will show the girl how likely it is that she, too, will miss her mark."'"

Perry took out his slingshot and sent a rock into the sky. If there'd been a roll up there he'd have knocked it down.

"'Tiger was irritated that I'd said he couldn't hit the roll. "Throw one up, Flora," he said, "See if I can't hit it. I'm good at this, you know." I did and he missed. A bald eagle nesting in a nearby tree saw the roll and opened its wings, as if thinking about going after it itself. I'd only brought four rolls and fancied eating one, so I told him I'd throw just one more. It was still rising when he steadied his bow and shot. He missed again and said, "Don't say anything, Flora. Throw up another." I sighed and bent to get another roll, when the one I'd just thrown came down and hit Tiger on the nose. We both laughed, but then the arrow came down, too, and hit him in the forehead.'"

"Yer lyin', Richie, a roll can't stay up in the air that long," said Perry. Then he snatched the binder out of my hands and ran down to the beach with it, his butt sticking out behind him like two hams in a sack.

"Bring that back!" I shouted, but he sent a rock into the dirt at my feet.

I danced around like a coward in a cowboy movie until another rock flew past my ear, and then I ran into the cave. Five minutes later, when I peeked out again, all I could see was the bay and the limbs of the nearby trees. Both Perry and my grandma's binder were gone.

WHEN I GOT HOME, COLD AND SWEATY in my swim trunks, Dad had just come back from his run and was cold and sweaty and irritable, I guess because his run hadn't gone well. He'd been a champion runner in high school and liked to remember his glory days. New glory days were few and far between for my dad.

"Go change, Richie," he said, "I don't want you dragging that beach crap into the house."

He was sitting on our couch with a glass of scotch. When I told him that I'd knocked the beach crap off already, he pinched his stomach and said, "I'm getting fat."

"You're not getting fat, Dad," I said, "You're sitting down."

I sat beside him, took his glass, and sipped from it. Have you ever tasted scotch? It's incredibly awful, but the face I make when I sip it usually makes Dad laugh and go get me a Coke. This time when he brought the Coke back, he said, "What are we gonna do now?"

Grandma was his mother, of course, and he'd loved her as much as I had. At her funeral, he said in front of everyone that he liked the way she died because it kept our "goddamn ordinariness" at bay. I'm not kidding, he said "goddamn ordinariness" just like that. And then he said that all summer long we'd been having trouble with a mole who kept burrowing into our yard and eating Grandma's chrysanthemums. We'd tried flooding it out, tried blocking its hole with stones, but nothing had worked. So Grandma decided to load her .22 and sit on our porch and wait. The way Dad told it, when he got up at 5:00 A.M., she was already out there, so all he could do was sit beside her. Grandma wouldn't let him talk, but after a few minutes she said, "Here's our Mr. Mole, soft shoulders filling up the diameter of his hole"; then *CRACK!* went her rifle and Mr. Mole slumped down.

"Here's our Mr. Mole, soft shoulders filling up the diameter of his hole" were Grandma's last words, since her heart stopped as soon as the mole's did.

MRS. KANT, THE TEACHER I HAD for ninth-grade English, told us that the *wherefore* in "Wherefore art thou, Romeo?" didn't mean "where" but "why." So Juliet wasn't asking where Romeo was, as we all thought, but "Why are you, Romeo? How come you have to belong to an enemy clan?"

Mrs. Kant was the best teacher I ever had, especially since her other almost full-time job was taking care of Mr. Kant, her husband, over on the other side of the lighthouse. I'd been to see her a few times this summer. Pitiful as it is, she was a pretty good friend. Mr. Kant was a college professor before he started having strokes. The Kants have a daughter, but she lives in a dormitory at Annie Wright, so she isn't much help.

I'm saying this now because after Dad and I had dinner, I said I thought I'd take a bike ride. My idea was to go find Perry and get the binder back, but I decided to talk strategy with Mrs. Kant first, since she knew Perry from school.

The Kants' house wasn't large, but it had a deck that faced the beach and they were always out on it. I sneaked around so I wouldn't have to go into their yard, where they kept a couple of peacocks. I got to the beach okay and was about to announce myself when Mrs. Kant said, "Sit tight, Herb. I'll go get your ice cream."

I slipped down under their deck. Its spotlight cast Mr. Kant in the center of a circle of light on the beach. He was decades younger than my grandma but in ten times worse shape, except for the fact that Grandma was dead. When Mrs. Kant came back with the ice cream, Mr. Kant said, *"Ut esy, Ev A brak zel. Ut won ut on."*

"Let's leave the seal alone for a while, Herb," said Mrs. Kant. "We still have hope."

Mr. Kant was a burden and Mrs. Kant was the bearer of

it, that's what he was saying. And the seal was on his medi-cine bottle. I knew it because I'd been there often enough to understand Mr. Kant pretty well. I also knew that that was not the time to show myself.

ONLY A FEW OF THE BROWN'S POINT HOUSES were on the water, and most of those were like ours, high up on a bank. They're expensive, but when Grandma built ours, it cost five thousand dollars. It's been paid off for thirty years, and these days the taxes are higher than the mortgage payments used to be. Dad says that's ironic, but what I think is ironic is that Perry's house is worth about one thousand dollars now. It's an ugly three-room box, plunked down on the roadside like it was moved from somewhere else.

It only took five minutes for me to ride over there from the Kants' house, but as soon as I got close, I ditched my bike and cut into the woods, where Perry's got a tree house his dad built, beneath which, last winter, he set traps to try to catch weasels. He said that in the winter weasels turned white and if he caught enough of them, he was going to make his mother a white weasel coat.

I needed a plan to get the binder back. I had three bucks in my shoe and thought I might try buying it back, though it would set a horrible precedent. As I went toward his house, I had to wonder why I was bothering to sneak if all I could think of was buying it, but really it was because of this girl I was in love with, Precious Smiley, who lived across from Perry. My dad said her parents should be shot for naming her Precious, but I'm here to tell you she could have been named

Dogshit Smiley and every boy in school would have thought it was the coolest name around. When I looked at her place, I could see her father, Howdy, standing in his shrubbery and staring at Perry's mom, who was sitting in her doorway, drinking beer and reading a book.

"What are you looking at?" she asked, but quietly enough that Howdy couldn't hear her. Next she said, "Who's there?" and this time I knew she was talking to me, since I'd stepped from my hiding place and waved at her.

"Richie," she said, "Perry's not home, but come over here a minute."

"Has he been home?" I asked. "I lent him something that I need to get back."

"Lent him something, eh?" she said.

She had a tough manner, Mrs. White, but I had always liked her.

"Yeah," I said, "It's a sort of book."

I wanted her to say I should go into his room and have a look, and when she didn't, I said, "We had my grandma's funeral," hoping for a little sympathy.

"Let me ask you something, Richie, and if you can answer correctly, I'll see if I can find your book. It's an easy question. Who sucks hind tit?"

"Huh? What?"

She nodded behind her to a flimsy kitchen table. "See that stack of bills in there? Go and get them for me."

"Go and get your bills?"

I thought maybe Perry was hiding behind the door, but I hurried in, scooped up the bills, and ran back out. "Here you go," I said.

"Count them for me, will you?"

"One, two, three, four, five," I said, "five bills," but she shook her head. "I think it's six," she said. "Count them again."

I didn't need to count them again, but I did finally look at the bills, and right there in front of me, typed out five times, was the name Loretta White.

"How *is* old Jack?" she asked. Then she got up and went into the house and came back with the binder. "Here you go, Richie," she said, "And sorry to hear about the old bird's death."

Once I got my hands on the binder, I figured I'd better get out of there fast, till "old bird" leaked into my head. She must have read what Grandma wrote, since Grandma called it "Old Bird's Diary" herself.

"It's not nice to snoop," I said.

Righteous indignation had been Grandma's specialty, but all the Lillys were good at it. Mrs. White, however, simply got out her keys, locked her door, got into her car, and drove away. And when I turned to look at Precious's house again, a voice nearby said, "What happened, shithead, my mom bawl you out?"

"She told me Howdy Smiley wants to get into her pants," I said.

It was a dangerous thing to say, but Perry had fewer friends than I did, so he let it pass.

"Ever been in Howdy's basement?" he asked. "He's got this old Ford flathead down there that Precious says he wants to put in my mom's car."

Pants, car. Same difference. "Come off it, Perry," I said. "Precious won't give you the time of day."

He picked up a rock, always a bad sign, so I followed him into the Smileys' side yard.

"That's Precious's window," he said. "See that flower on the sill?"

I would never admit it, but I knew Precious's window better than anyone. I knew that the flower was an artificial daisy in a thin brown pot and that when she closed her curtains, she left it between the curtains and the glass. I knew her room had yellow wallpaper, which you could see if you stood on a particular stump. I knew it all from passing by; I was no Peeping Tom.

"Yeah, I see it," I said. "So what?"

"If the flower's on the left, it means come in, and if it's on the right, it means her father's on the prowl."

"It does not!" I almost shouted.

"Okay, smart-ass, which side is the flower on now?"

"It's on the left, but I know her dad's home, 'cause I just saw him. So it doesn't mean shit what side it's on!"

I wasn't sure why I was so upset, but I was.

"Yes it does. Her father's laid off, so he's always home. The left-side flower means he's busy, that's all. Now look again. What else do you see?"

I saw a muddy yard and a rusted wheelbarrow filled with rain, Howdy's truck, and a sheet-metal toolshed. I saw Mrs. Smiley's planters and what used to be a doghouse but now stored wood, since Precious's dog, Roger, got killed when we were in fifth grade.

"I don't see anything," I said.

"Is the back door open or closed?"

"It's closed—or no, it's open a crack."

Perry was as happy as he ever got. "That means the coast is clear. You go first. Go down in her basement and don't make any noise."

I was scared but stepped into the clearing like I wasn't. When I got to the house, I pushed on the door, but it caught on a throw rug. I peeked through the crack and saw a light at the bottom of the stairs, so I pushed harder and squeezed inside. The door leading up to their kitchen was closed, and hanging from a hook beside it was Precious's winter jacket. She was too big for it now, if you know what I mean, if she tried to zip it up.

"Hello?" I whispered, "Anyone home?"

"Down here," said a girl's high voice. "Hurry up, honey, I'm cold."

Christ on His big wooden cross.

"Hi, Precious," I said, "it's Richard Lilly."

Why I had to use both my names, I didn't know. One thing about Precious, she'd been the prettiest girl in school since forever, but she was also kind, with never a bad word for anyone. So when she didn't speak again, I held on to my faith in her and went down to frame myself in their recreation room's door.

"It's Richie," I said again.

"Oh, honey, I'm cold," said Perry White.

High on the wall behind him was an open window, level with the ground outside. He was leaning against the wall with tears in his eyes and his mouth open. Precious was in a bean-bag chair, wearing an angora sweater.

"I'm sorry, Richie," she said. "It was his bright idea, the little dope."

She looked like she hoped I'd see the humor in it, but by then Perry'd started to snort. He'd be the richest kid on earth if snot were gold.

"Quit it, Perry," said Precious, "If my dad comes down here, I'll ban you from my basement for life."

"Yeah, Perry, quit it," I said.

"I saw you talking to Perry's mom, Richie," said Precious. "How come you didn't come over on your own?"

"I guess because my grandma just died."

Precious stood and came across the room to me. "I'm sorry," she said, "I remember her from your birthday parties."

When she put a hand on my arm, I was struck by my best insight of the summer: Precious Smiley was bored! That's why she let Perry come over. Oh, boredom! What a wonderful thing in the hands of a beautiful girl! But if I was going to use it, I had to act fast.

"Listen, Precious, do you still have your bike?" I asked. Then I told her that I thought Mr. Kant was going to kill himself.

Precious looked skeptical.

"I'm not kidding. He wants to take an entire bottle of medicine," I said. "He'll be dead any minute if we don't help."

I wished I hadn't said it—I felt like one of the Hardy Boys—but once I had, there was nothing to do but tell her how I'd listened to the Kants from under their deck. Precious's concern grew, neither of us glancing at Perry. This is what you do when you fish for salmon: first you set the hook; then you reel them in.

"Okay, let's go over there," she finally said. "You two wait outside."

She pointed to the window, as if we'd have to climb out that way, but Perry understood her better than me and reached up and pulled it closed.

"I'VE GOT A BOOK I NEED TO RETURN TO HER; that can be our
excuse," I said when we leaned our bikes against the Kants'
garage. I held up the book I'd packed after dinner.

"What if she won't let us in?" asked Precious. "Or just
takes the book and closes her door?"

I didn't know how to answer that without giving away the
fact that I'd been going over there all summer. Perry saved
me by saying, "Why would she do that? What could be worse
than sitting around all the time getting old?"

That gave Precious courage again, but I'd forgotten to tell
them about the Kants' two peacocks, and when we stepped
inside their gate, one of them jumped in front of us with his
feathers out.

"Mother of Jesus!" she said.

We tried to walk around him, but he pivoted with us,
first left, then right, until Mrs. Kant opened her back door.
"George! Gracie!" she yelled, since she didn't know which peacock was bothering us.

She got some grain and came down into their yard. Once
the peacock was out of the way, she put her hands on her hips
and said, "Hello, children, to what do we owe the pleasure?"

"What's up with Mr. Kant?" asked Perry. "He still alive,
or what?"

Mrs. Kant's expression didn't change, but Precious slugged
Perry hard.

"All right now," said Mrs. Kant. "It *is* a little bit late, you
know."

"I'm bringing back your book," I said.

Mrs. Kant loved to talk about books and Mr. Kant used to love to talk about birds, back when he could talk.

"I only meant if Mr. Kant was home, we'd like to say hi," said Perry.

"Lord, son, when is he ever not home?" said Mrs. Kant. Then she led us around the outside path to their deck.

"Guess what, Herb, Richard Lilly's here again," she said. "Isn't that nice? This time he's brought Precious Smiley and Perry White with him. They were in Richard's class at school."

When Mr. Kant swung around and started singing, "How Much Is That Doggie in the Window?" we all laughed like crazy.

"You kids tell Herb what you've been up to," said Mrs. Kant. "I'll go get some Cokes."

Precious and Perry were beginning to look like they wished we hadn't come, basically because Mr. Kant was drooling all over himself.

"Precious Smiley, don't you have a middle name?" he asked, his voice understandable for once.

"It's Donna," she said. "And I'm gonna use it, too, as soon as high school starts."

I looked at Perry and Perry looked at me. With a name like Donna, the world would be her oyster, both in high school and beyond.

"Good," said Mr. Kant. "We should call ourselves what we feel like calling ourselves. Now you, Perry White, what's your middle name?"

Since he was beginning to sound like a strangled cat again, I didn't think Perry would answer, but he said right away. "I don't tell no one that."

"Ah, a secret middle name. I've got one, too," said Mr.

Kant. "Tell you what. I'll tell mine if you tell yours. Mine's Bilge, I'm Herbert Bilge Kant."

He coughed up something orange, but his middle name wasn't Bilge; no one had a name like that. I could tell that Perry was worried, because by saying it without waiting, Mr. Kant had held up his part of the nonbargain. Perry knew he could threaten me into silence, but he wasn't so sure about Precious. He was savvy enough, though, to speak before any more tension built up. "It's Frank," he said, "Named after a singer my mom liked."

"Frank Sinatra?" asked Mrs. Kant, back with the Cokes, and Mr. Kant said, pretty clearly again, "I want to tell you something, young man. Are you listening to me? Because I don't want to have to say it twice." He waved a hand in front of Perry's face. "This is the day of the reckoning of names. Precious Donna Smiley, Perry Frank White, and Herbert Bilge Kant. From today, we all get new starts."

"What about Richie and Mrs. Kant?" asked Precious.

"I don't have a middle name," said Mrs. Kant, "but my maiden name is Thomas."

She barked out such a loud laugh that I laughed, too, though I didn't know what was funny about Thomas. It wasn't as lame as Darrell, which was my middle name. When Mr. Kant looked at her, the goodwill drained from his face. I nudged Precious. This was why we'd come, to save him from himself.

"I think it's time for you to go," said Mrs. Kant. "Bilge here needs to rest."

The corners of her eyes had tears in them. When none of us made a move to leave, she said, "What?"

"Another book?" I asked, but Perry leaned down to speak

into Mr. Kant's face. "It ain't true, is it, what you said just now?"

"What?" asked Mr. Kant, grumpy and garbled as hell.

"That from today we all get new starts. 'Cause lemme tell you, if I don't get one pretty soon, I doubt I'll last as long as you do."

The tears in the corners of Mrs. Kant's eyes moved out to fill them entirely.

"Richie's grandpa killed himself, too," said Perry. "Shot himself in the head with an arrow. If I get around to killing myself, I'm gonna swim out in the bay till I can't swim no more. I'll struggle like hell till I go down."

"Why don't we do that, Herb?" said Mrs. Kant. "Struggle like hell till *we* go down. Life's not over till it's over; we shouldn't have to learn that from a child!"

We made our way back through their kitchen, all of us ready to get out of there. But Mrs. Kant forced a copy of *Huckleberry Finn* on Perry and, on Precious, an English novel about sisters trying to get married. She gave me *The Grapes of Wrath*, with her name on the inside cover, from back when she was a girl: "Eva Sylvia Maria Thomas."

So Mrs. Kant had lied. She had *two* middle names, just like Grandma.

DAD WAS WAITING FOR ME WHEN I GOT HOME, beer bottles on the coffee table surrounding our phone. "What's with the binder, mister, and what's this about Grandma writing stuff down?" he asked from out of the dark.

I hadn't seen him, and I jumped, letting the binder slip out from under my shirt. When I gave it to him, he went to the window with it. He was still wearing his running clothes but had pulled Grandma's afghan from the couch and was wearing it, too, like a shawl.

"How much of this have you read?" he asked.

"Just the part about Tiger Lilly's death," I said, "but is there something in there about you and Mrs. White?"

Before he could answer, I realized that "what's this about Grandma writing stuff down?" was like that "old bird" thing at Perry's house. Our phone got bigger among the beer bottles. "Did Mrs. White call you?" I asked.

"She did, and she laid down the law. There's nothing new about any of this, Richie. I want you to know it happens to a lot of people. . . . Look, are you sure you didn't read more? Because Loretta read it all and she isn't very happy about it."

"What are you saying, Dad? Was Perry's mom your girlfriend?"

He took off Grandma's afghan, folding it like Grandma always had. In the car coming home from her funeral, he'd said we shouldn't let our lives go downhill, that we should honor Grandma's memory by keeping things the way she liked them, and I guessed folding the afghan was part of it.

"If you haven't already read about it, then yes, she was my girlfriend. Ours was one of those deeply painful loves that only kids can feel, as I'm sure you'll find out in a few years' time."

"I don't want to find it out," I said. "I'm doing fine not loving anyone."

I didn't mean that the way it came out.

"We'll see, but when Perry's mom broke up with me, it

hurt like taking a bullet," he said. "I hung around her house every day for a month, until her father chased me off."

"If she broke up with you, then how come she gets to lay down the law?"

"Because for her, it was like taking a bullet, too. We were in love like Romeo and Juliet, Richie, but when World War II broke out and I joined the service, she didn't want me carrying our love into battle. She thought breaking up with me was the greatest sacrifice she could make. We promised each other we'd meet after the war, but between Pearl Harbor and the end of high school, she started dating this army guy, and a week after we graduated, she married him. That was when I wrote what I wrote on my binder. It made me want to fight like hell during the war."

He picked up a beer bottle and drank from it. "But time passed and I met your mom down around Fort Bragg, where I spent the whole damned time."

One of Dad's regrets was that he didn't get to fight like hell but was trained as a drill instructor instead. "Down around Fort Bragg" was where my mom lived now.

He sat back down on the couch. "The month after your mom got pregnant with you, my dad died in the crazy accident you read about, and I came home for his funeral . . . and that's when Loretta and I suffered a relapse."

He tried to find my eyes, but I'd stayed in the darkest part of the room. If "relapse" meant what I thought it meant, I didn't want to hear more.

"We met at her house. Her husband was in England, her father in the navy, her mother always working, so we had the place to ourselves. It was Valentine's Day and I'd taken her flowers from my dad's memorial service."

He went on to say it happened only once, that Loretta was laying down the law because Perry and I both had a right to know, and that while he was telling me, she was telling Perry. More words came out of him, but I ran back outside, jumped on my bike, and zoomed off into the night. Perry's birthday was November 14, nine months after Valentine's Day, 1945.

IT WAS A LITTLE AFTER TEN WHEN I GOT BACK to the Kants' house, with two beers I had filched from Dad's stash. Since the tide was high, I couldn't sit under their deck, so I climbed into a madrona tree in the next-door lot. Their bedroom curtains were closed, but I could see inside over the top of the curtain rod. One of the madrona's branches was close enough to the house for me to reach over and pry off the beer bottle caps on a protruding nail. "Loretta sucks hind tit!" I yelled into the night.

Mrs. Kant pushed the curtains aside and cupped her hands against the glass. I was higher in the tree by the time she opened the window.

"Don't tell me it was nothing, Herb. I heard what I heard, and I know who said it, too," she said. "It was Perry White."

She stuck her head out. "Perry, go home! Your mother deserves better than to have an ungrateful son calling her names!"

She closed the window and curtains, and I drank both beers and almost fell out of the madrona.

The lights were off at Perry's house. I'd drunk the beers fast, so I wasn't feeling great, but I still couldn't help wondering if Perry was buried under his covers in his room, hating the idea that we were brothers. Mr. White had left his mom, which meant his mom was single, and my mom was down around Fort Bragg. I looked over at Precious's house. If Grandma knew about Dad and Perry's mom, and therefore about Perry and me, then a lot of the neighbors probably did, too.

It wasn't until I looked back at Perry's house that I finally saw Perry himself, sitting up in his tree house.

"Hi, Richie," he said. "Are you happy or sad right now?"

"I don't know," I said. "I'm still digesting it."

"Yeah, well I've digested it and what I think we should do is join the band in high school and take up the same instrument, like trombone. My cousin plays trombone and says they have sword fights with their slides."

If Perry had a cousin, did that mean I did, too?

"Now that I think about it, how about the sax?" he said. "But I get the bigger one, since I'm older'n you are."

He wasn't older; I was, by a month. He jumped down from his tree house, as quiet as a panther in the forest.

"What's a saxophone sound like?" he asked.

"I don't know, Perry. What does anything sound like? You know what a trumpet sounds like?"

"Course I do," he said. "Who doesn't know that?"

"Well, it doesn't sound like a trumpet."

I nearly said it sounded like a bird in flight—something Dad liked to say about his Charlie Parker records—but Perry's mom's car came up the street just then. She parked, got out, and lit a cigarette.

"She don't let me smoke but smokes herself," Perry said.

In the flash of the lights from her car, I'd seen his beady eyes, like the eyes of someone who would torment a weasel before taking its fur to make a coat. And in what he said next, I saw those eyes again, though it was dark.

"Listen, dipshit, we ain't brothers. I ain't nobody's brother, and you're dumber'n a skunk if you think I give a damn about the saxophone."

His mother peered into the woods. "You boys come here," she said. "I don't guess this'll be easy, but the truth is better than lies."

"Not if it ain't the truth," said Perry.

He stepped into the clearing, like Billy the Kid before a gunfight. "My dad's my dad," he said. "I ain't no Lilly; I'm a White."

"Your dad was your dad, for the years we had him," said his mother, "but now you've got me, Richie, and maybe Richie's dad, if you can come to terms with it. He said he'd like to take us to a Giants game. How would you feel about that?"

The Tacoma Giants were the AAA club for San Francisco, and Dad had tickets for when the big club came to play.

I stepped out of the woods, too. "Word is, Marichal's pitching," I said.

"My dad could pitch better'n him," said Perry. "Who do you think taught me how to throw rocks? He coulda been better if the war hadn't got him."

He looked so forlorn that I thought he might say that thing about swimming out into the bay again, when who should come outside just then but Precious, her father behind her with his hands on her shoulders.

"Precious, we're going to a baseball game," I said. "You wanta come?"

"I wouldn't mind," she said. "When's the game?"

"Evening, all," said Howdy.

No one spoke to him for such a long time that Perry's mother finally muttered, "Howdy, Howdy," like the neighbors always did to make him mad.

"I'll find out when it is and call you," I said. "Don't go to sleep yet; wait by your phone."

"And I'll drive *you* home," said Mrs. White. "It's too late to be riding your bike."

It wasn't too late to be riding my bike; we all rode our bikes anywhere and anytime. But if Dad was as single as Romeo and she was as single as Juliet, a well-timed car ride might be just the ticket. She jangled her keys, not at me but at Perry. "You coming, too?" she asked.

"What's in it for me?" he asked. "And what am I s'pose to call Richie's dad?"

"We live next-door to Winnie; that's what's in it for you," I said.

Mrs. White threw her cigarette down, opened her car door again, then looked at Perry and me. Not at the two of us together, but first at one of us and then at the other, like she was seeing if we looked alike.

Then she got in her car and started it.

AT OUR HOUSE, even though it *was* kinda late, Dad had showered, shaved, put back on the clothes he'd worn to Grandma's funeral, and was waiting for us in our backyard. Behind him, a couple of Grandma's candelabras sat on our picnic table. There were wineglasses and bunches of flowers from Grandma's funeral, too. It meant that when Dad and Perry's mom had their relapse back in 1945, he'd brought her flowers from his father's funeral, and now, as they were about to have their second relapse, his mother's funeral provided the floral arrangements.

When we went up onto the porch, I opened our back door fast so that Perry and I could go where we wouldn't have to watch their second relapse right before our eyes. We'd watch it, but from behind Grandma's curtains. That was a whole lot better than being there. If you don't believe me, just ask Romeo. Once he came out into the open, things went downhill fast.

As soon as I could drag our phone into the dining room, I called Precious, even though I didn't know the details of the baseball game yet.

"Richie?" she said.

Out the window, I could see Dad and Mrs. White sitting on opposite sides of a plate of little sandwiches, which we'd also brought from Grandma's funeral.

Precious said "Richie?" again but I just sat there, with both of us breathing on opposite ends of the telephone line. Do you know how that can be? I knew it, and I swore that Precious knew it, too. But she didn't, I guess, because she hung up without saying anything more. Perry'd found Grandma's afghan in our living room by then and was wearing it like a cape. He ran past me a couple of times as Superman, then sauntered by as Clark Kent. The real Clark Kent, George Reeves, killed himself last year, just after Perry and Precious and I finished eighth grade.

Outside, Dad and Perry's mom were drinking wine. I had the thought that "Loretta sucks hind tit!" might become a family joke, something we told one another over the years, but the thought went away when our phone rang. . . .

It was Precious, of course, wanting to know what happened. I let it ring three times, since that was the number of times that Grandma said was necessary for a person not to seem anxious.

But my anxiety showed anyway, I think, in the tone I used to say hello.

The Dangerous Gift of Beauty

[2001]

MARY FROM THE JAGUAR AGENCY sometimes thought of herself as Gloria Trillo, who sold Mercedes-Benzes on *The Sopranos* and became Tony's mistress for a while. She thought of herself that way because men bought Jaguars from her much more readily than they did from any of her male-counterpart salespeople, and because Annabella Sciorra, the actress who played Gloria Trillo, also starred in the movie *The Hand That Rocks the Cradle*, which was filmed at 808 North Yakima Avenue, a few blocks away from Mary's home, in Tacoma, Washington. During the filming of the movie, in fact, Mary had walked down to watch the goings-on, and once saw Annabella standing in the shade of an oak tree, thinking her actress thoughts.

Selling Jaguars in Tacoma at first had seemed oxymoronic to Mary, since Jags were expensive and Tacoma was a working-class town, but the agency's owner said he knew what sold luxury cars and that her look, which was sexy in the way of a trimmed-out librarian, was it. He said, "Let me worry about oxymorons," gave her the job, and the rest is local Jaguar-selling history.

Whenever Mary thought of Annabella Sciorra, she also

tended to think of Sister Wendy Beckett, the British art-critic nun who said, "God did not give me the dangerous gift of beauty" on TV. Mary, who'd been in bed with Earl, her lover, drinking wine and eating crackers when she heard it, reacted as if Sister Wendy Beckett were speaking directly to her. *She* had the gift of beauty, dangerous or not, and this semi-cloistered art critic was asking her what she was going to do about it. It was a turning point for Mary, who pointed at Sister Wendy Beckett's television image. "What if she *had* been beautiful?" she asked Earl. "How would it have changed her life, and how would the lack of beauty have changed mine? If I were Sister Wendy, would you be here in bed with me, Earl, drinking this wine?"

She knew she'd said it wrong but let it stand.

"What?" asked Earl, sopping up the wine she'd spilled. And then he said, quite fatally, "You know as well as I do that in *this* world, physical beauty dictates."

Earlier, he'd said he loved her like Galileo loved the nighttime sky, but this told her that he didn't so much love *her* as the shell she lived in. So she got out of bed, pulled on some jeans and a T-shirt, went outside to the "loaner" Jag she often drove, and cruised on over to 808 North Yakima, where she'd seen Annabella Sciorra that time. There were lights on in the house, but she parked at the curb anyway and walked up onto the lawn.

"Who is the me that I want Earl to see if the me he sees isn't me?" she asked the wraparound porch.

She hoped that Annabella might materialize and answer her, but even without it Mary knew that including Earl in her question was inessential to the power of it. Earl was just a placeholder.

There was a gap in the curtains covering the windows on the left side of the house, beyond a chestnut tree. She glanced back down at the loaner Jag, then stepped into the shadows by the window to peek through the gap in the curtains and think about her question. "Who is the me that I want Earl to see if the me he sees isn't me?" It was a serious moment, but she couldn't help noticing that the cadence of her question bore a strong similarity to "How much wood could a woodchuck chuck if a woodchuck could chuck wood?" And that, in turn, caused a lightness of heart to invade her that she hadn't felt since before the dangerous gift made her the target of men from one side of town to the other. "How much wood could a woodchuck chuck if a woodchuck could chuck wood?" Yes, it was identical to her Earl question.

Mary saw a man sitting reading in the room of the house visible through the gap in the curtains. He wore jeans and a T-shirt, too, with his bare feet crossed at the ankles and, like Mary and Earl at Earl's house, he had a glass of wine on a table beside his chair, with the nice addition of a few slices of cheese on a plate. He was a handsome man, easily her equal on the beauty scale.

Mary heard the faint sounds of singing coming from his stereo, and beyond him, through an archway at the far side of the room, she saw a hallway bathed in shadows and light, like in the Edward Hopper picture that hung behind her boss's desk at the Jaguar Agency. It was strange, but she got the idea that in the world in general her question—"Who is the me that I want Earl to see if the me he sees isn't me?"—was an integral part of life, while in the room where this man sat reading, it was not. Perhaps she got that idea because he had a reading lamp behind him—its cord stretched across the floor—making it look like he was out of himself. Other than the chair and the stool and reading lamp, the room was empty.

Mary's childhood home was two blocks over and one block up. She'd walked along Yakima Avenue countless times during the years she lived there. She'd even trick-or-treated at this house, climbing onto its porch while her mother stood down on the parking strip, just about where the loaner Jag was now. Her mother had had the dangerous gift, too, and had been bereft when it left her.

Inside the house, the man put down the wineglass that he'd apparently picked up when Mary wasn't looking. And now, with his book on his lap, he was staring at the window, slightly above her head. Though she'd been standing still, she froze. How humiliating to be caught like this, a Peeping Tom, a Peeping Mary, whose beauty screamed that it wasn't peeping but being peeped at that she was born for.

When he stood and came to the window, she had the thought that sexual intrusion—which, after all, was the bludgeon of a Peeping Tom—truly was a crime and that she should be ashamed of herself. What right did she have to intrude upon this man, who had not intruded on anyone, save, perhaps, those who lived in the book he was reading? But she held her ground, her eyes at the bottom of the obtuse triangle formed by the aging curtains. If he caught her, she'd make no excuse, like saying she had car trouble or needed directions.

Time passed, with Mary outside looking in and the man looking directly at his own reflection, maybe seeing new wrinkles in his face or perhaps simply pondering whatever had caught his attention in his book. So much time passed, in fact, that Mary's eyes began to water, until she finally did the unthinkable and rapped on the window with the bent middle knuckle of her left hand. She could see the man's thoughts ride back up into this ten o'clock Sunday evening.

"Hello?" he said, turning toward his front door.

"No, out here!" called Mary. "I'm in your side yard."

The man swung around again and pushed back the curtain.

"Oh," he said, "hi," as if thinking that someone had knocked on the front door had been silly of him.

"I was just passing by and remembered the *The Hand That Rocks the Cradle*," said Mary.

"I didn't live here then," he said. "Lived up in Seattle."

"Yes, well, that's where they pretended the movie took place. It was Tacoma, though; even Wright Park was in it. No one wants to give Tacoma credit for anything."

The window had a double pane, so their voices felt both distant and small, as if coming from people who had said those same words long ago, like maybe during the actual filming of *The Hand That Rocks the Cradle*. The male star of that movie, Matt McCoy, had been Annabella's husband in it, but Mary couldn't picture him. She closed her eyes to bring him closer but could only see the man who looked through the window at her now, who was handsomer than Matt McCoy was anyway.

"I know it's an odd request, but do you mind if I stay out here awhile?" she asked. "You know, sort of get my bearings?"

He looked back at his lamp and chair and stool, then once again at Mary. "This house is the Lourdes for fans of that movie," he said. "You're about the sixth person who's come around since I moved in. But knock yourself out."

He closed the curtains and went back to his reading before she could say that she wasn't a fan of the movie but had been sent by someone who was an absolute fan of Lourdes, Sister Wendy Beckett from TV.

Mary returned to the chestnut tree. The loaner Jag was on the street, the man was in his living room, and under the tree was a chair quite like the one she'd seen him sitting in inside, wicker and comfy-looking, with armrests and even a plastic sort of all-weather pillow. She hadn't noticed the chair when sneaking up to the house, but here it was, ready for indoor or outdoor use, a chair for all seasons, like Paul Scofield in the movie *he* was famous for. Sir Thomas More standing up to Henry VIII, and Sister Wendy Beckett explaining the meaning of art . . . Such connections were beautiful, with no element of danger in them at all.

Mary sat down in the chair, crossed her legs, and asked herself what her life meant. Down on the street, that loaner Jag meant something. It meant fine craftsmanship, precision engineering, but was *she* finely crafted, did *she* have precision engineering, past the skin-deep effect that had made her so much money? Twice she'd gone home with new Jaguar owners, giving them the prize they'd hinted that making such a purchase would necessitate.

Ten o'clock on Sunday night. Earl was surely beginning to worry. Maybe he'd called her cell, which, she realized when she felt her jeans, she had left in the Jag. Her own apartment in Old Town was closed and dark, rain was threatening, and the pleasure of the woodchuck comparison was dissipating fast. "Okay, Sister Wendy, what's it all about?" she asked. "My heart's so heavy sometimes."

She didn't expect Sister Wendy to answer, but a shadow came across her eyes when she looked at the rain clouds, giving her the sense that someone had heard her, plus the strength to ask a second question. "Why can't I just love and be loved in return?"

"That's the essential lyric in 'Nature Boy,' the Nat Cole hit from 1948," said the man from inside.

Her first thought was, Here we go again, and sure enough, he was carrying his chair, identical to the one she sat in, plus two big umbrellas. Did she have to get hit on every day of her life?

"I never got a living room set. I just keep taking one of these chairs inside and bringing it back out again," he said.

He put his chair beside hers, but not too close. When he gave her one of the umbrellas, she thanked him in her most guarded voice.

"Here's a coincidence," he said. "I was just reading about this time in 1956 when Nat King Cole got mugged on the streets of Birmingham, Alabama. No respect for his greatness among the racists."

"Don't kid a kidder, mister," said Mary. "You were reading no such thing."

"Don't kid a kidder" had been her mother's expression.

"I was," he said. "I've nearly finished his biography, and I was listening to his recordings when you knocked on my window, so maybe you asked yourself that question because you heard it in his song."

He sang a line from "Nature Boy," making her remember the ethereal tune. Could it be true? Could her most recent question not have come from Sister Wendy Beckett but from Nat King Cole?

"It's a good question, no matter who made me ask it," she said.

"I guess," said the man, who told her his name was Steve.

He opened his umbrella and leaned so far back in his chair that he looked like a laid-back lifeguard. He said, "Half of life is disappointment and missed opportunities."

In any other situation, such a comment would have seemed maudlin to her, but he said it cheerfully enough, and she was sitting under *his* tree, after all, as unexpected a place for her to be right then as Paris, France. He was right to bring the umbrellas, too, since a fine rain had started falling. She opened hers and sat back like he was. "How long have you lived here that you don't have a living room set yet?" she asked. "I saw that you put your Edward Hopper up, so you must have been here for a while."

She remembered as soon as she said it that the Hopper was in her boss's office at work. It showed a woman naked from the waist down, sitting on the floor by a bed.

"A year last week," he said. "Lost all my furniture in the divorce. That's my half a life of disappointment. Married twenty-four years and I'm forty-eight years old now."

Earl had a living room set, a dining room set, three bedroom sets, and a kitchen set, and there was a croquet set on his lawn. Even when he played croquet, his narcissism came out.

"Did you ever even see *The Hand that Rocks the Cradle?*" she asked.

"Got it on DVD. When I bought this place, the movie was part of the sales pitch. At closing they gave me a copy."

Mary's intention had been to sit here late into the night, waiting for an answer to her question, but now she sat back up. "You mean you've got the movie inside right now?"

They each carried a chair into the house, leaving the umbrellas on the porch. And sure enough, the book on the floor next to the plate of cheese was *Velvet Voice*, Nat King

Cole's biography. The man's TV was on a cheap metal cart, with the DVD player on its top. It, plus a guitar in an open case and a globe of the earth, Mary hadn't been able to see from the window. He also had plenty of DVDs. He looked back at her as he searched for *The Hand That Rocks the Cradle*, to say he had four loves: books, movies, music, and vino. She liked the way he said *vino*, though she would have thought it an affectation had Earl said it that way.

He found the DVD, put it in his machine, and walked over to hand her its case, which bore a photo of Rebecca De Mornay, torn down the middle to make her seem evil, plus another of Annabella Sciorra looking calm and healthy, a lover of ordinary life. Matt McCoy was there, too, but back a little, since his was a minor role. Mary wondered if the man she sat with now—if Steve had played a minor role in his marriage, and also whether he would like to play a fuller one in whatever life awaited him.

"Okay, ready to roll," he said, "This amarone is perfect for horror films. Would you like some?"

He pointed at the wine bottle on a tray, where two glasses sat, both of them recently washed.

"Do you really think it's a horror film?" she asked. "I always thought it was a thriller."

"Thriller—horror film—okay, here's the truth. They gave me the DVD when I bought the house, but I've never been able to watch the whole thing through."

That made her laugh. She wouldn't have watched it, either, sitting in the very house where all the violence had taken place. At least not alone. At least not without familiar furniture surrounding her. *The Hand That Rocks the Cradle* would be about the world's worst movie in such a situation, but it was a great first-date movie, would make a terrific story for a couple to tell their children later on. Her parents' first date, she remembered, had been going to see to see *Psycho* at the Roxy downtown.

When he asked her what was funny, she said, "I was just thinking of the improbability of things, that's all."

She meant the improbability of *everything*, of birth and death and all the mistakes in between, but when he smiled, it was clear he thought she meant the evening they were experiencing together, which, of course, was also pretty high on the improbability scale.

He'd turned on more lights when searching for the DVD, so now she got a better look at him. Yes, he was as handsome as a movie star from the old days, as handsome as Cary Grant, and, like Cary Grant, there was no duplicity in his face, no hidden agenda, only this befuddled aspect.

"Here we go," he said, pouring them both some vino.

The film's opening shot was of the outside of the house with its porch and large front yard. She saw the parking strip where her Jag sat now, and she saw the oak tree where she'd spied Annabella. She also saw the chestnut they had sat under, with their umbrellas open and the rain coming down.

Steve sat beside her just as the camera moved inside to the wide and inviting staircase near the front door. For the longest time, no one spoke in the movie; perhaps three full minutes passed while the camera ventured upstairs and down, outside and in, until finally people entered the frame, first Annabella, making breakfast for her family, then her husband and daughter in an upstairs bathroom, singing a song by Gilbert and Sullivan.

Mary decided that tomorrow in her apartment in Old

Town she would do her own spring cleaning, maybe even take her furniture outside so she could better get at the walls and floors. Maybe she'd put a sign up saying YARD SALE, then sit out there in one of her chairs. She'd have to call her boss, tell him she was taking the day off, and she would call Earl, too. He didn't deserve the treatment he got from her. He deserved a clear explanation.

A mentally handicapped man came sneaking around the side of the house in the movie, much like Mary had sneaked up on the window on this Sunday night. The man had been sent by a charity organization Annabella's husband contacted, to do repairs in preparation for the arrival of the baby Annabella was about to have. But his sudden appearance made Annabella scream and drop the glass of orange juice she was holding, shattering it all over the floor. The handicapped man wasn't dangerous—by the movie's end, he would be the family's savior—but Annabella's initial fear foreshadowed the danger that would soon arrive in the person of the undeniably beautiful Rebecca De Mornay.

Mary glanced at Steve, reluctant to buy new furniture, unable to watch this movie in the house in which it had been made, yet sitting here reading Nat King Cole's biography. And singing her the opening lines of "Nature Boy." Maybe when the movie ended, she would ask him to sing it again, or perhaps she would ask him to take that guitar from its case and play her something of his own invention, since she seemed to know that was what the guitar was for. Or maybe they would simply carry their chairs back outside and she would drive on home.

But whatever might happen later, now she wanted to concentrate on the movie, so she could see the beauty of this house and the street she had walked down as a child. She sipped her wine and nodded to show him her appreciation of it. It was a terrific wine, far better than the one she'd spilled in Earl's bed when Sister Wendy had let her know that it was time her real life got started, that there was no art at all in selling Jags.

Let's Meet Saturday and
Have a Picnic

[1999]

THIS IS A DIFFICULT STORY TO TELL after so many years, not only because my memory is fading but also because of all these interruptions. Nurses, they call them, but they're really only immigrants from who knows where—the Philippines, Nigeria, Vietnam . . . I asked one young woman when I first got here if she was Ethiopian, but she insisted I call it "Eritrea." She even wrote it on my napkin for me, using an *E* instead of the *A* that I thought it began with. I shouldn't be hard on her, though, since my name is spelt with a *K* not a *C*, and I've spent my life correcting people. It's Kurt, not Curt, and my last name is Larson. I'm eighty-nine years old and am living here at Tobey Jones, a nursing home for the semi-well-heeled near Point Defiance Park in Tacoma, Washington.

The Eritrean woman's name is Ruth, so I guess she grew up Christian. She calls me "Mr. Kurt," and not long after she wrote her country's name on my napkin, I became her favorite resident. She comes into my room quite often now to hold my hand and talk. I haven't been able to figure it out. Either she's a saint or she's practicing her English, but either way she asks me interesting questions, which is more than I can say for family members, like my son, Lars, or his son Lars Junior. They come, stay for twenty minutes, surrounding me not with the faces and voices of my loved ones but with nodding flowers, fragrant as the smell of death. Eighty-nine years old. A woman two doors down is also eighty-nine, and insists on calling us both eighty-nine years *young*.

It's 1:00 A.M. and Ruth is working the night shift out of homicide with her partner, Frank Smith. Ha ha. No, that's the beginning of *Dragnet*, a great TV show from the 1950s. It *is* 1:00 A.M., though, and Ruth *is* working nights, which she likes because it's quiet and she can come in for longer stretches to sit and call me "Mr. Kurt." Ruth's beautiful, I should say, with a narrow face and long cheeks and breasts I would have died for until I was eighty-two. Now I have only the memory of dying for them.

"Mr. Kurt," Ruth whispers. "Are you awake?"

I'm sitting up in bed with my lamp on, reading *War and Peace,* but I answer her nicely. "Why yes, Ruth, I am. Come on in, dear, have a seat."

"Mrs. Truman's on the prowl again. Want me to close your door?"

Mrs. Truman is the other eighty-nine-year-old. She sometimes mistakes me for her husband.

When I nod, Ruth latches the door, then opens a stepladder that leans against my window, locks its legs, and sits beside me on it. The stepladder was in my kitchen until Lars, my grandson, brought it here so he could put up fancy curtains. Ruth's posture is perfect on the stepladder. "I'm not intruding?" she asks, one finger pointing at *War and Peace.*

I'm more than halfway through the book, at the Napoleonic

Wars part, and I've been thinking of those who died before me, legions upon legions of them, most around Ruth's age.

"It can wait," I tell her. "You look tired, Ruth."

She's brought her lunch and is trying to open it quietly. It's a homemade something or other from Eritrea, and she tears off a piece and hands it to me. I've always liked foreign food, even before the current ethnic restaurant craze, but Ruth's lunch tastes like a spongy bandage with hot sauce on it.

"I'm not tired," she says. "I bet I get more sleep than you do, Mr. Kurt."

She has a bottle of water with her and cracks its seal. The curtains Lars Junior put up are hanging from the window behind her. Ruth was in my room recently when he came over. Lars Junior is a fool with women, has messed his life up with a lot of them, yet he can't see the beauty in Ruth. He has taken over my business, an automobile agency, while his father, my son, spent his life delivering milk.

"After the war, I fell in love with a Korean woman even younger than you are now, Ruth," I say. "Would you like to hear that story, or would you rather have me finish the one about my septic tank?"

I'd started my septic tank story in the dining hall, an inappropriate place for it, I guess. Mrs. Truman was at my table and spit some mashed potatoes onto the front of Ruth's uniform. "The love story, Mr. Kurt," she says, "If it's good, when I fall in love, I will remember you and tell it to my husband."

I like that. I'll be dead, but my name will be uttered in kind remembrance at Ruth's house. One mention of it there, it seems to me now, is better than having it live on forever on the sign above my automobile agency.

"It was 1954," I tell her, "so how old was I then, Ruth, forty-four?"

"You're a maths wizard, Mr. Kurt, a man who can add up taxes in his head. You know better than me how old you were."

"Okay, I was forty-four then, yes, and so unhappy that I rejoined the army after my divorce. I was one of those men who fought in World War II *and* Korea, and was stationed there after it, helping with the mop-up."

Ruth laughs at *mop-up,* saying, "Korea was your Mrs. Truman, Mr. Kurt."

"Actually, Korea was barren and burned by the Japanese and people lived in hovels and there were war orphans everywhere, Ruth . . . 1954, my God."

"Eritreans and Somalis lived in hovels in Nairobi," says Ruth, "stealing and scheming and holding their hands out for alms."

That made me look at her. "But you weren't one of them, right?" I say. "You got a job in a modeling agency."

I was after facetiousness, but Ruth heard sincerity. "I believe what most Americans believe," she says. "We must pull ourselves up by our own feet."

"In 1954, a lot of Koreans believed that, too. If there were jobs at a U.S. base, people stood in line to apply for them."

"I was like the ugly stepsister beside those models," says Ruth. "Yet here I am with a real good job, while they are still dreaming of pipes."

She tears off another bit of sponge bread and gives it to me. "Will you let me tell this story, Ruth?" I ask. "Let's save Nairobi for tomorrow night.'"

Ruth looks down. "Okay, Mr. Kurt. It was 1954 and the people needed dignity and work."

"Yes, they did; that's a good way to put it. But some of the women, like the models in your agency, played the only cards dealt them—by that, I mean their physical beauty—and worked serving drinks to men. Outside the gates of the military bases, there were actual prostitutes, but my friends and I were far more interested in going into town and finding what they called *gisaeng,* like the *geisha* in Japan. Have you ever heard of them?"

"Singing and dancing!" says Ruth. "With them, prostitution was out!"

"Singing and dancing and flirting and touching. All the high arts, Ruth. And we were lucky enough to find a place called the Pusan House sitting on the edge of a river, and expensive . . . oh my gosh . . . if we'd tried to go there at night, we'd have had to pay a month's salary. So we went on weekend afternoons, and the owner took pity on us."

Ruth's eyes are as dark as coal and as bright as the fire coal brings to us. When any kind of entrepreneurship is at issue, she's charged up.

"No one else was there in the afternoon and we couldn't speak Korean, but the same three *gisaeng* always came to sit with us, feeding us tomatoes and strawberries and working out a rudimentary method of communication, English phrases and Korean phrases and pointing out body parts. It was always the same three young women, Ruth: one for me, one for my friend Paul, and one for Paul's friend Felix. They pretended to love us, but for me, at least, the love I felt was real. I was just plain gaga over Chung-ja, Ruth, the one who sat with me."

"Felix was Paul's friend but not yours? Only three men and already there is a distance."

"Felix isn't the issue here. His story left with him when his tour was up."

"Felix is gone, but his name remains in your story, like yours will at my house."

That moves me greatly. "Oh, Ruth, do you think love can be defeated as easily by a difference in age as by distance? Do you think the love of one's life might be born fourteen years after him?"

Actually, Ruth was born some fifty years after me, but that seems too great a number to state. She's as moved as I am, though. She knows what she knows and bears that knowledge with composure.

"Love can't be defeated by anything, Mr. Kurt," she says. "Who do you love in that book you are reading? Think how much older she is than yourself."

The moon shines through a gap in the curtains Lars hung, laying a small moon highway across my bed. In *War and Peace* I love Natasha, of course. People have been loving Natasha since before I was born, and now I'm closing in on death and love her, too.

"One day, after Paul and Felix and I had been going to the Pusan House for a while, we decided to invite our three *gisaeng* up into the mountains, and through a series of gestures and looks we gained their acceptance of our invitation, forming a sort of conspiracy with them. We, after all, were Americans, and, like on the moon highway there on my bed, we might drive them out of the misery of postwar Korea."

Ruth makes legs out of two of her fingers, leans forward on the stepladder, and stands them on the moon highway. I make legs out of my fingers, too, but they remained upside down in my lap.

"In order to be sure they understood us correctly we spent hours teaching them to say 'Let's meet Saturday and have a picnic' in English. We made them repeat it and repeat it, with my girl, Chung-ja, easily surpassing the others in clear pronunciation. She was the prettiest, too, I haven't said that yet, and though you can't see it now, I was better-looking than either Paul or Felix.

"Let's meet Saturday and have a picnic," says the woman standing on the moon highway on my bed. The moon has shifted, moving the entire highway, and Ruth's finger woman, too, close enough for me to right my finger man and walk him up to where he can better see his beloved waiting for him.

"All the following week, I was of two minds. One—I'm not afraid to say this to you, Ruth—was that it would be fun, booze and sex in the burned-down mountains for a man from Tacoma, Washington. But two, the other mind, told me that I would take Chung-ja to the U.S. embassy in Seoul and make her my wife."

"Only the single-minded save themselves," says Ruth.

Her highway woman turns away, so I make my finger man step toward her. The act of leaning forward in the bed is hard on my back, which is broken and sore and the reason I had to come here in the first place. Seeing me in pain moves Ruth to bring her finger woman off the safety of the moon highway and across my blankets, until she's standing near my finger man, looking at him steadily in the dark.

"Finally the day of reckoning came. Paul and I went shopping for beer and soda, the freshest bread, and fruit—oh my, we had such mounds of fruit that it would hardly fit in our backpacks. Felix, meanwhile, brought a bottle of scotch and a couple of packages of condoms. We went to our appointed meeting place at our appointed time."

"But the girls didn't come," Ruth says.

"How did you know? Can you feel the disappointment that I felt that day?"

"No," says Ruth, "I simply remember such things from the modeling agency."

IN *War and Peace,* most of those with steadfast hearts are rewarded for their goodness. There is time for that in novels, with the characters forever on the cusp of things, while I, Kurt Larson, have no cusps left, except at the nubs of my worn-out teeth.

Ruth takes three days off, leaving me alone with my thoughts. Lars and Lars Junior come to see me, talking their talk and looking at their watches. Lars Junior visits twice as often as his father, but it is his father whom I want. His mother turned him against me somehow and I was never able to win him back.

On the night Ruth returns, the two Larses arrive with her at 7:00 P.M. Dinner is over and I am sitting with Mrs. Truman in the TV room, not expecting them, not even expecting Ruth till midnight. I have just told Mrs. Truman the septic tank story again, hoping she might spit up on another woman's birthday cake, when they walk in, a Lars on either side of Ruth, who looks refreshed after her three days away from Tobey Jones.

"Hi, Dad!" says my son. "Look who we found in the hallway!"

Lars Senior is emphatic. Though deafness surrounds me, and I, too, tend to shout at my coevals, my own hearing and eyesight are less impaired than those of either of the Larses. I may have the look of a broken-down mule, but I can hear and see and smell death coming. Not like poor Mrs. Truman, who smiles now, thinking that Ruth and the Larses have come to see her.

"Hello, Ruth," I say. "Hello, Lars and Lars Junior."

Ruth hasn't put on her uniform yet, is wearing Eritrean dress, some kind of wrap, gold or dark yellow, with a leafy blue pattern on it. She looks fabulous, like in a poster for Eritrean Airlines. "Hello, Mr. Kurt," she says. "And how are you this evening, Mrs. Truman?"

Mrs. Truman says, "One morning a wide brown lake appeared in our front yard."

That is the beginning of my septic tank story. Lars Senior looks at her and then at his watch. He once admitted in a fit of rage that he became a milkman to hurt me, since I had spent a lot of money sending him to college and graduate school, where he did all the work but his dissertation for his Ph.D. in geography. I don't know how he came up with milkman as a way of hurting me, but it worked.

"Mr. Kurt—" Ruth says, but Lars Junior interrupts her.

"Grandpa, Ruth and I have something to tell you. We've been seeing each other, and tonight's Ruth's last night here at Tobey Jones. She's coming to work for me at Lars Larson Motors."

Lars was my father's name, so I named both my company

and my only son after him. "Seeing each other?" I ask. "Does this have anything to do with my stepladder?"

Ruth smiles. When Lars put my curtains up, she'd steadied the ladder for him, though it had only three steps and didn't need steadying. I thought at the time that Lars was a dunderhead for not noticing her, but I guess I was wrong.

"Well, criminy, Ruth," I say, "what did Lars say you'd be doing at the company?"

I feel choked up but hide it well.

"Accountancy," says Ruth. "That is what I did at the modeling agency."

"Accountancy," Lars Junior repeats, like he's never heard anything so cute in his life.

Lars Senior is looking at his watch again and sees me catch him at it. Lars retired from delivering milk a few years ago and is finding it difficult to know what to do with himself. "I know, Dad," he says. "Time is supposed to heal all wounds, but it hasn't done it with us, right?"

Maybe seeing his son fall in love again broke something loose in him, because this is the first time since he became a milkman that Lars has confronted the issues between us, and I'm as stunned at that as I am by the coming loss of Ruth. It's the age-old nursing home dilemma, how to love the life you lived and not the one that escaped you.

"What did you do, Ruth, give Tobey Jones a one-day notice?" I ask. "I thought two weeks was customary. And yes, Lars, time went on holiday with us, but it's not too late for us to catch it."

Lars Junior is standing close to Ruth now, as if making his announcement gives him the right of encroachment.

"I did give them two weeks' notice," says Ruth. "It's you

whose notice is shorter, Mr. Kurt. I thought that two weeks of thinking about this might not be so good for you."

"One day *is* better," Lars Senior says. "In our case, what good did forty years' notice do, Dad?"

Was Lars a milkman for forty years?

"It didn't do any good," I admit. "But to work for a man you're involved with, I don't know about that, Ruth."

My eyes so unexpectedly fill with tears that I look at Mrs. Truman, as if she is responsible for them. Mr. Truman lived at Tobey Jones, too, but died two weeks before my arrival, thus giving Mrs. Truman two weeks' notice on the transfer of her affections to me.

"I would like to come to your room tonight," says Ruth. "I would very much like to hear the end of our story."

She says it like I might not want her to come to my room, and when I nod in a jerky kind of way, tears land on my gnarled hands.

"Okay, then," says Lars Junior "I'll take off till your shift is over, hon . . ."

He's talking to Ruth, of course, his tone open and cheerful, ready for whatever a life together might bring.

"This is going to surprise you again, Dad," says Lars Senior, "but if you don't mind, I'll hang back a bit, stay a little longer just for tonight."

Mrs. Truman looks up and says, "Of course you can stay, Harry. You know as well as I do that you should never have gone away in the first place."

AT MIDNIGHT, I'M ALONE IN MY ROOM with another book in my lap, this time *Middlemarch*, open to a section where Miss Brooke's strength of character is in evidence. *Middlemarch* and *War and Peace* have been my touchstones since I came to Tobey Jones.

Mrs. Truman is in the hallway in her wheelchair, staring through my open door. On the lenses of her glasses I believe I can see a projection of the images that penetrate her thoughts. She is watching Mr. Truman, ill with one of his many diseases. Twice now, Ruth has walked past. Before she comes to visit me, she'll roll Mrs. Truman into her room and put her to bed, removing her glasses and the images pulsing across them. Lars's glasses were bright with memory, too, earlier, when he lingered in the TV room.

"May I come in?" Mrs. Truman calls from the hallway.

"No, Mrs. T., you may not. I'm Kurt Larson. Your husband, Harry, is dead."

Actually, her husband's name wasn't Harry, but that's the name she has given him now.

Earlier, in the TV room, Lars waited until Ruth rolled Mrs. Truman out of earshot before he said what he'd stayed to say, which was, "I know a lot of time has passed, Dad, but I want to get involved with Lars Larson Motors. My name is over its door and . . . well, it's my goddamn legacy."

"Why not ask your son?" I told him. "He's the company president."

Maybe that was churlish of me, or—what do they call it now?—passive-aggressive, but this issue of Lars's joining Lars Larson Motors was what caused our falling-out in the first place. It was 1967 when I made him an offer to join our sales force and work his way up. I knew he might refuse, but you'd have thought selling Jaguars was a crime against humanity, that we packed every new model with Agent Orange, by the way he articulated his refusal.

"I did ask him and he told me I'd be welcome," said Lars.

Out the windows of the Tobey Jones TV room, I could see the trees of Point Defiance Park, where generations of Tacomans have gone to swim in Puget Sound, look at zoo animals, or stop at some secluded spot along the Five Mile Drive to wax their cars. I hadn't remembered it until that second, but we'd been there ourselves, my son and I, in the shade of some pines, when I asked him to join our sales force. The shade and the trees are still there, of course, while I am nearing the end of my life and, a few years into milk-man retirement, Lars is at the end of his rope.

"Then what's the problem?" I asked. "You wanted to start in accountancy?"

Mrs. Truman hasn't gone away and Ruth hasn't come to get her. I don't think Ruth will learn to love my grandson, though she might believe it now. What she *will* learn to do is add up sales taxes in her head.

"Okay, Mrs. Truman. You can come in," I call, "but you have to leave again when Ruth gets here."

The planes of her glasses come up. It's like watching the movement of the Hubble Space Telescope.

"Okay, no more flippancy," I told Lars in the TV room, when he didn't respond to my accountancy dig. "What do you want to do at the company, and why start now? Did you tell Lars Junior you had anything particular in mind?"

Lars was looking out at Point Defiance Park, too, possibly remembering the same day I did.

"Don't laugh, Dad, but I'd like to take over the advertising, put myself on TV, see if I can't increase our revenues. I'm a natural at stuff like that."

It has taken Mrs. Truman time to find her hands in her lap and move them to the handles of her wheelchair. Also, she's forgotten to put her feet on the footrests and they've turned in, pigeon-toed in multicolored socks, like the feet of that witch in *The Wizard of Oz*.

"Didn't you used to scoff at those ads?" I asked Lars. "Didn't you like to say they played to our lowest common denominator? Something like that?"

"That's because they were never well done. I have a really classy idea in mind, Dad. We're selling Jaguars, after all, not goddamn Kias."

"Jaguars and Volkswagens," I reminded him. "'Master Craftsmanship for Any Pocketbook' has been our slogan since I started the company."

"Yes, and for forty years I've had to read it on the license plate holders on half the cars I came up behind in my milk truck. How do you think that made me feel, Dad? My father and my son are out making money, while I'm stuck watching cartons of milk and cottage cheese come forward on my conveyor belt."

"Do people still order cottage cheese?" I asked. "And television ad campaigns are expensive, Lars. For Volkswagens, it might make sense, but we get by on our name alone when it comes to Jags."

"The operative part of that sentence of yours is 'get by,'" Lars said.

"You look bad, Harry," says Mrs. Truman now. "I wish you'd let me take the burden from your shoulders like I did in the old days."

She has finally worked her way to the side of my bed.

"Don't forget now, Mrs. T., as soon as Ruth gets here, you're on your way."

I want Ruth to take the burden from my shoulders, not Mrs. Truman, which goes to show that I haven't learned any more about life than Lars Senior has, though I'm my son's senior by a couple of decades.

Lars's ad campaign idea, as he told it to me in the TV room, consisted entirely of himself in various sets of clothing, first old hippie garb, then his milkman uniform, then in a series of progressively more expensive suits, from the leisure suits of the seventies to suits made of cotton and wool and cashmere, which the dealership would apparently buy. He said that as a hippie he'd step out of an old VW bus, as a milkman out of a Beetle, hurrying off to deliver an emergency milk order. In the leisure suit, he'd hold a tiny milk bottle to his lips, so the viewers would know it's him, and so on and so forth as he worked his way up to cashmere and our most expensive cars. He wants to call the whole campaign, "We Will Sell No Car Before Its Time."

Lars stayed in the TV room with me for an hour. He said that "We Will Sell No Car Before Its Time" was a better slogan than "Master Craftsmanship for Any Pocketbook," because no one used a word like *pocketbook* anymore.

"What is the question you asked about love last night?" Mrs. Truman asks. "Can love do what, Harry? What did you say about it?"

As she comes closer to my bed, she pulls her feet up so they're suspended in midair, like two socks hanging from a clothesline. "You asked if love could penetrate the generations," she says. "Only you didn't put it that way. . . ."

"Can love be defeated as easily by a difference in age as by distance," I say, but softly, since Ruth is in the doorway now and she's the one I said it to before, not Mrs. T.

"Yes," says Mrs. Truman. "That was it precisely."

Ruth has come to apologize for keeping her Lars Junior secret from me. She has come to tell me that fifty years is too much difference, that though she feels a kinship with me, it would never work, that yes, love can be defeated by age.

I try to remember where Mrs. Truman was when I posed my question to Ruth, but I can only remember her looking high and low for Harry.

"Shall I take you back to your room now, Mrs. T.?" asks Ruth. She uses her nursing home voice, the one she never uses with me.

"No!" says Mrs. Truman, gripping her wheelchair, like she's forgotten our deal.

"She might as well hear the end of my story," I tell Ruth. "After all, when you are gone, who will be left for me to talk to but Mrs. Truman?"

"Oh, Mr. Kurt!" says Ruth.

There is real pain in her voice, like all this means something to her. "Do you love Lars Junior?" I ask.

"Of course she doesn't love him," says Mrs. Truman. "Love's great enemy is ambition, and she's ambitious, Harry. I know because I was ambitious, too."

Once Mrs. Truman brought a photo album to the TV room and sat showing me pictures from her youth. She hadn't been pretty, but there'd been a likable quality about her, a look that ran across her nose and eyes. A boy had been in some of the photos with her, standing behind her and giving her looks of love. That boy's name truly had been Harry.

"Love grows like kudzu," says Ruth. "Love can be learned."

Ruth lived in Mississippi before moving to Tacoma, and she often mentions kudzu as a metaphor for life's difficulties.

"Love does grow," Mrs. Truman admits. "But only about an inch a year."

Ruth is wearing her uniform now, but she hasn't removed her Eritrean sandals. Tobey Jones buys its employees' uniforms, like Lars Larson Motors will presumably buy Lars Senior's series of suits, if we allow him to do the ad campaign.

"Accountancy is my love," says Ruth, but I can see now that she's only following moves as if upon a chessboard, and I wonder if she's really better off than the models who followed their dreams in Nairobi. It's a question I would have asked her if she'd given me the two weeks' notice I deserved.

"It broke my heart when Chung-ja didn't show up for our date that day," I tell both Ruth and Mrs. Truman. "Paul and Felix didn't like it, either, but they soon wandered off to look for other women, while I just sat there brokenhearted."

Ruth finds the stepladder and places it about halfway between my bed and the door. I get the feeling that when she leaves, she'll take it with her. "What happened next?" she asks. "Did you go back to her bar?"

"Yes, but the owner wasn't friendly. She said that Chung-ja had quit. And two months later, I got my second set of discharge papers."

"Harry was killed in 1944," says Mrs. Truman. "His parents got a Silver Star and a Purple Heart, brought to their door by a couple of men in uniform."

I can see Harry clearly in her photo album, thin, with short hair, already balding slightly. I wonder what will happen to the album when Mrs. Truman dies. Will that be the end of Harry, or will someone in her family pick it up, telling his story to the next generation?

"So that's it?" asks Ruth, shifting her weight. "That's the end of your story?"

"Almost, but not quite. Four years later, in 1958, I went to Japan to try to form a partnership with Mitsubishi. Lars Larson Motors was just getting started and I thought the Japanese would one day make great cars."

It was true, I had thought that, but though I wait for Ruth or even Mrs. Truman to acknowledge such prescience, neither of them says anything. Ruth's own prescience weighs on her, while Mrs. Truman is back in her photo album.

"I failed; I couldn't form the partnership. But one weekend I flew over to Korea to have a look around. The Japanese get more credit for it, but Koreans are hardworking, too, and were busy rebuilding their country after the horrible war they'd suffered through."

"Koreans are tough," says Ruth. "I've had two of them here as supervisors."

She seems distant now, as if she already has one sandaled foot out the door, so I focus on Mrs. Truman, who, when she feels me looking at her, glances up, her glasses no longer reflective but simply showing her magnified eyes.

"I stayed in Seoul for a couple of days, then took the train to the town I used to live in, and who should I meet as I was coming out of the station but my old friend Paul, who had remained in Korea for a couple more tours of duty."

"Oh, Paul, so good to see you!" Mrs. Truman says. "How have you been, Paul?"

Maybe it's the scorched terrain of her brain that gives her

this unnatural empathy, or maybe she has had it her whole life long.

Ruth brings the stepladder over so she can sit by Mrs. Truman. Even on her last night she'll be diligent, following Tobey Jones protocol. By that, I mean if Mrs. Truman gets too excited, she'll take her back to her room.

"Yes, Mrs. Truman, it was Paul, all right, and he looked the same as he did the last time I saw him."

"Did you tell him that?" she asks. "One thing I've learned in life, if you think someone looks good, you ought to tell them. Life is just plain short of compliments."

"I did, and I took him up on it, too, when he offered to buy me a drink for old time's sake. Paul was an afficionado when it came to Korea, loving both its high and low life, and that night he was drawn to a low-class bar not two minutes' walk from where I met him."

"Some men are drawn to bruises, others to beauty marks," Mrs. Truman says.

Ruth puts a hand on the back of her wheelchair. I'm surprised to see that there are tears in her eyes.

"As we walked along, it was like going back in time," I say. "All the work the Koreans had done to rebuild their country was out along the main roads, but the back streets were still war-torn. We saw bombed-out buildings and orphans sitting on piles of rubble. Disease and poverty were everywhere, but Paul put his arm around me and, I swear, started singing 'Who's Sorry Now?' at the top of his voice."

At first, I think it's Mrs. Truman who sings along with Paul, but it's Ruth. Her voice is good, like an Eritrean Connie Francis.

"Paul took me into this horrible place called Saxophone

Heaven, where laborers and street kids sat listening to a band made up entirely of saxophone players standing in the middle of the floor below one of those twisting ballroom balls, with hundreds of little mirrors, so that light was cast around the room. The floor was wet and women danced in the light from the mirrored ball, turning in circles with their arms up, as if holding dance partners. They wore placards with numbers on them, so if you wanted one of them, all you had to do was call out her number and she'd be yours."

"That is not the world depicted inside either of your books," says Ruth. She picks up *Middlemarch*, opens it, and reads from the beginning, "Miss Brooke had that kind of beauty which seems to be thrown into relief by poor dress."

"I had the kind of beauty that couldn't be thrown into relief by anything," Mrs. Truman tells us.

"Paul and I took a table at the side of the room. Paul had learned Korean well by then and ordered beer and told our waiter that we didn't want any of the floating women, that we weren't in the market for sex slaves."

"He said 'sex slaves'?" asks Ruth. "Just like that?"

"That's what he told me he said. The waiter looked tough, like he'd just as soon kick our asses as take drink orders, but when he heard Paul's Korean, he drew a line in front of our table with the toe of his shoe, making a bunch of hopeless women turn and dance away. Clearly, he was saying he would beat them if they came back."

"That was unkind," says Ruth. "The models in my modeling agency—" but Mrs. Truman interrupts her.

"What did the saxophone players like to play?" she asks. "I was always partial to 'Deep Purple,' by Earl Bostic. Did they happen to play that?"

"Actually, they played only three tunes: 'Too Young,' by Nat King Cole, 'You Send Me,' by Sam Cooke, and, of all things, 'Old Black Joe.' And no matter which of the songs they played, the dancing women sang along. It was when the band was playing 'Too Young,' in fact, that one woman danced across the imaginary line on the floor and sat down next to Paul, staring across the table at me like I had just caused her great insult."

Mrs. Truman tries to sing 'Too Young' until Ruth puts an arm around her, tears making inroads down her face.

"At first, I thought she wanted to hurt me and I was about to call that waiter, but Paul's face crumbled when he saw her. *Paul's face crumbled, not mine!* Until, that is, she leaned across the table, touched my arm, and said, 'Let's meet Saturday and have a picnic,' in perfect English."

"Chung-ja!" Ruth cries. "It was Chung-ja trapped inside that woman!"

"She had a placard around her neck with 'fourteen,' written on it," I tell Ruth. "And, of course, I was fourteen years older than she was."

"Your grandson is fourteen years older than me, too, Mr. Kurt," says Ruth. "Are you telling me this story to give me some sort of message?"

Actually, I'd begun my story before I knew about Ruth and Lars Junior, but are they really only fourteen years apart? Harry and Mrs. Truman, I knew from her photo album, had been about the same age.

"Poor Chung-ja," says Ruth. "She fared worse than most of those Nairobi models. What did you do when you discovered who she was?"

"That waiter came over to throw her out, but Paul said we

were friends from the days when the ravages of life did not yet have us by the balls."

"Paul was a poet," says Mrs. Truman. "A better man than you thought he was."

She forgets she can't walk and puts her stocking feet on the floor and pushes against the wheelchair and stands and turns in little circles with her arms up. Ruth stands, too, but when she tries to get Mrs. Truman to sit back down, Mrs. Truman lashes out, scratching Ruth's cheek along the tracks of her tears. That makes Ruth call Al, a Tobey Jones orderly who was just then passing by. Mrs. Truman likes Al, so she sits when he tells her to and lets him roll her back into the hallway. Ruth has to follow them, since Al isn't allowed to be alone with Mrs. Truman at bedtime.

I expect Ruth to come back soon, so while I am waiting I pick up *Middlemarch* and open it, to a spot held by one of our Lars Larson Motors bookmarks, *Master Craftsmanship for Any Pocketbook*. It's a much better slogan than "We Will Sell No Car Before Its Time."

In *Middlemarch,* things have grown complicated and Miss Brooke is being asked in various ways to forget what the Brooke name stands for. She won't do it, of course, she never does, no matter how many times I read *Middlemarch.*

In a while, I put my book aside and fall into the lightest of slumbers and remember as if it were a dream what happened after we left Saxophone Heaven that night. It was 11:30 and raining and I didn't have a place to stay and Paul was in high spirits, talking in Korean to Chung-ja. Eleven-thirty and raining, with the midnight curfew coming fast. I needed to find a room and Paul had to get a taxi back to the base and Chung-ja seemed to think we would have our picnic that very night, that, though four years had passed, our love had merely been unplugged, and we could plug it back in. When we came to a spot where taxis were waiting, Paul said something in Korean to Chung-ja, and then said to me, "If you run out of ways to communicate with her, Kurt, just sing one of those three songs and point."

"Too Young," "You Send Me," and "Old Black Joe."

Maybe Paul said the same thing to Chung-ja, for as soon as he left she took my hand and very clearly asked, "Why do I weep when my heart should feel no pain? Why do I sigh that my friends come not again?"

Those are the initial two lines of the second verse of "Old Black Joe," the little-known heart of everyone's story.

As we looked for an inn, the rain increased. We didn't have umbrellas, and the first four inns we came to didn't have vacancies. Oddly, however, by the time we got to the fifth inn, the accelerated years of Chung-ja's difficult life had begun to fall away. I knew then that our first instincts had been correct, that we could have been good for each other, we could have had a decent life, that she could have provided the help I needed at Lars Larson Motors, most particularly, even back then, in accountancy.

When I awake in the morning, a storm is beating against my Tobey Jones window, and Mrs. Truman is in the hallway in her wheelchair. "Wake up, Maggie," she says. That tells me she's been alone in her room for hours, with no Ruth and no Al, with no Harry and no Mr. Truman, and with nothing to do but listen to the oldies station on her radio.

Eighty-nine years old we are, while Chung-ja would be seventy-five—still fourteen years younger than both of us.

Anyone Can Master Grief
but He Who Has It

[1979]

RALPH, THE ENGLISH TEACHER, lunched every Sunday at Knapp's restaurant up on Proctor Street in Tacoma, Washington, and one particular Sunday, as he was sitting beside the ruins of his meal, a woman approached him. "Aren't you Ralph, the English teacher," she asked, "from the English department at the University of Puget Sound?"

Since he *was* Ralph, the English teacher, or had been before his retirement, he could do little but admit it. He'd never actively disliked the word *professor,* but back in the sixties it had been fashionable for students to call their professors by their first names, and he had gotten used to it.

The woman said she'd taken a class with him, and had also seen him out and about, occasionally, for a night on the town. She told him she was at the restaurant celebrating her mother's seventieth birthday. Her mother stood nearby, and when the woman pointed at her and she came forward, Ralph stood out of his booth.

"We're the Kants," said the woman. "I'm Immy and Mom

is Eva. I'm sure you remember my late father, the ornithologist Herbert Kant? He taught at UPS, too."

"My gosh, Immy," said Ralph. "I remember you well. Sorry I didn't recognize you. You took world lit from me."

"Shakespeare," said Immy.

"I was an English teacher, too," said her mother, "though my highest level was ninth grade. And we had you out to dinner once, before Herb's illness."

"I'm about to have pie," Ralph said. "Come, both of you, join me. . . ."

He remembered Herb Kant as if it were yesterday, for Herb had broken his heart.

A waitress came by with pie menus. Blackberry for Ralph, apple for Immy and Eva. Two pieces of pie but three forks.

WHEN EVA KANT CALLED A FEW DAYS LATER to invite him out to their house, Ralph grew troubled. Retirement was retirement, and he wanted to spend it with his thoughts and his poetry. But he hadn't thought quickly enough to turn the invitation down, so half a week later he dressed in his good linen jacket, with a poem he'd written for the occasion folded in its inner pocket. And he also decided to take his dog, Jip, as a hedge against too much intimacy. Jip was good at that.

The Kants lived on the beach at Brown's Point. On his way out, Ralph stopped to buy a bottle of wine. To arrive with nothing save the poem in his pocket seemed rude, even for a reluctant guest. But the stop made him late and he had to stop again to consult a map—how could he not remember where Herb had lived?—which made him even later and therefore somewhat flustered when he pulled up behind the house. When Jip understood that they were near water, he pressed his nose against the window, and when Eva Kant came outside, she said, "What a good idea, you've brought your dog," though her face belied her enthusiasm. "Well, come in," she said. "Herb is out on the deck."

"Herb?" said Ralph, while Jip danced up on his toes.

"Oh, don't worry, it's only his likeness, a gift from his best student ever, shipped to us a few years after Herb's death."

Herb's best student ever had been Ralph's undoing, but he managed a simple nod. "Do you mind if I walk Jip first?" he asked. "He'll go nuts if he doesn't get to explore the beach."

"Take that side trail and come up to the deck when you're done," said Eva. "Immy's out there, too."

When Ralph found Jip's leash, Jip sat down nicely—it was the only bit of training Ralph had managed to impart—but once the leash was fastened, he tugged Ralph toward the trail, forcing him to lean back radically to give Eva Kant the bottle of wine. She took the handoff nicely, as if it were a relay race baton, then walked back into her house.

FOUR GLASSES OF WINE—not from Ralph's bottle—stood on a tray on the deck, not far from where a life-size and perfect likeness of Herbert Kant sat in a wheelchair with his legs crossed, when Ralph and Jip came up the outside stairs some ten minutes later. Herb's face had the same preoccupied look and lopsided grin that Ralph remembered. He wore a long-sleeved blue shirt, beige chinos, argyle socks, and shiny brown penny loafers. His hair was slightly mussed, as if the wind had caught it, his elbows rested on the arms of the wheelchair, and his fingers were laced in his lap. He also leaned forward, as Herb had been wont to do when pretending to listen to someone make some point.

Immy wasn't on the deck when Ralph and Jip got there, but she joined them soon with appetizers. The floor of the deck had a thick glass window in it, put there years ago so Herb could watch the water sloshing around beneath him.

"High tide was Dad's favorite time of day," Immy said.

She gave Ralph a glass of wine, handed one to her mother when she came out to join them, and took one herself. Jip turned in circles, trying to find a place to lie down.

"You know, Goethe's Faust also traveled with a dog," said Eva. "People believed his dog turned into a servant, so it's really not so strange that we pour a glass for Herb when we're out here drinking in the evening. You don't find that strange, do you, Ralph?"

Ralph said he didn't find it strange, never mind her non sequitur. He had the impression that she would also say that it wasn't strange to have her dead husband out on her deck in a wheelchair, but Immy spoke first, quite as if she'd lifted the word *wheelchair* from Ralph's thoughts.

"We use it to take him in at night, or when the weather's bad," she said. "Temperature control's important when dealing with taxidermy."

"Please, Immy, how many times do I have to ask you not to use that word?" said her mother. She turned to Ralph. "It isn't taxidermy, of course, but that student studied taxidermy with Herb, and now he's head of human reproductions at Madame Tussauds in London."

"He caught Dad's personality pretty well, don't you

think?" said Immy. "That is, if you believe that personality resides in one's physicality. I bet you do. I bet you can name all kinds of examples of it in literature."

"Richard the Third, Ahab, Tiny Tim, the Hunchback of Notre Dame," said Ralph. "Their personalities all lead back to physical deformities."

He blushed, fearful they'd think he was showing off, but Eva only picked up the wine bottle and refilled her glass. "Tiny Tim's deformity didn't defeat his cheerfulness, though," she said. "Quasimodo's bummed him out, it's true, yet it also gave him his nobility. . . . But I don't believe deformities in literature equate very well to those we find in real life. In life, I don't think there's much catharsis. We just keeping on keeping on."

Ralph took courage from that, took it to mean that no cathartic moment was likely to come today, but when Immy said, "Dad kept on keeping on for a decade after he started having his strokes," her mother harrumphed.

"How would you know? You were off getting married and divorced while I sat out here trying to talk your father out of killing himself," she said. "He would have done it, too, if he could have managed on his own, but I wouldn't be a party to it. Are there examples in literature where a person won't help another person kill himself, Ralph?"

Ralph couldn't think of one and said so. He felt the poem in his pocket—its subject departed loved ones—but he didn't feel that now would be a very good time to pull it out. "You certainly have a beautiful view," he said. "Do you eat out here often?"

"Are you trying to tell us you're hungry?" asked Eva. "Is that your way of saying you'd like to get this over with?" But when Immy said, "Mom . . ." she once again grew cheerful.

"Ralph, do you like meat?" she asked. "I failed to ask you on the phone."

"I don't deny myself any sort of food," said Ralph.

He rocked back on his heels, like he would if their deck were a boat. Surely she wouldn't say that he hadn't denied himself with Herb.

"That's good, because we're having Dad's favorite," said Immy. "Prime rib, Polish sausage salad, carrots and peas, and ice cream for dessert."

Those weren't Herb's favorites. His favorite had been salmon with wild rice.

"In fact, I'll run in and see how things are going," Eva said.

When she left them, Immy sat next to her father. Ralph sat down, too, crossed his legs, then quickly uncrossed them. "I first met your father at one of our brown-bag colloquiums," he said. "He was presenting on bald eagles, the numbers of which had been steadily declining around Puget Sound."

He wanted to say that the meeting had changed his life, that it alone proved that life had cathartic moments, but instead he asked, "Do you ever see bald eagles around here anymore?"

"Rarely," Immy said, "though your question would have pleased Dad."

Ralph looked at Herb, in the hope of seeing a pleased expression.

"I suppose you take him in at night not only because of the weather but also so he won't get stolen," said Ralph. "I know nothing of these things, but it seems his student did a pretty good job."

Oh, how he'd hated that student, had wanted to get a death grip on his throat.

"He did a *beautiful* job," said Immy, "right down to the blotches on the backs of Dad's hands."

"Liver spots," said Ralph. "I've got some of those."

He put his hands out in front of him, turning them over and back.

"Dad had a scar on his abdomen, and it's there, too," Immy said. "I hate to think how the student knew that. His name was John Hancock, by the way, and he signed his work with great big letters, just like our famous forefather."

Ralph drank some of his wine, his hatred of John Hancock roaring back in, just as Eva came back outside. "Another few minutes," she said. "Now you have to tell me if you want to eat inside or out. Can you manage a little chill, Ralph?"

The only chill he felt came from thoughts of John Hancock. "I can manage out here," he said, "and the deck will be better for Jip."

Jip looked up when he heard his name.

"We could leave where we eat up to Dad," said Immy. "Whatever else it might be, John Hancock's version of him is a pretty good weather vane."

She reached over and took off her father's right shoe. Ralph could see Herb's toes through the creases in his argyle sock.

"Immy," said Eva. "How many times do I have to tell you not to say 'it' when talking about your father?"

"He's a good weather vane," said Immy. "His right big toe is an actual thermometer, Ralph. It turns blue if it grows too cold for him, red if it grows too hot. I guess John Hancock knew about our deck."

She pulled off Herb's sock to reveal five fleshy toes, none the least bit blue or red. She rubbed her father's right big toe.

"When I had a fever last month, I thought about sticking this in my mouth," she said.

"I used to tell my students that trashy talk would get them nowhere," Eva said, "but I never thought I'd have to tell my daughter."

"Sorry, Mom," said Immy. "Guess I got my sense of humor from Dad."

"Eva, I wanted to ask, when you taught English, what did your students read?" Ralph asked. "Anything remotely Shakespearean?"

He hardly cared what her students read, but he *could not* take any more of Herb's toes.

"*Romeo and Juliet*," said Eva. "I used to think if I heard another 'Wherefore art thou?' I'd scream, yet now I find myself screaming for no good reason."

"Hardly for no good reason," said Immy. "Your husband died a decade ago, yet here he still sits. I keep saying you should go to Paris, take a cruise. . . . Ralph, will you please tell her seventy's not too old to do something like that?"

"It's not," Ralph said. "I'm nearly that age and I'll be heading back to Oslo soon, where I once had a Fulbright scholarship."

When Eva went inside to check the food again, Immy put her hands to her face, but soon enough she asked Ralph to put her father's shoe and sock back on while she helped her mom. He didn't want to do it. By the time Herb needed help dressing himself, he'd left Ralph for John Hancock. Still, he picked up the shoe and sock. To his surprise, the sock was warm, and when he looked inside the shoe, he saw that it was from Thom Browne, a shoe store he had introduced Herb to. When he glanced back into the house, Eva was taking the food off the stove and Immy was stacking plates, so he put the sock down, took off his own right shoe, and slipped his foot into Herb's Thom Browne. And when he stood to test how it felt, Jip took off down to the beach again with Herb's sock in his mouth.

THE PRIME RIB WAS PERFECTION, the Polish sausage salad phenomenal, especially if you mixed it with the peas and carrots. Ralph had never tasted anything like it, and said so.

"Dad used to eat it all mixed up like that," said Immy. "He felt that otherwise the sausage was too salty."

Herb sat there smiling his crooked smile. Jip was still down on the beach. Ralph had put Herb's shoe back on him without the argyle sock, hiding the fact that the sock was missing by crossing Herb's other leg. Herb's joints had moved fluidly, his knee in Ralph's hand, even after all these years, as familiar as Ralph's own. If Eva or Immy noticed the missing sock, they didn't show it, but tried to make the meal go well.

"We don't stand on ceremony here," said Eva. "If you want more of anything, Ralph, help yourself."

She nodded at a side table, where the meat sat on a platter, the Polish sausage salad filled a bowl, and the carrots and peas roamed around on a plate of their own. "I will," Ralph said.

"Herb had the most amazing metabolism. He could eat this way every day and still not gain weight, while my hips got bigger with a single bite," Eva said.

Ralph laughed dutifully, his eyes on Herb, who'd insisted that his wild rice and salmon be cooked without salt, and surrounded by lemon wedges.

"You look fit, too, Ralph," said Immy. "What keeps you so trim?"

"I skip a lot of meals," he said, "don't get much chance to have a great one." He pointed at his food with his fork.

It hadn't been chilly when they decided to eat outside, but at about the time Jip came back from the beach, with no sock in evidence, such a powerful wind came up that Eva and Immy both started to carry things inside without a word. So Ralph stood to push Herb in after them. He had to put Herb's feet on the wheelchair's footrests, but Herb did not complain. Jip did, though, when Ralph told him he had to stay outside.

"He can go in the laundry room, if you want him to," Immy said. "There's a basket there that Charlie used to sleep in. . . . Charlie was Dad's old pointer."

Ralph knew Charlie. Herb had taken him to Ralph's house often.

"Herb didn't even like Charlie," said Eva. "He'd go to any length to see some stupid bird, but Charlie could stare at him all day long and he would never notice."

In Ralph's memory, Charlie had been Herb's beloved partner in bird-watching. He'd often thought of Charlie when trying to train Jip.

"It was the same with me," Eva said. "I was as loyal to Herb as anyone's dog, but all he wanted from me was a good meal every night, then help when he decided to kill himself. Sometimes marriage is a crock, Ralph. I hope you get that."

Immy went to open the door for Jip. Though Herb's argyle sock hadn't been in evidence when Jip came up from the beach, there it was again, hanging out of his mouth. Immy used it to pull Jip into the laundry room.

"Bring clean socks when you come back!" Eva called. Then

to Ralph, she said, "You're probably wondering why I keep Herb around after all these years, especially given what I just said about my marriage."

"Not at all," said Ralph. "Loneliness can make us do a lot of strange things."

He wanted more prime rib, so he took her at her earlier word and reached over to the side table to spear a slice of it with his fork.

"When John Hancock sent him to us, he was in a box as big as a coffin," said Eva. "And the postage, my God, it was nearly four hundred pounds, even back then. So though I was shocked when I saw him, at first I kept him so that John Hancock's efforts wouldn't go to waste. And also because I was afraid he might come visit."

Ralph stifled an impulse to say "Fuck John Hancock."

"Am I right in thinking that after while you got used to him," he said, "that he became a kind of solace to you?"

"And close the laundry room door!" shouted Eva.

Her voice had a warble in it, and when she looked at Ralph, the warble was in her entire face. "Am I right in thinking that after a time you got used to the loneliness?" she asked. "That it became a solace to you?"

Ralph looked at her evenly. He wanted to care for this woman but didn't like her much.

"You know, *solace* and *solitude* have the same root," he said. "And what I came to understand was that 'wanted' solitude is a blessing, while 'unwanted' solitude is a curse. And yet they are the same thing."

When Immy returned and saw the pain in both their faces, she said, "Mom! You asked him already? The two of you were in here talking about this while I was dealing with a dog?"

Her irritation was greater than her mom's had been.

"Ask me what?" said Ralph.

"I've decided to start living my life again with a modicum of dignity," said Eva. "That means disabusing myself of any residual belief in Herbert's love, and *that* means sending him home with you, Ralph. I've done my duty; now it's time for you to do yours."

When Immy, who'd brought fresh socks, knelt and nudged her father slightly, his chest fell forward, his arms slipped off his lap, and his hands fell down on either side of his feet, but Immy simply sat him up again. When she finished putting his shoes and socks back on, she nodded at her mother.

"I learned about you and Herb more than a year before Herb died," said Eva. "When I was cleaning his boat, I discovered your letters in his tackle box. You think you know a man. . . . I never confronted Herb with the letters—he was too sick by then—but after he died I shared them with Immy."

"You did know him, Mom," said Immy. "It was just that that kind of love, back then. . . . Dad didn't know how to deal with it."

She looked at Ralph. "I wasn't shocked by what you wrote, and after a while Mom wasn't, either, when she thought back over their lives together. She knew him, she just hadn't let herself know she knew him, if that makes any sense at all."

"But the letters were to Herb from me," said Ralph. "He didn't write them."

He could have said that Herb's letters to him were as often expressions of hatred as love. He could have said that Herb had been awful to him, but Herb was sitting right there, staring with his lopsided grin.

"There were letters from John Hancock, too," said Immy. "Angry ones. They made me think that the letters Dad wrote him were 'Dear John' letters in more ways than one."

"He never wrote me a 'Dear Eva' letter, at least," said Eva. "Perhaps that meant he loved me. But in any case, I've packed his bag with three shirts, three pairs of pants, and six pairs of socks."

"All of the clothes were really Dad's," Immy said.

"You may think John Hancock took Herb from you, Ralph, but John dressed him in jeans and a paisley shirt for the trip over here, for crying out loud. Can you imagine Herb in paisley? He'd turn over in his grave."

Immy left the room, coming back quickly with Herb's suitcase.

"You don't absolutely *have to* take him," she said. "We're not giving ultimatums here, but if you don't, we're sending him to Davy Jones. Mom's met someone, and I won't have my father sitting here ruining it for her."

She met someone? She wasn't going to Paris, but she was taking up with someone else?

"It was all so long ago," said Ralph. "It killed me to get over him once, so I'm sorry, Immy, I don't think I can take him. But Davy Jones? Why such a radical solution? Why not donate him to the university? He could sit in the room with all the stuffed birds, be a sort of gatekeeper. And I'd be glad to help make that happen. I still have a bit of pull."

That he didn't have pull, that once he retired he'd hardly set foot back on campus, was an issue he would deal with when he got back from Oslo. Until then, Herb could wait in his place, scare the devil out of the dog sitter.

"That would certainly put him in his element," said Eva, "and he *was* an emeritus professor."

For the moment, everyone smiled. Immy mentioned the ice cream, but nobody wanted it.

When it was time for Ralph to leave, they took Herb out to his car with very little fanfare, sitting him cross legged in the passenger seat. While Immy buckled his seat belt, Eva insisted that Ralph take the wheelchair, too, so they put it in the backseat with Jip.

"Good-bye," said Immy, "and thank you for doing this for us."

"You're welcome," Ralph said.

Eva thanked him, too, and forced upon him the same bottle of wine that he had brought. "You're going to need this," she said.

IN THOSE DAYS, YOU COULD STILL GET BACK to Tacoma proper on 11ᵗʰ street, with its many waterways and bridges. Along the way, there would be several opportunities for Herb to meet Davy Jones, if Ralph decided to introduce them. He did slow down when crossing the Hylebos bridge, and again when he got to the mouth of the Puyallup River. The Eleventh Street Bridge was his favorite, with it slabs of suspended concrete that acted like thick, slow guillotines when the bridge had to go up. He stopped for a moment, looked at Herb beside him, then put his car in gear again and drove on home, where he got out of his car, let Jip out, too, then went inside by himself to look out the window at Herb. He thought of driving him over to the university when the hour grew late enough, of dropping him off in front of the science building. But in the end, at just after midnight, he went outside again, got Herb's wheelchair, lifted Herb into it, and rolled him inside. It galled him to think that in order to rid himself of the pain this man had caused him he would have to go to Oslo twice, but as he opened the bottle of wine Eva'd returned to him, and poured two glasses, that was what he did think.

In a moment, he took his poem from his jacket, smoothed it out on his knee, then laid it on the fledgling flames of a fire he'd just started in his fireplace. Loss was the subject of his poem, the departure of loved ones. The moment he did it, he was sorry, but the flames were far too hungry for him to retrieve it. Still, the title of his poem was the last to curl and brown, so at least he could read that: "Anyone Can Master Grief, but He Who Has It." It was a title he'd stolen from Shakespeare.

A few moments later, he heard Jip at the door and got up to let him in.

Jip bounded over to lie down in the warmth of the fire. He looked up at Ralph with love in his eyes, but he didn't seem to notice Herb.

The Dancing Cobra

[1985]

RON AND BILL WERE FRIENDS who had been dating Sally and Beverly for almost a year, during which time neither couple was alone much, though Bill and Beverly talked on the phone daily and had occasional wrestling matches in Beverly's living room when her mother wasn't home. They were young, this quartet, and thus far had remained somewhat circumspect, though desire raged in them all.

One cold evening, when Bill was picking up Beverly (Ron and Sally were outside in Ron's father's car) and Beverly kept him waiting, Bill happened to open a linen closet, which was in an upstairs hallway, where he wasn't supposed to go if Beverly's mother wasn't home. He wasn't looking for anything, just sliding his hands in between the pleasing folds of sheets and towels, when he came upon Beverly's mother's vibrator, which he pulled out just as Beverly was about to open her door. He shoved the vibrator in his pants and ran downstairs to sit on the couch, where he belonged. He would not have taken it if he'd had time to think, but, of course, time to think changes us all.

The smell of Beverly ballooned before her when she came downstairs slightly after him. Maybe tonight would be the night. Both Bill and Beverly hoped so, though they hadn't talked about it.

At first, Bill couldn't wait to share his vibrator discovery with Ron, but by the time they got to the drive-in movie they were going to, he'd decided to keep quiet about it. When the movie started, Ron and Sally scrunched down in the front seat while Bill pulled the vibrator out of his pants and put it inside one of the shoes he had just taken off. Beverly saw him do it, or rather, she saw him rebutton his pants, and said something he had longed to hear her say for weeks by then, which was, "Why not let me do that?" Ron, in front, heard it, too, and looked at Sally with a firmly set jaw.

Meanwhile, back at Beverly's house, Beverly's mother came home. She was single, a hardworking woman who had just turned forty that day. The vibrator was a birthday gift she'd bought for herself and tucked away in the linen closet for a spectacular celebration she was thinking of having that night. When she opened the front door she called, "Beverly!" though she knew her daughter wasn't home. Beverly was a wonderful daughter and would have stayed to celebrate with her mother had her mother not insisted that she go to the movies with Bill. Her mother was an admissions counselor at the University of Puget Sound, the deputy director of Admissions, so one can well imagine that to have bought the vibrator, and now to actually have it in her house, was an act quite contrary to those she performed during her workday. She hadn't yet used it, but she'd unpacked it and loaded it with batteries and turned it on and off a couple of times. It said, *Bzz, bzz.*

In the kitchen, while putting down her bundles, she found a cake that Beverly had made that afternoon, with "Happy Birthday, Mom!" written on it. The mail was there, too, a card from her ex, a few bills. Forty. She was forty years old. At school, the fathers of prospective students were close to her age, some of them single, but she rarely dated, had locked herself up in her work and in Beverly for so long that when men did occasionally ask her out, she nearly always turned them down. She sometimes wondered why she was so reluctant— she'd been outgoing and friendly growing up—but there it was, forty years old and no one in her life. And then she saw the vibrator ad tacked to the back of a bus stop. And now it was upstairs in her linen closet.

But of course it wasn't; it was nestled in Bill's shoe, on the floor of Ron's father's car at the drive-in movie, where Beverly had her hand down Bill's trousers. Beverly had never done this before and was tentative, wanting to please Bill and to satisfy her own vital urges and curiosity. It was a strange thing to touch, both hard and soft at the same time, like a piece of snipped-off garden hose. Was she really going to let him put it in her? She imagined it lying up against her powdered thigh.

For his part, Bill moved about in spastic pleasure, hoping not to embarrass himself. And Ron, who *knew* what was happening in the backseat, had repeatedly taken Sally's hand and put it between his legs. She'd firmly retrieved her hand each time and was getting irritated. She didn't mind kissing Ron, and she liked letting him put his hands beneath her sweater, but she wasn't going further, not now, probably not ever with Ron. So Ron grew frustrated and suddenly sat up. "Come on, Bill," he said, "let's go to the concession stand for popcorn and Cokes."

Bill didn't want to go to the concession stand, but the moment Ron spoke, Beverly pulled her hand out of his pants, and as long as Ron continued to stare at them, she wasn't putting it back. So he sighed and said, "God, Ron, your tim-ing's not great, but okay."

The excitement of what Beverly had done, and his genuine love for her, made Bill forget about the vibrator in his shoe until he bent down to put his shoes back on. And by then, Ron had the door open and the light came on. So Bill could either go buy popcorn in his stocking feet or shove the vibra-tor under the seat in front of him. Oh, why had he taken the thing in the first place? He pushed it under the seat and slipped into his shoes, but in his irritation, he shoved it so far forward that it hit one of Sally's ankles. He and Ron were gone by the time Sally reached down and closed her fist around it.

Back at home, Beverly's mother was preparing her other birthday treat: a rare red steak with a baked potato and a glass of good wine. After that, a piece of Beverly's birthday cake and then a hot bath. And *then* her clandestine date with Mr. V., *if* she had it in her to do such a thing. All during din-ner preparations, she thought about it. She always tried to be mindful in everything, from her role as an admissions coun-selor to cooking well every night for herself and Beverly, but the idea of what sat in her linen closet disrupted her mindful-ness tonight. She forgot to set the timer for her steak (which was eight bucks a pound) and she left the wine corked for too long. She didn't exactly hurry—her date with Mr. V. was for ten o'clock, not sooner—but when the phone rang at 8:30, it was jarring, accusatory. So she decided to let her answering machine take the call.

"Hello, Donna?" said a man's voice, "Happy birthday, Donna. If you're there, pick up."

It was a voice she knew but couldn't place, a voice with a cloak of warmth around it that made her take her hand off her wineglass and put it between her knees. Whose voice was it? Who knew about her birthday? He waited for the longest time, half a minute, maybe, before hanging up. In the silence that followed, she remembered that there was a way to discover the number of whomever had called most recently. She had to look in the phone's instruction book to learn how to do it, but it worked, first try. The number was full of sixes and threes, like a code. When she had the thought that she might like to hear that voice again, at right around ten, it was like an electric shock. The number was 636-3663, and the area code was the same as Donna's.

It was cold outside but warm in the drive-in movie's concession stand, and warmer yet in the car, where Ron had left the engine on while they'd been gone. And the vibrator was warm in Sally's hands while she sat there thinking about Ron. Was he so insecure, did he have such fragile confidence in himself that he had brought this thing along for help? Did he plan on using it on her? She wanted to be outraged, but by the time the car door opened again, she decided to bide her time and tucked the vibrator out of sight.

"What did we miss?" Ron asked, but Bill only took his shoes off again and snuggled up next to Beverly. There was a blanket behind them, so he pulled it down and covered them, in the hope that they might get back to what they were doing. He had forgotten about the vibrator, for his mind was entirely taken up with Beverly, about whom he had come to a decision during his long wait in the concession line. This touching was fine and he wanted more, but he also wanted to tell her that they should go no further tonight, not in the backseat of Ron's father's car, but should do it properly in her bedroom tomorrow, when her mother was out.

Back at her house, 636-3663 was quickly becoming Beverly's mother's mantra, playing havoc on her mind, while the vibrator played just as much havoc on Sally's. So while Beverly's mother finished her dinner and washed the dishes with as much mindfulness as she could muster, all the while thinking that the phone call was either from Hal in Chemistry, Frank in Buildings Maintenance, or that new guy, Lou, from her very own office, Sally was in the throes of antithetical emotions, incensed and intrigued at the same time. At first, she kissed Ron so hard that he almost spilled his Coke and did upset their popcorn. "Sorry," he said when they both got their fingers buttery picking it up, but Sally said, "Never mind that," slipping one of those fingers into his mouth, her other hand around the now buttery vibrator. How dare he bring this! she said to herself. Unlike Beverly, Sally wasn't a virgin, though she hadn't enjoyed the experience with her previous boyfriend, Ned. She thought of Ron as a stopgap, someone to help her get over Ned, but here she was, about to let this new passion for him get the best of her, when suddenly her fingers hit the switch that turned the vibrator on. *Bzz,* it said, with such unexpected encroachment that Ron sat up and started messing with the heater knobs. *Bzz, bzz.* Sally pressed down hard but had difficulty turning it off.

At home, though it wasn't yet ten, Donna went down to the basement to dig out the vibrator's packing box. She hadn't read its instructions—she'd been far too nervous unpacking it—but she didn't want to hurt herself by misusing it on her birthday. What if she got it stuck in there or kept it on too long, or even, God forbid, electrocuted herself? She laughed as she took the box upstairs and set it on the edge of the tub.

ASSISTANT ADMISSIONS DIRECTOR DEAD AT FORTY. She could see the headlines now.

She put bubbles in her bath, lit candles around the tub, took off her clothes, and slipped down into the churning water while music played in the background. The music was from a classic rock radio station she liked and the Beatles were just then singing, "I get by with a little help from my friends." That made her laugh, as well. She was a good-looking woman, only forty, for crying out loud. Oh, why couldn't she put a name to that voice on the phone?

She picked up the box and for the first time really looked at the cover drawing: an anthropomorphic snake with a row of sibilant *S*'s coming from its mouth. The vibrator's name was "The Dancing Cobra," with the slogan "Find Your Own True Happinessss at Home" written in undulating letters. "Ssss, my ass," she told it, and then her phone rang again, not only downstairs but here between the candles, right on the edge of the tub. She didn't normally bring her phone into the bathroom with her, but she had tonight, pulling it from her bedside on a terrifically long cord. "What if it's him?" she asked the snake on the box.

She had her wineglass in the bathroom, too, and took a sip while she counted the rings—three, four—until she heard the answering machine clicking on downstairs. "Yes, hello?" she said, grabbing the phone beside her and sitting up in the tub.

"Donna?" said that same man's voice. "You're there; you're home. . . ."

"Yes, I'm home. Who is this?"

She reached over and turned down the radio.

"It's Richie. . . . You know, from back in high school and

Brown's Point. I know this is weird, but I got you a birthday present and wondered if I might bring it over."

Richie from high school? Richie from back when she was a kid? My God, she hadn't spoken to Richie in twenty years. How did he know about her birthday? She looked at the photo of the dancing cobra.

"Richie," she said. "What a wonderful surprise. How *are* you?"

"I'm well. I'm back in town. I'd dearly love to see you."

"Well, I don't know, Richie," she said. "It is kind of late, and Beverly isn't home."

She laughed and put a soapy hand to her brow. She hadn't talked to him in twenty years and still she wanted to tease him. Had she really said, "Beverly isn't home"? "Of course, Richie. I have no idea why you'd get me a present, but of course you can bring it over. And is 'Richie' still okay?"

"'Richie' will do," he said. "So what do you think? Is ten too late?"

Ten o'clock, the witching hour.

"Ten's perfect," she said, "I'll give you a piece of birthday cake."

When he hung up, she dropped "The Dancing Cobra" box, then picked up a bar of soap and started to wash, her heart skipping around the edges of the tub. Richie from high school, Richie from all the way back to Brown's Point was calling her and telling her he wanted to bring her a birthday present.

When she stepped from the tub and looked at "The Dancing Cobra" box, some soap fell from her body and landed on the snake's mouth, making it look even more obscene than it had when it arrived in the mail.

Back at the drive-in, in the movie itself, a woman was sitting in the cabin of a boat with her legs parted and her panties showing, her face bemused and taunting. "You think you're man enough, Johnny?" she said as she raised and pointed a pistol. The camera switched to Johnny. "What do we have here?" he said.

That's what Sally imagined herself telling Ron while holding up the vibrator. True, while Ron had been kissing her, she'd just about decided not to say anything, to take the vibrator home with her—but what did he think, that he was going to shove it in her and make her think it was him? What a fool Ron was! How could she have seen anything in him in the first place?

"Get your hands off me, Ron, and take me home," she suddenly said.

"Huh?" said Ron.

"You heard me. Take me home, you pervert. Damn you, Ron, what kind of girl do you think I am?"

"Sally, what the hell?"

"Just start the engine and drive! I've half a mind to tell your father what goes on in his car."

"How come they're fighting?" Bill asked Beverly when the engine roared to life.

"Search me," said Beverly, "They should learn to get along, like us."

They were under the blanket. holding each other and smiling, their hearts as light as Ron's was heavy. When the car lurched away from its parking space, however, slamming over the drive-in's speed bumps, they both sat up. "Hey, Ron, slow down," said Bill.

"Get your own goddamn car!" bellowed Ron.

Bill reached up to touch his friend's shoulder, but Ron was in no mood to be cajoled. "Get your hands off me or I'll kick you out right now," he said, "And Sally, you can go fuck yourself."

"Don't mind if I do," Sally said.

She was far too pleased with her own cleverness and barked out a couple of laughs, and though Beverly remained dumbfounded, that made Bill remember the vibrator. He leaned down to search the floor, inside his recently removed shoes, and everywhere. He reached so far forward that he brushed Sally's ankle.

"What happened, Bill, you lose a contact lens?" asked Beverly, while Sally punched Ron's shoulder. "Creep!" she cried. "Weirdo!"

Ron was furious, but as they roared along the highway, he tried to slow down. All he needed was another speeding ticket and he would lose his driving privileges. "You must be on the rag or something, Sally!" he yelled.

"That's right, blame me! Sexist! Pig! Big man Ron, can't get it up without help!"

But she had gone too far. She couldn't steal the vibrator now without trouble. So she nearly pulled it out to wave at Bill and Beverly. If she did that, though, Ron might really go crazy. So she let out an agonized "Ohhh!" and shoved it back under the seat.

"Got it!" said Bill, pretending he'd just found his contact lens.

"Want my hand mirror, sweetie?" Beverly asked, but Bill shook his head and feigned putting the contact back in his eye. And after that, they sat with their shoulders touching, until Ron pulled up in front of Sally's house, reached across to open her door, and screamed, "Get out!"

Meanwhile, Donna had parted her curtains and was peeking out at the quiet street. Not only was there cake but there was sherry, too, and she'd gone around the living room fluffing pillows and straightening Beverly's various pictures on the walls. It really was overkill to have so many photos of your child. There must be four dozen, she realized, and vowed to put some of them away. Richie would think she didn't have a life of her own.

She wanted to part the curtains again, but when she heard someone pull up outside, she went into the kitchen instead to plug in the coffeepot. Coffee went better with cake than sherry, and gave less of an impression that this was a date. Richie, my God. She put the sherry in the cupboard and returned to the living room to open the door.

Beverly and Bill were coming up the walk and behind them Ron had just zoomed away when another car, an ancient 1950s MG, pulled into the vacated spot. Beverly and Bill looked as bedraggled as the MG, which was spotted with lead and primer. Richie sat behind the wheel, a large package in the seat beside him. He killed the engine and got out, not by opening the door, but by stepping over it. She would *not* have recognized him.

"Sorry, Mom," said Beverly, "but Ron and Sally were freaking out." Richie, meanwhile, reached back into his car to pick up the box.

"Don't you know it's winter?" Donna called, "Doesn't that thing have a top?"

"No more double-dating with those two," said Bill.

When Donna looked at him, her eyes were drawn to the

bulge in his pants. She thought, Poor Bill, and resolved to have a talk with Beverly. She didn't want her daughter making the same mistakes she had.

"It's got two tops," said Richie, "a hard one and a soft one."

He had come up the walk behind Beverly and Bill, struggling under the poorly wrapped box.

"I didn't know you were having company, Mom," said Beverly, "Bill and I will go upstairs."

"It's not company; it's Richie, from when I was growing up," said Donna. "And no, you won't go upstairs."

She put a hand up to fix her daughter's hair, smiled at Bill, and made the introductions. "There's cake, it's my birthday, an old friend has popped in, and I've got this mysterious present. You really shouldn't have, Richie."

"Should have, shouldn't have . . . I've been thinking the same thing all week."

Bill helped Richie with the box, which was so poorly wrapped that it began to unwrap itself before they got it inside. Richie had another gift, too, smaller and flat. They brought the box into the living room and put it on the coffee table. Richie smoothed its paper and Beverly said she'd run up and change her clothes and come right back down.

"I'll go with you," said Bill, but when Donna gave him a look, he sat on the couch.

"I know it's odd, my coming over like this," said Richie.

"Well, you can make up for it by helping me get the coffee and cake," Donna said, drawing him into the kitchen with her.

When he was alone, Bill dug the vibrator from his pants, looked around for a place to hide it, then shoved it in his pants again when Beverly came bounding down the stairs. She saw the bulge and said, "Wow."

"You guys stay put," called Donna from the kitchen.

"I really have to go to the bathroom," said Bill.

Donna and Richie brought the cake and coffee into the living room on an old tea tray. While Richie arranged the candles on the cake, Bill started up the stairs.

"There's a bathroom down here, Bill," Beverly said, but he waved and kept on going. Beverly and Donna smiled at each other, and when Beverly turned off the overhead light, Richie lit the candles, which wavered in the room until a much relieved Bill came back down to join them.

"Now make a wish, Mom," said Beverly, "And blow out the candles."

"Gosh," said Donna, but she closed her eyes and wished as hard as she could for Beverly's eternal happiness.

When the candles were smoking toward the ceiling and she finally turned her attention to Richie's gift, it nearly unwrapped itself again.

It wasn't new, no newer than his car, but it delighted her like nothing else could have. It was an ancient record player with a one-inch shaft in its center, made especially for playing 45s, just like the one that had sat in her parents' basement when she was a girl.

"Well, I'll be damned," she said. "All I need is my old beanbag chair."

"It works," said Richie. "Here, now open this one."

He gave her the other gift from under his arm.

"You truly shouldn't have, Richie," said Donna.

"You might remember that I never knew how to be subtle," he said.

While Donna opened the second gift, Beverly dished up the cake and Bill helped Richie put the phonograph by an electrical outlet on the floor.

"Oh, Richie!" said Donna, holding up the odd-looking record.

"What is it, Mom?" asked Beverly, "Bing Crosby singing 'White Christmas'?"

"It's *the best* two-sided single from 1958," said Richie, "by a guy named after me. I'm sure your mother knows it."

"Know it? Ha!" said Donna.

"Well, what is it?" Beverly asked again. "Hurry up and put it on."

"Yeah," said Bill.

Donna slipped the record over the phonograph's shaft and watched it fall down and start spinning, forty-five revolutions per minute. She laughed again. The tune was "La Bamba," by Ritchie Valens, killed in a plane crash when he wasn't much older than Beverly was now. Donna and Beverly both knew the words and leapt together, singing like crazy. *"Bam-ba Bamba! Bam-ba Bamba!"* Richie sang, too, while Bill took a bite of his cake and made a wish of his own—that Beverly's mother would leave them alone tomorrow.

Though they all loved it, Richie hadn't bought the record for "La Bamba" but for its flip side, a dreamy slow-dance tune called "Donna," and as that side started, he took Donna in his arms, and Beverly took Bill's cake plate from him, and the four of them danced. When "Donna" ended they played it again, and then a third time, and then they returned to "La Bamba."

Though it hadn't started out like it would be, this was a life-changing birthday for Donna. She and Richie were hardly ever apart after that, whether at her house, cooking and listening to music, or at his, working on the MG in his garage. And the next day, Bill got his second wish when Donna did leave them alone, going out early to poke around with Richie in an auto-wrecking yard. Beverly took him to her bedroom, the promise of the drive-in movie kept during the clear light of day.

In the quiet afterward, and also later, when Donna and Richie came back, everyone thought they could hear a vague buzzing, as distant as a fly in a jar. But no one mentioned it, for each of them believed it singular to themselves, while each also began to believe that they had found their own true happinessss at home.

The Women

[1995]

I

THAT FALL, I TOOK MY DOG RUNNING at Wright Park daily, but while other dogs checked each other out by pressing noses to genitals, Bovary held his up high, like he might were he on the cover of *The New Yorker*. Maybe naming him Bovary did it, I don't know, but he'd lately been distant when it came to other-dog encounters, preferring the company of humans, just as I, I suppose, had lately preferred the company of him. A boxer he met that day growled, in fact, when Bovary refused a friendly romp and bit the boxer on his snout for his trouble.

We were in the park again a few days later, me in my jogging suit and Bov in his regular nudity. It was sunny, so we were sitting outside a nearby coffee shop after our run when a woman going into the shop gave me a look that said, I have a dog, too. Maybe I'd like this guy. She didn't have her dog with her, mind you, nor did she speak, but I have found that dog owners often know one another through a certain invisible vibe. I smiled and nudged Bovary, hoping he'd do the same, but by then a storm had invaded the woman's face.

"Hold on a second, what's your dog's name?" she asked.

I said his name was "Balzac," without thinking twice.

A half an hour later, we ran into her again, this time with Rocky, the boxer Bovary had bitten a few days before. Rocky'd been with a dog walker the first time we met him while she, the woman, was off teaching yoga at Stadium High School. The dog walker'd described the encounter, giving the woman Bovary's name, plus a pretty good description of me, I imagined, judging from her coffee shop suspicion.

"Hi again," I said, while Bovary barked, *"Bonjour."*

I should have said already that he's a large and reddish poodle and comes from a line of trufflers.

"Look, his name's not Balzac; it's Bovary," I said. "I had a dog named Balzac as a kid. I guess I must have flashed back to him."

My dog when I was a kid was Otis, the only dog I ever loved as much as Bovary. Women brought the liar out in me—or so say my ex-wives.

"Well, whatever his name, Rocky's been beside himself since their fight," the woman said. "He's had enough of fighting to last a doggy lifetime."

I glanced at Rocky, who didn't look beside himself but crisp and squared away, like every other boxer I'd ever seen in my life. I liked dogs who didn't face the world with so much blankness in their expressions.

"The dog walker's my neighbor," said the woman. "She tells me what goes on."

She was a dead ringer for Debra Winger, this woman, the best of the actresses I never seemed to see anymore.

"Your neighbor's a dog walker, but what does *her* neighbor do?" I asked, I thought, rather cleverly. It was then that she told me about the yoga teaching. I, in turn, said I was a lawyer who was running for judge, even pointing across the street at an ANDY FOLLETT FOR JUDGE sign on someone's lawn. My only other bit of notoriety was that Ted Bundy had been in a class I'd taught at the Puget Sound law school back in 1973. I told her that, as well.

Bovary and Rocky sauntered on ahead of us while the woman apologized for her coffee shop aggression, said a bad breakup had put her out of sorts, and agreed when I surprised myself by asking if I could call her. She gave me a pale pink card with only *Mariah Spring* and her phone number written on it, plus a sketch of a woman in a yoga pose. I determined to wait three days, which I'd heard was a rule of thumb, but when I broke down and called her that evening to ask if she'd like to take a drive with me up to Mount Rainier, she seemed happy to meet at our park the following Saturday. During the week, I gave Bovary three baths, twice washed my car, got a haircut, and bought a new pair of hiking shorts. It seemed an eternity, but when the day finally came and Mariah saw how clean my car was, she said right away, "It didn't occur to me that you might not want Rocky along."

She made no mention of my haircut or shorts. "Not true!" I said. "I'm in this as much for Bovary as myself," and when I showed her that I'd layered my car's backseat with a mound of worn and comfy blankets, she smiled her Debra Winger smile.

I had in mind a drive up to Paradise Inn, a hike among the wildflowers, and a slow trip back to my house for some cold sauvignon blanc and some very cool Miles. My second ex-wife used to tell me that I didn't know how to connect with what she thought and felt, past the introductory seduction of wine and jazz, but wine and jazz was still a good start, was it not?

Mariah looked great. Though I'd told her we'd be hiking, she wore a khaki dress that buttoned from top to bottom, engendering in her a certain wash-and-wear athleticism. Her body beneath the dress was toned, the muscles in her legs and forearms dancing around like little cloistered versions of Baryshnikov. During our drive, she told me the parts of her story that first dates allow: a happy childhood, popularity in school, and marriage to a football player whose career was ended by a wayward tackle, causing both a spiral fracture of a femur and the spiraling demolition of their relationship. She took up yoga before her marriage and started teaching it after.

At Paradise Inn, we parked away from other cars, letting Rocky and Bovary off their leashes so they could romp where romping wasn't allowed. Mariah took my hand, caressing its palm with her nails. She said, "It's third and long in my life, Andy, and I'm afraid to call an imaginative play."

That would have been poignant, its intimacy thrilling, but I heard *tired* instead of *third*. "Yes, yes. Who's life isn't tired and long?" I almost said, but caught her actual words in time. So I asked instead, "Did you sue for the football metaphors in the divorce?"

"I sued for Rocky and a few hundred bucks a month," she said. "I don't know what it is, but the law isn't the law when it comes to athletes. Cops and judges love them."

"I won't love them when I'm a judge," I said.

Rocky and Bovary had gone into the woods by then, but Bovary soon came running back out with his tail up behind him at a forty-five-degree angle. His nose was up, too, making him a pointer at both ends.

"Uh-oh," said Mariah, "I hope they didn't have another fight."

Rocky had stopped at the tree line, his head cocked off to one side.

"Good boy!" I shouted, then said more quietly, "It's not Rocky this time, Mariah, but morels! We have to follow his tail back into the woods."

Mariah seemed to think I'd said *morals* and squinted at me.

"No, *morels*. Mushrooms! I can tell their variety from the angle of his tail."

If you know the ground cover of a Pacific Northwest forest, then you know that it can have a mossy carpet, built up over centuries primevally. Bovary led us back past the place of Rocky's confusion to at least fifty morels standing behind a giant Douglas fir, an entire family of them out for a stroll.

"It's like a magical city with domed roofs!" said Mariah. "You can almost see Rapunzel staring down from the window of that one, Andy!"

She pointed and laughed and swung my arm. Since I swung her arm, too, for a second we were like a couple of discus throwers warming up together at a track meet. She knelt beside Rapunzel. *"Help me. I'm trapped in here!"* she made Rapunzel say. It was the mushroom proxy of every human voice.

When I said, "If we had a sack, we could take them back to my house, eat them with the sauvignon blanc," Mariah unbuttoned the entire bottom of her dress, pulling its sides up into a makeshift basket. The morels were oblivious to the doomsday scenario until we plucked Rapunzel first, then ravaged their town.

Though I'd parked away from others, a man was leaning against my car when we came out of the woods. Mariah's dress, with the bottom looped up, made it look like she was naked from the waist down. "Who's that, the leash police?" I asked while Mariah said, "Oh no, it's Kahuna! Let's go back in the woods for a while."

"What, the football player? You mean you were married to Kahuna Kamakuale?"

Everyone knew Kahuna, who'd been a Seahawks star. But before Mariah could pull me back into the woods, Rocky ran *to* Kahuna, joy written all over his foolish boxer face. Bovary ran, too, and when he got there, Kahuna kicked him.

"Hey!" I shouted, causing Mariah to throw an arm across my chest like a parent with a kid in a car. She also dropped her dress, spilling morels all over the ground. I picked up Rapunzel, and was about to throw her at Kahuna, when two other guys appeared from behind my car, both of them carrying clubs. Their faces were round and as huge as his, with horizontal lines climbing their foreheads. It wasn't until Kahuna nodded to them, however, that I saw the things they carried weren't clubs but ukuleles. And as soon as they started strumming them, Kahuna broke into this terrific falsetto version of "Over the Rainbow." It was a straight-out theft from Iz Kamakawiwo'ole, but I had to admit it sounded great.

"Enough, Kahuna, that's not fair!" Mariah cried before going over to stand in front of him in a strange hypnotic sway.

And not five minutes later she and Rocky were headed back down the mountain in Kahuna's BMW, leaving me and Bovary alone.

"I've learned life's lessons slowly, too," I said, "and as judge I'll try to remember that, aim toward leniency if the law allows. Does that answer your question?"

I stood in front of a gathering of twenty at a campaign rally at the old Normanna Hall up on MLK. The question had come from a middle-aged black man with his arm around his sullen son. The election was a week away, and two weeks had passed since my humiliation up on Mount Rainier. I'd seen Mariah at the back of the hall when I started talking, but I made it a point of honor not to look her way.

The man and his son lingered after my speech.

"What do you think, Junior, should I vote for Judge Follett?" asked the man.

"Not Judge yet," I said, while Junior said he didn't care who his father voted for.

"You'll care if you end up in court," said the man. "Now tell him what you did."

"Stole some drumsticks from Ted Brown Music."

Mariah came up to us, but I kept my eyes on the kid.

"I guess you got caught," I said. "What's your stand on shoplifting now?"

"Answer the man, Junior," said Mariah.

Junior's eyes left the floor, where they'd been glued. "What are you doing here, Ms. Spring?" he asked, while to me, he said, "I already promised about a million times that I won't do it again."

"In that case, if you were in my courtroom, I'd send you home with a warning," I said. "*And* make you pay for the drumsticks."

When Junior and his father left, I gave Mariah a suspicious look.

"He's in my 'rescue yoga' class," she said. "He's not as bad a kid as he wants to be."

I went to the podium to get my speech. I'd had three such events since I last saw her. My opponent said on television that candidates for judge shouldn't campaign, but I wanted people to know where I stood.

"What *are* you doing here, Ms. Spring?" I asked when I turned back toward her. "Tired of the Wizard of Iz?"

"What's a girl to do when you won't answer her calls?" she said. "I guess I came to apologize."

"How's Rocky? And seriously, tell Kahuna that if he kicks my dog again, I'll be the one going on trial—for murdering him."

"If you have a message for Kahuna, you'll have to deliver it yourself," she said. "I haven't seen him in a week and I won't be seeing him again. And *Wizard of Iz* . . . ha! Good one, Andy."

When she smiled and took my arm, I felt a weight lift off my chest. We had stepped out onto the street.

"'Rescue yoga,' huh?" I said. "What other kinds of yoga do you teach?"

"Oh, lots of different kinds," she said. "'Cheerleading yoga,' so the little idiots won't start breaking bones; 'stress-reduction yoga' for teachers after a difficult day; and 'don't be such an asshole yoga' for the football players."

A bunch of football players came into my mind, standing around semaphorically. Would that I could read what they spelled out.

"Browne's Star Grill ain't what it used to be, but it's right up here," Mariah said. "We could stop for a drink if you like, maybe get things back on track?"

I thought about how certain people say "ain't" when they want to sound spontaneous or carefree. Mariah and I had found great spontaneity before Kahuna's arrival on Mount Rainier, but neither of us had been carefree. My cares were tied up in two bundles: one containing my failure in two fraught marriages, the other my desire to help set things right in the world at large by becoming a judge.

I didn't know what Mariah's cares were, but I hoped I was destined to find out.

"IT WOULD HELP IF YOU'D STOP CALLING IT 'prophetic,'" I said a month later, on the evening of the day that Junior *did* appear before me in court.

"Come on, Andy," Mariah asked, "are you going to give him the leniency you promised, or what?"

"I didn't promise, and drumsticks aren't the issue anymore."

For me the best of Mariah's yoga techniques turned out to be "don't be such an asshole yoga," which I discovered when she gave me a yoga mat to celebrate my victory in the election. We'd just put our mats away, in fact, and were about to walk our dogs when the subject of Junior's day in court came up. Mariah didn't live with me, but she stayed at my house on weekends and on Wednesdays, the day it currently was.

"Did you let Junior out on bail, at least?" she asked when we finally got Bovary and Rocky on their leashes.

"I did, but his dad didn't have money enough even for a bail bondsman, so I don't know if he's actually out."

I hadn't been a judge long enough for good courtroom

management. I knew the law but was still learning the system's nuts and bolts.

"Are you going to make me ask what Junior's accused of? Really, Andy, he was one of my favorite yoga kids."

I didn't want to tell her, not only because it seemed a violation of Junior's rights but also because I didn't want to see her disappointment. But I said rather quietly, "Assault and grand theft auto. He and another kid knocked a man down, took his car, and went joyriding. It's a serious charge, Mariah. What's worse, or almost worse, the other kid is still at large and Junior won't give him up."

"Oh hell, *I'll* give him up," she said. "It's got to be Tyrone Wiggins. He was in rescue yoga, too, but an absolute jerk. Get him out of Junior's life and Junior might have a chance."

When she took out a plastic bag, I moved ahead of her with Bovary. We'd grown close in a month, Mariah and I, but both of us still picked up our own dog's shit.

THE NEXT MORNING, I DISCOVERED that Junior *was* still in jail, and told the investigating officers about Tyrone Wiggins. They looked him up, found him asleep at his mother's house, arrested him, and brought him in. He said yes, he'd been riding in Mr. Simonetta's car, but that Junior'd been the one who knocked Mr. Simonetta down. Junior said Tyrone did it, which Mr. Simonetta confirmed, so when the prosecutor turned her focus on Tyrone, I let Junior off, on the condition that he write a letter of apology to Mr. Simonetta, do five hours a week of community service until the end of the school year, *and* find an after-school job. Junior's father, a baker, brought me a strawberry shortcake that afternoon as thanks. I took the shortcake but shared it with everyone in my office. Junior's dad and I sat on my uncomfortable couch. When he asked how Mariah was, I said, quite unexpectedly, "She'd be the woman of my dreams if I weren't too old or she too young."

I haven't said yet that 16.8 years separated Mariah and me, I guess because of the embarrassment. But to have a woman of my dreams, rather than to want to be the object of hers, as I'd always done before . . . that was unexpected, too, and pleasing.

"She's not too young, but you're too old if you think she is," said Junior's dad. "You've got to strike while the iron is hot, man, not go around second-guessing yourself. Biggest sorrow of my life is that I did that with Junior's mom till she got tired of it and flew the coop. Just let the woman know your future'll be dark without her. And build yourselves a life together in a house that neither of you lives in now. That way, you'll be building fresh memories, not living among your old ones."

Over the course of the rest of that day his words—"build yourselves a life together in a house that neither of you lives in now"—simply would not leave me alone. I'd lost houses to each of my ex-wives and was currently living in the back house of a lawyer friend, while Mariah, it turned out, had been renting a room from her dog-walking neighbor since her divorce. Neither of us had any money. . . . I'd been a lawyer and now I was a judge, but the two divorces meant I seemed always to be starting from scratch.

I had a terrible and a wonderful idea before I left my office, which I determined to share with Mariah that evening. You will remember that I mentioned Ted Bundy's having been in a law school class I'd taught. Well, that was a bit of a stretch, for I'd been an adjunct at the law school, only tutoring a few of the first-year students in lawyering and criminal law. Lawyering dealt with legal problem-solving skills, criminal law with blameworthiness as a precondition for criminal liability. What I didn't mention was that Bundy stayed after a tutorial session I had given one evening to ask if the opposite of blameworthiness wouldn't naturally be blamelessness and to insist that if a person were held blameless, then there could be no criminal liability. I thought that was obvious, but his interest had been so intense that I went into a rambling, youthful spiel about the insanity defense, with him standing there staring at me. I remember feeling sorry that I'd gone on like that, but I forgot about it until a few years later, when his infamy made him the talk not only of the town but of the entire country.

And then, for a time, I grew obsessed with him. I learned what he liked in women—long straight hair, parted in the middle—read everything I could find on his victims, even memorized their names: Lynda Ann Healy, age twenty-one, attacked while sleeping; Donna Gail Manson, age nineteen, kidnapped while walking to a concert; Susan Elaine Rancourt, age eighteen, abducted from Central Washington State College. Once I even stood in the flower bed of a house on North Fourteenth Street right here in Tacoma, where, it was suspected, he'd pulled his first victim from her bedroom back in 1961. Ann Marie Burr had been eight years old, her house on Bundy's paper route. Ann Marie's murder has never been solved.

After Bundy's execution, my interest in him waned, but whenever his name came up, I felt it breach the surface of my consciousness again, like the back of a whale might breach the surface of an otherwise-calm sea. How could someone be so heinous, so heartless . . . and more specifically, how could I not have recognized such consummate evil when it stood in front of me asking a question?

A couple of nights *before* Junior's father visited my office, I had read in *The News Tribune* that a local Realtor was trying to sell Bundy's childhood home . . . nearly selling it and failing, nearly selling it and failing . . . with the price plummeting each time a prospective buyer discovered who had lived there. The paper also mentioned strange occurrences, like the words *help me!* and *leave!* written some mornings in the condensation on the windows.

Pranks, of course, but when I told Mariah that I thought we ought to buy the place, fix it up together, and try to live there, what do you think she said?

2

IT WAS A MODEST, BOXY AFFAIR, only fourteen hundred square feet, but with a fenced backyard where Bovary and Rocky might better get to know each other. The current owners—not the Bundys—priced the house at eighty thousand dollars, but we got it for thirty-five, which we managed to pay with what little we'd saved, twenty thousand from me and fifteen from Mariah, decided on the theory that the law was more lucrative than yoga teaching, which was true, of course, over the long run.

The street the house sat on, tree-lined and full of people going about their business, produced a cadre of kids on bikes, come to greet us on the afternoon we got the keys and opened the place to the cold November rain.

"You really moving in here?" one kid asked.

His bike formed the point of the V of the bikes of his friends.

"Yep," said Mariah. "Any advice you want to give us?"

"Maybe don't do it?" he suggested.

His friends turned into a flock of nodding Canada geese.

"It'll be a while yet. We've got to get things shipshape first," Mariah told them.

We'd come in both our cars, packed with supplies we'd bought at Gray Lumber and thought necessary for the repairs we could do ourselves. Buckets, mops, sandpaper, scrapers, primer and paint, paintbrushes and rollers, two stepladders, drop cloths, gloves, and turpentine.

I walked back past the kids, ready to begin unloading.

"He still comes here," the lead kid said, and then he and his flock flew down the road.

"I think we just discovered who's been writing on the windows," said Mariah, "*and* we've got the antidote."

She nodded at her car, which Junior had just gotten out of. We'd hired him for after school and weekends. We were paying him five bucks an hour, twenty-five cents above the minimum wage.

"Want me to sleep here tonight so I can chase them off?" Junior asked.

"No," I said, but I could see Mariah brighten.

"You have to get your dad's permission first," she said.

The house had four bedrooms, one in the basement, which the Realtor said had been Ted's. His mother and stepfather had slept in the largest of the upstairs bedrooms; the others had been occupied by his stepsisters. Mariah and I would turn those into a yoga room and an office. We'd already hired someone to refinish the hardwood floors everywhere but in the bathrooms and kitchen, where we'd replace the linoleum with tile later on. Today and over the weekend we planned to rip out a terrible carpet, scrape and patch and prime the walls, and do what we could with the basement.

"We'll get pizza at the Cloverleaf for dinner," I told Junior. "You can call your dad from there."

For the next couple of hours, Junior and I pulled up the carpet in the living room and bedrooms, and carried it to the backyard. Then I put Junior to work removing four decades' worth of carpet tacks while Mariah vacuumed and washed the kitchen cabinets and I opened a door next to the one that led to the backyard and made my way down to the basement.

The stairs were laid with the same orange shag that had ruined the living room, but the light in the stairwell was soft, as if someone had wanted the mood down there to be mellow. More carpet spread out on the basement floor for four or five feet, but after that was bare cement. To my left were the hookups for a washer and dryer, to my right a door that led, I had to think, to Ted's childhood room. Had he had his paper route when he slept here? Had he come back one morning in 1961, the scent of Anne Marie Burr still on his clothes? I put a shoulder against the door and pushed it open.

The room was grimly neat and had a dankness that told me, as the Realtor had, that the owners after Bundy's parents hadn't used it. Though I flipped a light switch, there was no bulb in the overhead fixture, and the long, thin window at the top of the far wall was covered with a stained and yellowed bedsheet. I sensed that to reach up and pull it down might contaminate me, but that was what I did, with barely a pause. The only light in the room, after all, came from beyond that sheet, and from the door that I had left ajar.

The moment I touched the sheet, two of my fingers poked through it, tapping against a window that seemed colder than the day outside, and sent something awful pulsing through me. The urge was strong to fling the horrid thing away, but I held my breath, bunched it against my chest, and turned and left the room with as much sense of carriage as I could muster. I walked up the stairs and out through the yard to dump the sheet in a garbage can in the alley. A cat crouched nearby, drinking from a puddle. When I finally took another breath, the cat looked up, its dark eyes shining.

Once in the backyard again, I saw Mariah through the kitchen window, standing on one of our stepladders and running a nozzle of the vacuum cleaner along the kitchen's narrow crown molding. Could I go in and tell her I'd changed my mind? That I'd been wrong? That we should find a better garden in which to plant the seeds of our love?

No, I could not, for Mariah and I hadn't talked about love. We had talked about wanting to find a refuge from the storms that had caused us both such havoc.

The air in the yard was fresh and wet and cleared my head a bit, letting me walk back past the soggy carpet and around the side of the house to where I could view that basement room from the outside looking in. I had left its door open, so I could dimly see an obtuse triangle of light spreading across the floor, with echoes of it forming a series of lines, faint and climbing the opposite wall.

As I stood there looking at it, Mariah called me.

"Andy, are you still outside?"

"Can you come here a minute?" I asked. "I'm around the side of the house."

She must have stepped back into the kitchen to turn off the vacuum, for suddenly I could hear the pop and clang of Junior pulling tacks and throwing them into a bucket.

"You've changed your mind," she said when she got to me. "You think we're in over our heads."

There wasn't any judgment in her voice, only intuition, and the thoughtfulness of someone who doesn't stand in the way of another person's confession.

"What do you see through this window?" I asked.

She stepped into the flower bed, knelt to put her hands against the window, and rested her face against her hands. "I see a bed and nightstand, and a ceiling that's too low to let you stand up straight. I also see a room I wouldn't want to go into."

She put her hands down and looked at me. "Is that what you see, Andy? The terrible amount of exorcising that's ahead of us with this place? Exorcising and, I guess you'd call it, courage?"

"Look at the lines running up the wall," I said. "The light from the door is making them. They remind me of the lines in someone's notebook."

She put her hands against the window again.

"Oh yes, I see them," she said.

LYNDA ANN HEALY, DONNA GAIL MANSON, Susan Elaine Rancourt . . .

I'd told Mariah about my Bundy obsession when I'd

suggested we might buy the place, but I hadn't told her that I'd memorized his victim's names. So when we got to the basement with a marking pen we'd bought to label boxes, at first I spelled only those three while Mariah wrote them on the wall.

"It's Lynda with a *y*," I said, "and Ann without an *e* at the end."

Junior had come to the basement after us, to stand in the doorway and watch.

"Whose names are those?" he asked.

"Come in, Junior," I said. "Don't block the light."

"They are his victims," said Mariah. "Kids just like you, Junior, only girls."

Junior put his tack bucket down and asked Mariah for the marker, his demeanor utterly serious. When I said and then spelled Roberta Parks, Brenda Ball, and Georgann Hawkins, he wrote them as steadily and as clearly as Mariah had the first three. That made six names, so I took the marker and added two more: Janice Ann Ott and Denise Marie Naslund. I guess I thought it would be liberating to do such a thing, but it was punishing, each name a fist to the stomach. I put the cap back on the marker.

"The list goes on," I said, "but I don't think I can."

"Oh, but you must," said Mariah. "Now that we've started, we have to write them all."

I took the cap off the marker again. Nancy Wilcox, Melissa Anne Smith, Laura Ann Aime, Carol DaRonch, Debra Jean Kent.

When I said, "They all died in 1974," Mariah took the marker to write "1974" at the edge of that wall. She then went to the opposite wall, stood on top of the bed, and waited for me to give her more names.

Caryn Eileen Campbell, Julie Cunningham, Denise Lynn Oliverson, Lynette Dawn Culver, Susan Curtis.

"Is this supposed to make us feel good?" asked Junior, for he had also felt that stomach punch.

"It's supposed to free the house from the hold he's got on it," Mariah said.

I'd memorized the names of Bundy's victims six years earlier, at the time of his execution, but knew them still, as if, as they say, by heart.

"Margaret Elizabeth Bowman, Lisa Levy, Kimberly Diane Leach. Kimberly was only twelve years old."

"I got a cousin who's twelve," Junior told us.

Mariah wrote those last three names, making twenty-one in all, not including those who survived him, nor those whose names Bundy hadn't known.

Before we left the room I took the marker to write the name Ann Marie Burr across the floor.

3

EATING PIZZA SEEMED ABOUT AS FAR from something we could do after that as spending the night in the house did to Junior. So we washed our hands and arms to our elbows, closed and locked the doors, and Mariah drove Junior home, with me following behind her. When she happened to pass the Cloverleaf, however, she put her turn signal on and pulled in and parked. So I did also.

"They've got a section in the back for underage people,"

she said when we got out of our cars. "It's ten o'clock and none of us has eaten, not since lunch."

Inside the tavern, people were sitting around with their sleeves rolled up. They wore work shirts and plaid shirts, with jackets slung across the backs of their chairs. And most of them had pitchers of beer on their tables, pushed to the sides by their pizzas. The bar itself was in the shape of a cloverleaf and occupied by solitary men, drinking and watching TV. We walked around them to the underage section, which was just then closing for the night.

"You can sit out front if you don't order any alcohol," the cleaning person told us.

From what I remembered of Washington State liquor-licensing laws, that wasn't true, but we went back out to sit in a half-moon booth anyway, hunger and melancholy driving us.

A waitress came to take our orders, a Coke for Junior, water for Mariah and me, plus two large sausage-and-mushroom pizzas, the specialty of the house.

In the booth next to us, three women in their forties sat eating pizza with knives and forks and chatting about haircuts.

"I wore mine long for*ever*," one of them said. "Sometimes it takes a while for a person to know that it's time to give up on youth."

When she patted the back of her head, the other two smiled.

In the booth beyond them sat three more women, and beyond them four more, up to a total of twenty-two women. Was it an etiquette club? A sorority reunion? A meeting of AA, perhaps, since none of them was drinking?

I couldn't keep my eyes off the nearest three—Roberta

Parks, Brenda Ball, and Georgann Hawkins, I called them—*Georgann* the one who'd just cut her hair. What came into my mind as I watched her was the image of a vivacious brown-eyed girl, happy and dancing in the fall of '73, at a party at the University of Puget Sound. I even knew the name of the band that played, Blueport News, for I was also there, fresh from my law school tutorial. Had Bundy followed me, then, to spot this beautiful girl?

The people at the tables in the center of the room took no interest in the women, nor did Junior and Mariah. And the waitress, when she brought the Coke and water, didn't stop to look their way. Were the women our companions, then, conjured up at Bundy's house and brought into the tavern with us?

The moment that that idea struck me, the three nearest women, and then those beyond them, began to look sketched in black and white and posed like in old high school yearbook photos, their heads cocked oddly, their interest in the pizza minimal, while the other tavern patrons sat in living color, with animated bodies and voices.

I couldn't help thinking that I could break this spell, that they would either become members of the living world again or go back whence they came if I simply leaned past the boundary of our booth and said hello. And I couldn't help noticing also that Georgann's short hair was common to the others, that each had cut her hair, as if, through that one act, they might escape Bundy's fetish. Each, that is, save the farthest two, who weren't yet women anyway but girls. Their names were Kimberly Diane Leach and Anne Marie Burr.

When I tested my theory by leaning into their territory, the air grew instantly cold, as if I were still touching the glass in the basement, on the other side of that horrid sheet. Roberta and Brenda didn't look at me, but Georgann said, with barely a glance in my direction, "Each and every one of us was loved."

Back in our own booth, the woman I hoped would one day love me and a boy we both hoped would find his way in the world were eating their first slices of pizza, which the waitress had just then brought.

"Why are you all at the age you would have been had you lived," I asked, "while the girls at the end down there have remained at ages twelve and eight?"

"God only knows," said Georgann. "Maybe because they hadn't yet reached puberty? We like having them that way, but they don't like it very much."

The cold against my face was such that I thought it would freeze if I didn't lean back into the life I was trying to forge. But I also *had* to ask another question, needed to come away with some sort of truth. "Each and every one of us was loved," she had said. Could I ask if she meant only each and every one of *them,* or if I was included in it?

Georgann seemed to wait, but I couldn't ask that, couldn't ask a murdered girl for words of hope for myself. So I asked, instead, "Did we bring you with us, or were you here before we arrived?"

Immediately, I knew that that was another wrong question, that to ask about our influence on them rather than about something solely theirs, like were they still in pain?—or something important to everyone, like was there ever any justice in the world?—was a failure the likes of which I had exhibited in both my marriages.

But what could I or anyone else ever find to ask Georgann Hawkins?

When I leaned back into the booth with Mariah and Junior, the waitress was arriving with our pizzas. I'd been wrong in thinking that they'd started without me.

"Finally!" Junior said. "I'm starved."

"But it's worth the wait," said the waitress. "Can I freshen that Coke for you, hon?"

Before she headed back to the bar, she took a stack of bills from her apron, laying one on each of the other booths in calm succession.

And with that, the women pooled their money and grabbed the coats and scarves that they'd apparently placed beside them. Only the girls farthest from us stood quickly, but they weren't paying anyway, because they were still too young.

When Georgann got up, she looked at me. "I hope you enjoy your meal," she said. Then she lined up behind the others and they left the tavern, led by the two girls.

We ate our pizza in silence.

"We ordered too much," Mariah said after a while. "Junior, you'd better take the rest home to your dad."

Who knows why that made me think of the morels we had pillaged up on Mount Rainier, in that long-ago time when the only danger we had known came in the person of Kahuna. *Morels,* not morals.

Junior said his father would be thankful for the pizza, that after a hard day of baking he rarely remembered to bring any real food home.

Mariah and I smiled at "real food," though, slathered as it was with sausage and mushrooms, that was what Junior clearly thought the pizza was.

On our way out of the Cloverleaf a half an hour later, I

noticed that the booths the women had occupied were clean and ready for other customers.

I didn't think anyone had come to clean them, but I could have been wrong.

eHarmony Date @ Chez Panisse

(2011)

H E ARRIVED SO EARLY that he actually called the restaurant from the sidewalk outside, asking if he might
move his reservation up from 1:15 to 1:00 P.M.

"I'll try to work you in," the hostess said.

Good. To be sitting there calmly would be best. It
wouldn't do to arrive after her, nervous and sweating. Nor
would it do to arrive together, for he knew from her profile
that she was taller than he was—she was five ten against his
five nine and a half.

Once inside the restaurant, he glanced into the downstairs dining room. He'd intended to offer her dinner, but
his brother, Angelo, warned him away from such ostentation.
Dinner at Chez Panisse was too much, Angelo'd said, like buying a house when all he really needed was an apartment. He
thought about calling Angelo now to tell him about the reservation change, but when he took out his phone, he remembered Angelo's last bit of advice—"Be *with* this woman, Bert,
don't be elsewhere"—and powered the thing off once and for
all. Or until he was on his way home anyway.

When he walked upstairs to the café section, the hostess
sat him in a waiting area and gave him a glass of sauvignon

blanc when he asked for one. He would have another with lunch. Two glasses of slowly sipped wine was an accoutrement to conversation. Angelo had said that, too, but when he also said, "Like a belt holds up your pants, the wine will keep your face from falling down," Angela, Bert's sister-in-law, had shut Angelo up, kissing Bert and wishing him luck. Bert had met Angela first. He'd introduced her to his brother, and the rest had been years and years of sorrow on the one hand and gloating on the other.

"We can seat you now if the rest of your party will be here soon," said the hostess.

Those were her words, but her look said, Why don't we seat you, get your back against the wall so you can have some support?

She gave him the warmest of smiles, but was he that transparent? He'd been here twice before with dates but fully believed he'd been invisible. He walked behind her, not glancing at the other diners. His table (for two) was in a line of three such tables with not much space between them. He would have to remember to keep his voice down—another bit of Angelo's advice—and also not to eavesdrop.

"It really just floored me. I mean, forty grand a semester? Why couldn't she stay right here and go to Berkeley?" said the woman at the next table. It was as if *she* were his date and had chosen those words as an opening line, since he knew the subject well, having taught at Berkeley for the last twenty years. It made him think that, far from not eavesdropping, perhaps he should engage these lunch neighbors. Wouldn't it make him look at ease if his actual date saw him listening to the opinions of others and giving advice? When he turned toward the woman and peaked his bushy eyebrows at her, however, he saw immediately that she didn't even know he'd sat down. He also saw that half his wine was gone, and put a finger on the rim of his glass. He ate a piece of bread, then swept its crumbs onto his lap, though a waiter stood nearby with a crumb scraper.

SHE FOUND A PARKING SPACE A BLOCK AWAY, bought two hours' worth of parking from a nearby machine, and put the receipt on her dashboard. She didn't suppose she'd need two hours, but if the date turned out well and she lingered, she wouldn't want to get a ticket and spoil things. She'd had eleven Internet dates and told herself that she would quit at an even dozen. And, of course, a last date should not be rushed, somewhat like a last supper.

She was early, too, so walked past Chez Panisse twice. On every previous date, she had promised herself two things: to pretend that each was her first and to say what she thought, not what she guessed her date might wish to hear. She'd spent nine years pretending to interests she didn't have with Steve. That her marriage had ended in widowhood, not divorce, in fact, had forced her to pretend again. This time to the success of it.

During her first three Internet dates, she'd caught herself not only talking about her marriage but presenting the men with the very version of herself that Steve had invented, or, more fairly, that *she* had invented when trying to make Steve happy. She didn't mean to begrudge him. . . . Steve *had* had his good side, which, if she remembered correctly, was his left. She laughed as a man came along the sidewalk toward her.

When he looked at her, his eyebrows peaked, like the roofs of the birdhouses her father used to build up in Tacoma.

WHEN HE SAW HER MOVING across the dining room toward him, he stood up too quickly, knocking the table with his thighs. Some of his water sloshed out, but he'd drunk enough of his wine that *it* only frowned up the inside of its glass and then settled back down, somewhat like the grouchy expression she was trying to hide. She had already given him the nickname "Birdie," because of his eyebrows. He needed one of those hair clipper things she'd seen advertised on TV, not only for his eyebrows but also for his ears and the portals of his nose. He looked *very* Italian, though it said on his profile that he was only Italian on his father's side. Not that she minded . . . She liked Italians just fine.

"I'll have one of those," she told the hostess, pointing at the wine.

"Sauvignon blanc," said he, lest the hostess had forgotten.

"You'd better be Bert," she said. "I mean, what if you weren't? Wouldn't that be funny? What if you were some other Internet guy waiting for someone else?"

She couldn't help thinking, Would that it were so.

"I'm Bert to most people, Alberto to the members of my family," he said. "You know what I do whenever I get a little free time? I make my own salami."

Shoot me now, he told himself, while she thought, What if I called him Birdie out loud? He might think it was Bertie, a twelfth-date diminutive, an excessive amount of cuteness spilling out.

"Well, I'm Liz, though I used to be Mary," she said. "To *my* family, I'm Mary Elizabeth. My mother says I'm working my way down the syllables of my names, so I guess Beth is next."

She thought that was clever, and waited for him to acknowledge it. This didn't have to be a disaster, did it? But he was still in mourning over that salami comment. "I'm Bert," he said again, his eyebrows so evenly flatlining now that they looked like someone's just-clipped hedge.

Her wine arrived before she was properly seated, and when she scooted herself in, a bit of *it* sloshed out onto the table-cloth, making a Rorschach rabbit, she swore. Was this what they'd have in common? Thigh butts and sloshings, fat legs rocking the table? Not that her legs were fat; they were exactly what they had been when she was twenty.

"Your profile said you moved down here recently," he said. "How's it going so far? I've been here for twenty years myself."

He could feel himself pushing, and placed his fingers on the stem of his wineglass. She was actually *prettier* than her profile photos. When did that ever happen? Angela had told him that he looked like Tony Curtis in his profile photo, while Angelo said he looked more like General Curtis Lamay. Angelo was a World War II historian and also taught at Berkeley. Angelo had bullets from the Battle of the Bulge on his desk, which was what he'd been fighting all these years, Angela said.

"It's an experiment, moving here," she said. "I thought I could leave Tacoma behind, but I've brought it with me. Any fool could have guessed that would happen, but I'm not any fool. As you can see, I'm a very specific one."

Neither of them had any idea what that meant, but it was

certainly true that Tacoma sat within her like a bullfrog on a lily pad, croaking away. Now, however, it was her turn to ask him something. That was the unwritten rule of Internet dating. "Have you ever thought of buying one of those rotating eyebrow cutters?" came to mind, but she said instead, "Your profile listed your field as organic chemistry. When I was in college, organic chemistry used to scare the living shit out of me."

She paused, sorry for "living shit," then added, "You know, I have this theory that scientists often know the arts but that artists never know the sciences. Would you say that's true? Tell me something artistic, why don't you?"

She pressed the fingers of both her hands into the tablecloth. She'd never thought of herself as mean, but there it was.

"Actually, I think Beth suits you better than Mary or Liz," he said. "You have the softness of the *th* around your eyes."

He'd been thinking of saying that the whole time she'd been talking. He'd never said anything remotely flirtatious on his other dates, but Angela had told him just that morning to loosen up, to tell the woman she was pretty if he thought so, to tell her whatever came to mind.

When she peaked her own eyebrows at him, he said, "In chemistry Th stands for thorium. It was discovered in 1828 by Jöns Jacob Berzelius of Sweden. He named it after Thor, the Norse god of thunder."

"Glad you cleared that up for me, or I might have thought he named it after John Jacob Jingleheimer Schmidt," said Liz or Mary or Beth.

Oh God, she had to stop this. None of it was his fault. Except, of course, for the outdated photos on his profile. There ought to be a rule about those, some sort of statute of limitations. She said rather wistfully, "You've never been married, have you?"

"Married to my profession" was his usual reply, but something in the way she'd made fun of Jöns Jacob Berzelius made him turn off the tape recorder in his head. What did it matter what she thought of him?

"I had a close call once with the woman who is now my sister-in-law," he said, "but she chose Angelo and now we're friends. That is, not Angelo and I but Angela and I."

"Here's to close calls," she said, once more raising her glass. She reached across the table and tapped his wrist, as if saying, Hello in there, hello? Can we not both simply stop this, act like human beings for once in our lives?

"What about you?" he asked. "Are you still in love with your dead husband?"

THEIR WAITER HAD COME BY TWICE, so they fell into a moment's silence, both of them staring at their menus. The two hours of parking she had purchased now seemed to her like a prison sentence, while he decided he would let loose the force of his personality on her soon, which Angela always said was his great secret weapon. Their waiter loomed above them like a dirigible, so he asked for the daily special—an edible schoolyard garden salad, followed by spicy Monterey Bay squid roasted in a wood oven with chickpeas—while she decided on the yogurt-and-cucumber soup, then pan-fried sea bass, which didn't sound good but seemed to be the dish that most reminded her of this man. She smiled but felt meaner than she'd felt since Steve died. She had no idea what gave her this urge to make fun of him.

"They don't call it 'Chilean' sea bass here," she said once the waiter had left. "'Chilean' is code for 'unsustainable,' and an absolute no-no in this place."

She'd read up on Chez Panisse, and gave him a genuine smile.

"Do you think the actual Chile will turn out to be as unsustainable as its bass?" he asked. "I mean, one never knows with these fledgling democracies."

He felt like slapping his face. God what an imbecile he was! That wasn't letting loose the power of his personality but simply saying something banal! Everything he knew about Chile he had learned when watching TV coverage of the coal mine disaster. He didn't know how "fledgling" their democracy was, wasn't even absolutely sure it was a democracy.

"I sure hope not," she said. "I like their wine and I want it to keep on coming."

There, she had said something equally dumb. She thought to ask him if he believed the final *t* in Pinochet to be spoken or silent—to say that it, along with how to say Qatar, seemed to cause havoc with journalists around the world. But instead, she simply let him try to read her look, which didn't have any meanness in it for once.

"That science and the arts thing you said a moment ago," he said. "I think so, too, though it might seem arrogant of me to say it. But I wanted to ask, are you an artist, then, saying it in self-deprecation? If you are, you didn't say so on your profile."

He picked up the saltshaker, lining it up with the pepper mill. He clicked them together at their bases, making them do a little dance. He thought of that scene in *Fiddler on the Roof* where the Russians and the Jews had a dancing contest.

"If someone says he's a scientist . . . if he truly *is* a scientist, then, by definition, there is a world of study behind it," she said. "But to throw the word *artist* around is easy, don't you think? About like choosing yellow or blue from one's paint palette. The only thing worse than calling oneself an artist is calling oneself a poet. Or maybe *artist* is worse, I don't know."

My God, he had had that thought, too! He distrusted many of those in the arts for just that reason.

"Are you a painter?" he asked. He let his eyes move down to her hands, looking for flecks of paint.

"In Tacoma, I was in sales. For a long time Jaguars, and for another long time real estate," she said. "But yes, I'll admit to painting now. At least behind closed doors. Painter, I can live with; artist, I cannot."

"It seems to me that when doors are closed, we don't have to clothe ourselves like we do when they are open," he said. "What are your paintings like? Can you describe them for me?"

He moved the saltshaker and pepper mill apart, then danced them back together, no longer Russians, but in the kind of do-si-do of a square-dance couple. He didn't think of what he'd said as showing her the power of his personality, since he'd just come right out and said it, but he could tell the comment impressed her. And, indeed, she thought "when doors are closed, we don't have to clothe ourselves like we do when they are open," was exactly like something she might say. She had even written something like it in her profile. Was he reciting it back to her? Surely not. Oh, she had to stop this! Why was she suspicious of this man? Maybe she'd have a thirteenth date, end on a higher note, call it a baker's dozen.

When their first course came—his garden salad and her yogurt-and-cucumber soup—she finally gave some serious thought to his question. What were her paintings like? Could she paint one of them for him now using words? In sales, one obviously sold something. Would talking about her paintings therefore be selling herself, or would it be letting him see the clothes she wore when she was behind closed doors?

He took a bite of his salad and watched her. She reminded him of some of the graduate students he had had over the years, women who saw only chemical equations when they looked at him. She was far too beautiful for him, no question about that, but where did her beauty reside? Could he isolate it? In chemistry, in order to understand a reaction when many reactants were involved, the order of reaction was determined by isolation. In female beauty, then, in *her* particular beauty, what was the order of his reaction? Did it commence with the wonderful width of her mouth, the perfect smallness of her nose, or the dark and inquisitive eyes that darted about above them both?

When he said, "Mmm, fresh vegetables" out of absolutely nowhere, Farmer McGregor came into her mind, sneaking up on Peter Rabbit, and she looked at the tablecloth to see if her wine Rorschach rabbit was gone. It was not, but it had faded out of its rabbitness, was now actually something like the painting she'd been working on that morning: lines and squiggles, dark white on light white and falling dimly away from any representative reality. She decided that if it stayed there beyond their first course, she would not only tell him about her paintings but tell him everything she could think to tell him about herself, no holds barred. It was her final Internet date after all, unless she decided on a baker's dozen.

She picked up her spoon, slid it beneath the surface of her yogurt-and-cucumber soup, and lifted it to her mouth. When the soup's flavor hit her, she closed her eyes. "Lord, this is good!" she managed to say, while for him the closing of her eyes isolated them, proving that her beauty did not reside there, or not only there, at least. That the rest of her face, undone by the startling flavor, looked deranged, made him think of what she might look like during sex. But her beauty was not diminished in the slightest.

"In milk, there are two types of proteins," he said. "Casein and whey. When the milk goes sour, it curdles. The coagulating part is casein, and the watery substance is whey. It's a bit like the Indian dish raita, wouldn't you say?"

He was talking about her soup and she knew it.

"What I would say is it's fab-u-lous," she said. *"Muy fabuloso."*

She was ready to spoon some of the soup into his mouth, and had it not been for the sudden intrusion of Spanish, she would have done it. But *muy fabuloso*? Where had that come from? She'd never studied Spanish, not even in high school.

"Très fantastique!" he said. *"Très magnifique!"*

He looked at the saltshaker and pepper mill, thinking to turn them into French balladeers, but he kept his hands to himself.

"When I was a child, I used to love to paint clouds," she told him, "and I paint clouds these days, too. Not big puffy ones and not rain clouds, either. These days, they are unrepresentative; they're the clouds within my head."

That wasn't as good as his "when doors are closed" thing,

but it wasn't half bad. And it was true. She thought to say she painted clouds from both sides now, but decided it would be trite.

"Unrepresentative clouds," he said. "Sort of like petri dish formations."

She took another spoonful of soup. *Très magnifique! Muy fabuloso!* "Yeah," she said. "I guess so."

"I have a painting by Agnes Martin at home," he told her. "There is this little scrap of paper on its back, on which someone wrote, 'I can see humility, delicate and white. . . . It is satisfying just by itself.' I like to think that the writer of that note was also Agnes Martin. It has come to mean as much to me as the painting."

She looked from his eyebrows to the mottled fields of his cheeks, his nose like a dangerous ski jump. *I can see humility, delicate and white. . . .* He was not only not attractive; he was actively *un*attractive. His face seemed made from the leftover parts of a child's discarded Mr. Potato Head.

"I know Agnes Martin," she said. And then she said, "Tell me something. Where did you hang that painting? I mean, where exactly is it in your house?"

"As a matter of fact, I didn't hang it," he said. "It's sitting on my couch, staring out at me like some kind of abstract, uninvited guest."

Damn. Everything he said was better than what she could come up with. "You don't mean to say *over* your couch, but on it? Correct?"

He'd made that perfectly clear, but she wanted it perfectly clear again.

"*On* the couch," he said. "Yes."

"What's the painting's name?" she asked. "And what does it look like?"

"I don't think it's supposed to look like anything, but to me it looks like a piece of blank sheet music. Its name is *Acrylic on canvas.* From 1997. It's not a very good name."

She wanted to say that she would like to see the painting, not as code that the date was going well but because she really wanted to see it. An Agnes Martin. On his couch. Not over it. She imagined his ears as the sheet music's treble clefs when he stood in front of his couch looking at it. Treble clefs with two sharps after it, like the tufts of hair coming out of his ears. So what key was that? Two treble clefs as seen from the back. That is, if sheet music could have two treble clefs.

"I think I know that painting," she said. "It's gray on gray, like even though the sheet music hasn't been written on, it's been waiting to be written on for quite a long time?"

"Why, yes," he said. "It's exactly like that."

He flatlined his eyebrows again.

Waiting to be written on for quite some time . . .

He wanted to ask if she'd like to come write on it right that second, but of course they had only finished their soup and salad.

WHEN HE DELIVERED THEIR MAIN COURSE, the waiter said, "Sea bass and squid are nothing alike, but they live together in the same stretch of ocean," causing them both to believe he was making reference to their unlikeliness as a couple. The waiter's flourish when placing the dishes down convinced her that she was wrong, that it was just something he said, but

Bert felt insulted. *Très* insulted. Like d'Artagnan. The waiter needed a lesson in manners.

"I think what they really do is swim at the same depth," she said. "And I also think that one eats the other, since I often used plastic squid as bait when I went fishing at home."

To her surprise, Bert laughed, his facial parts collapsing into congress. "Fishing?" he said. "I used to go fishing with my dad."

She took a bite of her sea bass, which was nearly as good as the yogurt-and-cucumber soup, but she was on guard against another Spanish outburst. "And I with mine, but we never fished for bass," she said. "Salmon was our goal, cod our consolation prize."

He looked at his squid, a consolation prize against the size of her bass. When he took a tentative bite, what got to him first was its texture, which was firm but not tough, the little squid bodies and the little squid tentacles cooked to perfection. When the taste came to him half a second later, it was like a second chance to make a first impression. Squid weren't handsome, either. With their weirdly elongated bodies and capped heads, they looked, in fact, like uncircumcised penises, three of which graced his plate. His propensity to eat fast, Angela told him, was her first indication that she would choose Angelo, who ate as slowly as a cow chewing its cud. But before he remembered that and stopped himself, he'd already eaten two of the squid, the last one cowering on his plate.

She, however, was in a sea bass heaven. . . . "Splendid, splendid, splendid," she said. "What a place to bring me! I'll tell you one thing, of all my dates so far, this is . . ."

She was going to say "the best restaurant," but stopped, worried that "What a place to bring me!" assumed that he would pay. Had she actually accented the *bring*? On each of her previous dates, they'd split the bill, and they would this time, too. Also, to say that of all her dates so far this was the best restaurant could be taken to mean that the date itself was nowhere near the best she'd had, and that wasn't quite true, not because she saw a future with him but because, well, because she was having fun. She said, "My paintings aren't like clouds on a normal day. They aren't like clouds during rain, nor are they like clouds during thunderstorms. They're not . . ."

"They are not cumulus, cirrus, stratus, or nimbus," he said. "It's cloud's illusions you recall, you really don't know clouds at all."

At first, she stared at him blankly, then somewhat coldly, as if he were making fun. But she hadn't spoken a line from that song aloud earlier; she was sure she'd only thought it.

"They're cloud primal screams," she said, "like some of those early Coltrane solos. But they're still clouds, my friend, and I do know them."

She played with her carrots, lining them up above what remained of the sea bass like eighth notes for the Agnes Martin painting. She nearly said more about early Coltrane, but she had learned about Coltrane from Steve, and she didn't want Steve to have a spot at the table.

"No," she said. "I got that wrong. They aren't like primal screams but more like primal shouts, calming into primal conversations, I hope."

He thought that was absolutely brilliant.

"I know I'm not supposed to ask this," he said. "But 'calming into primal conversations . . .' Is that what we are doing now?"

Goddamn he's good, she thought, but she said, "You're certainly *not* supposed to say it." She tapped her wineglass. "Two more sauvignon blancs?"

Should she have said sauvignons blanc? Did it work like attorneys general? "I'm an easy drunk," she said. "Oops, I mean a cheap one."

But that was wrong, too, since the wine was fourteen bucks a glass.

"Angela reminded me not to eat too fast," he said. "She said that the last thing a woman wants to see is me gobbling down my food."

"That Angela," she said. "I hope you thanked your brother properly."

For a while they ate and drank slowly, both adhering to Angela's rule. When he took a bite of his last squid, she took a sip of her wine, and when she returned to her sea bass, he put his wineglass to his mouth. Their arms and hands moved in awkward unison, like the pincers of a crab after a stroke. For ten minutes this went on, their eyes and thoughts lively but every other part of them like wary drivers going through a school zone.

When the noises of the room came back to them, they heard a woman at a nearby table actually say, "Eat slowly, Peter," and that made them smile, as if eating fast had once been an issue with them, which they had long ago solved.

"An apricot tart with Chantilly cream," he told the waiter. "Two spoons, and . . . what do you think? Two coffees?"

"I'd love a cup of coffee," she said, "but unless you're

ambidextrous, we won't be needing two spoons. I'm not much for sweets."

"You think you're not," he said. "But this is a special occasion."

They had been there for ninety-seven minutes and most of the other diners were gone. When she asked the waiter if he recommended the apricot tart, he swooned like Cupid had just shot him through the heart. When he was gone, she said, "I'll eat some if you can tell me what Chantilly cream is. Otherwise, you're on your own."

"It's a light whipped cream with vanilla or brandy added," he said. "A sort of liquid version of Chantilly lace, I guess you could say."

He briefly thought to tell her its chemical formula, but he did not. Angelo always brought up history, always told people historical facts whenever anyone mentioned anything at all.

When the dessert arrived, almost instantly, it looked deflated, as if some dessert bully had pushed it down in its tart pan. It also looked old, its texture as mottled as the skin on his cheeks. The cream was not filigreed across the tart's top, either, like his Chantilly lace comment made her believe, but formed a small white pond beside it, like a long-unused swimming hole beside an ancient dock, forgotten since the kids grew up.

"Never judge a book by its cover," he said. "It might be a cliché, but that's what Angela did, and for a while I figured that's what you were doing, too, but you're not."

His look was so intense, the blue of his eyes so bore into her, that at first she didn't know what to do, except to quell the sudden urge to get up and leave the table. But when she found herself calling them "cobalt" blue, his eyes, she understood as clearly as if she had been one of them that this was the look he gave his organic chemistry students while they stared through their microscopes at life's most elemental parts. No, she was not going to judge a book by its cover. She was going to judge it by reading it, and that would take more than just this one dumb date.

They didn't eat the apricot tart until their coffee came. A couple of weeks earlier, she had dined alone at the recommendation of a friend, at a hole-in-the-wall Chinese place on San Francisco's Kearny Street. The food had been a disappointment, but when her fortune cookie came, it said, "Don't dine alone! Hell is *not* other people," and she'd kept it. She decided to tell him that now, so he could let her know that it was a play on the famous Jean-Paul Sartre line, thus providing a bit more evidence that scientists knew art. But when she opened her mouth, he put a spoonful of apricot tart with Chantilly cream in it.

"Just one bite," he said. "Think of it as chumming for salmon."

Like the yogurt-and-cucumber soup before it, the apricot tart demolished not only her face but all of the sinewy mess that her life had been until just about that moment.

He took his own bite of tart, letting its fabulous flavor unglue his rough features, until he looked to her like one of those early Cubist Picasso things that she had seen at SFMOMA on the same day she had gone to the Chinese place. *Hell is not other people.*

"Do you want to go to a movie?" she asked. "Or maybe sit in the park and listen to jazz?"

"Early Coltrane?" he asked.

"Actually, I like the straighter stuff," she said. "I am partial to early Nat King Cole. I even read his biography once."

When they left Chez Panisse, the weather had turned, not cooling down but warming up. He shrugged and said, "Sometimes you need a jacket, sometimes you don't."

When they got to her car, there was a ticket on its windshield. Two hours and five minutes she'd been gone.

Plus, of course, the twenty years in sales.

The Strange Detective

[2002]

O N HIS WAY BACK FROM SEEING his grandfather at Tobey
Jones nursing home, Lars Larson Junior took a detour
into Point Defiance Park, his elbow out the window of the
new VW Beetle he sometimes drove so rain would mat the
hair on his forearm. It was dead winter, but since childhood
he'd liked the cold, could run in it in a T-shirt and shorts
back then, or go to Owen Beach and trudge along among the
driftwood. Winter and driftwood and crashing waves, rain
and low cloud cover—this was what Lars loved.

Once inside the park, he intended to loop around the Five
Mile Drive, then head back to work at Lars Larson Motors,
but he changed his mind when he saw a sign for the very
Owen Beach he'd just thought of. He got on his cell, called
Ruth at his office to tell her he'd be late, then turned on the
radio. "Beechwood 4-5789" came out of the speakers, which
were as good as he told his customers they were—surround-
sound in a Beetle really was great. The car was a Lars Larson
Motors loaner, the oldies station set by whomever they'd lent
it to last, but Lars left it alone. Beach wood was what he would
soon be walking amid—the detritus of his life in Tacoma.

At Owen Beach, Lars was disappointed to see two other

cars in the parking lot. That meant he might run into other walkers, which was fine, he guessed, since the beach was public, but also not fine, because even solitary people sometimes liked to strike up conversations. He did note that the two other cars were American, a new Jeep Cherokee and an old red T-bird from too late a year to be cool, sometime in the early 1960s was his guess. The T-bird's tires were oversize, giving it the sense of a muscle car and making it look ridiculous.

Lars parked and took off his tie and reached into the back-seat for a parka. He still had his suit pants on but found his old Nikes on the floor and removed his business shoes and put them on. His suit jacket lay across the passenger seat so he could look nice later, when trying to sell cars. He got out, locked the VW, and headed down the beach toward the Point. The tide was coming in but would not be up to the driftwood line for at least another hour. "Beechwood 4-5789" was in his head. Can you really call someone up and get a date any old time? Such a jaunty view of relationships was nowhere near the truth of them in Lars's experience, but on a whim he took his phone out and called the number anyway. *B* equaled 2 and *E* equaled 3, so 234-5789. Only the lack of a 6 kept it out of sequence. It was very much like him to do such a thing—one of his ex-wives used to tell him so constantly—but no one picked up, and he didn't leave a message when the machine clicked in. No dates this time.

Across the bay, Lars could see the Brown's Point Light-house, a solid pillar in the otherwise wispy haze, with a few boats dotting the chop in between. Fishing was ruined, so only when the weather was good did he see even half as many boats as he had when he was a child. His grandfather had a story about fishing at the mouth of the Puyallup River during a salmon derby back in the 1930s, rowing along by himself and having an eighteen-pound Chinook jump into his boat. His grandfather won third prize in the derby, but those days were gone forever. And nothing had ever jumped in Lars's boat, even metaphorically.

He kept his eyes on the beach, stopping occasionally to look at something left by the outgoing tide. The wind blew around the Point with a vengeance, forcing the few boats he did see to hunker down. He decided he would walk as far as the clay banks before turning back. Nothing was happening at the dealership—his salesmen wouldn't be in yet and Ruth would be putting yesterday's accounts in order before going to the bank and then meeting him for lunch. Lars's life was nothing like he expected it would be, though he couldn't remember having any particular expectations.

A large swatch of unnatural color came bobbing along the beach toward him, worn by a man walking beside a woman and somehow putting the term *red dye number two* into Lars's head. He remembered the other cars in the parking lot, so he hurried to the top of the beach and got down behind a log. He hoped these other walkers would pass without seeing him, but as they got close enough for their voices to cut through the wind, he noticed that one of them was shouting. Lars scrunched down next to a sodden half case of Rainier beer, a few of the bottles broken but one still unopened. A blanket was there, too, stinking and wet, with an actual condom sitting on top of it. God, Lars thought, I might have hopped over this log and sat down on the thing! As it was, he only sat next to it. He watched the other walkers and stayed out of sight.

The guy was fair-skinned and huge, his jacket one of

those Pendleton things, woolen and soaking up the rain like the filthy blanket beside Lars. Two scarred hands came out of the man's jacket sleeves, and one of them gripped the arm of a woman half his size. She drove the Jeep, Lars guessed, while the T-bird with the oversize tires belonged to this guy. Lars wished he hadn't hidden, since his presence on this beach might have helped the woman who was getting shouted at, but he couldn't very well pop up now. He'd thought before that Red Dye was pushing her along the waterline but then realized as they reached him that he was making her walk *in* the water. "What the hell?" Lars said, but the wind swallowed his words.

"Now go in up to your cunt or I'll slam this rock down on your cheating, lying head!" shouted Red Dye.

His right hand held a stone, about the same pale color as his skin. Lars felt he had to act, to come to the woman's aid; he couldn't watch something bad happen to her and do nothing about it, but what? And right then, as if in answer to his question, his cell phone started ringing, making Red Dye and the woman look his way.

"Lars Larson Motors," said Lars, standing and nodding at the couple. Lars got stupid when he was nervous. Anyone could tell he wasn't behind his desk at the office. Still, he expected it would be Ruth, so he was surprised when a strange woman's voice said, "This is LaVeronica. Did you just call me?"

"Beechwood four-five seven eight nine?" asked Lars.

The woman laughed and said, "Is that you, Johnny?"

"Can we help you?" asked Red Dye from the water's edge.

"What do you know, it is you, ain't it, after all this time!" said LaVeronica. "But who else you talking to, Johnny?"

"Look," Lars said, "whatever you do, don't hang up. I'm in a situation here and might need you to call the cops."

Because of the wind, Red Dye couldn't hear everything Lars said, but "call the cops" came through well enough. "Hold on, mister," he said. "This has nothing to do with you. This is our own private business."

He looked like a pit bull pulling at his leash, so Lars pointed his phone at him. "Come out of the water," he told the woman. "Step over here by me."

He picked up the one full beer bottle and cocked it in his throwing arm.

"But if you want the cops, Johnny, why you callin' me?" asked LaVeronica. "I hope you didn't do it to trifle with me."

Lars was surprised to be able to hear her so well, until he realized that he'd pushed his speakerphone button, letting Red Dye and the woman hear her, too.

"Yeah, Johnny!" said Red Dye. "Why didn't you call the cops yourself? And don't trifle with the woman. That's what went wrong between Cindy and me, too much trifling."

"We're on Owen Beach at Point Defiance Park, where a man is assaulting a woman," Lars said into the phone. It made him sound like a reporter following a traffic chase. "This is Lars Larson, of Lars Larson Motors, not Johnny."

"Lars Larson? You mean the guy from TV?" asked LaVeronica.

"The guy from TV is my dad," said Lars. "Now will you please make that call, LaVeronica?"

"We don't need the police," said Red Dye. "Cindy, get out of the water. Lars Larson Motors, huh? That that place out in Federal Way?"

"Federal Way, South Tacoma Way, and somewhere else,

too, right, Lars?" said LaVeronica. "I wouldn't be messing with Lars Larson if I was you, mister whoever you are."

"I'm not messing with him," said Red Dye.

Cindy came out of the water and walked over to stand by Lars. "We don't need the police," she told his phone. "And do you know what? I went to high school with a girl named LaVeronica."

"What?" said LaVeronica. "Who's that talking now?"

"Cindy Ronkowski, from Wilson back in 1998. Ron Ronkowski's sister . . . Everyone remembers Ron."

"You a skinny white girl with big tits?" asked LaVeronica. "Skinny cute, I mean, not skinny skinny. And those tits were real."

"That's me!" said Cindy, "Hi, LaVeronica. We had English together, remember? Man, long time no see!"

"I've got tits like fruit baskets, but they never got me near as far as yours did you, not back then and not now. And it wasn't English, honey; it was biology. I even remember the teacher checkin' you out."

"God, Mr. Simons," said Cindy. "I haven't thought of him in years."

"Goddamn everything in life," said Red Dye.

"Okay," said Lars, "I guess we don't need the police quite yet, but stay on the phone, will you please, LaVeronica? You're the only weapon I've got besides this beer bottle."

"Sure I will, Lars. I can't believe I thought you were Johnny. And what beer bottle? I hope you haven't been drinking this early in the day."

LARS KEPT HIS SPEAKERPHONE ON while they walked back to the parking lot. He knew he wouldn't last ten seconds in a fight with Red Dye, but he also knew that his stomach would churn for weeks if he didn't resolve this thing in some honorable way. And to make matters worse, LaVeronica, who had stayed on the phone like he'd asked her to, wouldn't stop talking. She was actually *in* her car and headed for Owen Beach by then, so she could meet Lars Larson, the Johnny surrogate, and talk to Cindy about tit sizes. Lars knew that the danger to Cindy, or the *immediate* danger anyway, had passed, so he wasn't sure if he could explain why he still insisted on inserting himself.

"I don't go to Point Defiance much, but I'm headed down Pearl. That's right, ain't it?" asked LaVeronica.

If she'd said she was coming before she started driving, Lars would have tried to talk her out of it, but she was halfway to them now.

"That's right," said Cindy. "Once inside the park, just follow the signs."

Lars had set his cell phone on the hood of Cindy's Jeep and they were standing around talking to it. The rain hadn't stopped and another two cars had come down to cruise the beach before Red Dye finally unlocked his T-bird, got his own cell phone out, and called someone. This was all too ridiculous, even for Lars.

"It's me," said Red Dye. "I'm still with Cindy and now some fool is messing with us."

His tone was as cold as the day.

"Who's he callin' a fool?" asked LaVeronica. "He's the fool. Was he talking 'bout me just now?"

"No, he wasn't, LaVeronica," said Cindy. "He was talking

about Lars, and he's talking *to* his twin brother, Fred, the cause of all our grief."

"I can't get over how much Lars sounds like Johnny," LaVeronica said. "It made my heart do cartwheels when I heard his voice. . . . Hey, on my left now is the Goldfish Tavern. Maybe we should all meet there, work this out where it's warm and dry. I ain't sayin' nothin' 'bout you-all's taste, but this don't look like beach weather to a normal person."

"The Goldfish isn't open yet," said Red Dye, still on his phone. "But it's not a bad idea. Robin Hood here can buy us lunch. You wanta come, too, Fred? Screw things up a little more?"

"I could at least get out of these wet pants," said Cindy. "I've got dry ones in my car. How about it, Lars? You're the one who started all this chivalrous stuff." Lars looked at his watch, shocked to see that is was 11:30.

"And it is too open," said LaVeronica. "There are motorcycles parked in front and its sign is lit. I don't wanta incriminate myself, but I know an open bar when I see one, just not this early in the day. Should I pull in here, or what?"

BACK WHEN HE WAS MARRIED to his second wife, Lars used to go to the Goldfish to drink and play shuffleboard. In those days, there were actual goldfish swimming under the tabletops, beneath a scratched sky with beer mugs on it. It had been years since he'd been there, though, and he figured the goldfish idea had pretty much dried up.

LaVeronica's car surprised Lars, who led the caravan to the tavern in his loaner VW. He didn't know what he thought she might drive, but a bright red Prius stood next to the motor-cycles, with a big black woman leaning against the side of it. She had a scrunched-down face before she saw Lars, but then her face did the same cartwheel her heart apparently did when she thought of Johnny, and it flipped itself around into a fabu-lous smile. Lars waved, but Cindy, who drove in just behind him and just ahead of Red Dye, stormed out of her Jeep and into LaVeronica's arms.

"Now, now," said LaVeronica. "Things gonna work out fine."

Inside the Goldfish, which Red Dye entered first, three bikers sat at the bar discussing housing prices. Otherwise, the place was empty, so Lars and LaVeronica went to the table Red Dye found while Cindy walked into the ladies' room to change. "I don't think they serve lunch here," said Lars.

"We don't, but I can order pizza," called the bartender. "Individual deep-dish pie from up the street. Cook used to work at the Northlake Tavern."

He came to take their drink orders. LaVeronica told Cindy she looked great when she came back out of the ladies' room wearing new designer jeans and some cool green shoes. Her hair was combed out nicely, too, and drier than anyone else's.

"I got empathy, honey," LaVeronica said. "Went through this same unending pain with Johnny. It don't have to be this way, though. It only feels like it now."

Maybe so, but to Lars, Cindy's look said she'd stuffed her unending pain in the bag with her beach clothes. He was older than these women by a couple of decades, and he should be meeting Ruth so they could talk about their own unending problems. But back when he was fourteen years old, Lars had had trouble with some bullies, scarring his sense of himself for years. That was why he'd felt compelled to come to Cindy's aid—he had sworn he would never let it happen again, to himself or anyone else. Now, though, it all seemed futile and silly. No one came to anyone else's aid; in the end everyone just had to help themselves. Still, he waited until they ordered their beer and everyone but him had asked for various pizzas before he looked at Red Dye and said, "I don't know you, don't know your situation or even your name, but what possessed you to say such horrible things to Cindy down at the beach?"

He was pleased, felt he'd struck the right tone.

"What'd he say to her?" asked LaVeronica. "I mean, if it was only words, Lars, you know that old thing 'bout sticks and stones. Folks say lots of things they don't mean."

"He told me to get into the water up to my cunt," said Cindy.

"*What?*" LaVeronica turned her steely eyes on Red Dye. "You no-good dipshit! I ought to kick your head in right now, you, you . . . What *is* your dumb-ass name?"

"It's Red," said Red Dye.

"Really?" asked Lars. Another old wife, his first, used to tell him he had a fine-tuned intuition, often getting the sense of things before anyone else.

"You mean their mama named them Red and Fred?" asked LaVeronica. "No wonder they're so messed up!"

"Actually, she named them Frederic and Frederico," Cindy said.

That made Lars laugh. Frederic and Frederico. He remembered that Red had reminded him of a pit bull down at the beach and thought about getting one himself, or better, he'd get two, name them Frederic and Frederico. Except that if he ever got another dog, it wouldn't be a pit bull, the dog-breed equivalent of oversize tires.

Red didn't like Lars's laugh, but before he could say anything, the front door opened again. "Oh God, it's Fred," said Cindy, closing her eyes.

Lars kept his eyes open and saw double trouble filling the frame of the Goldfish's door. Frederic and Frederico. Fred didn't look exactly like Red because his hair was long and he had a beard. What he did look like was a man wearing a disguise, a devil in a hippie costume, a robber before a heist.

Fred surveyed the room, then came over to put a hand on Red's shoulder. Lars now noticed that he wore a single dangling earring with a Buddha at its end, as incongruous as a pirate tattoo on a ballerina.

"Does this mean one more pizza?" asked the bartender. "I'm just calling your order in now."

RUTH HAD WORKED AT TOBEY JONES NURSING HOME before joining Lars Larson Motors. She'd been Lars's grandfather's caregiver and sometimes went with Lars to see his grandfather now. Ruth was Eritrean and a trained accountant, so Lars didn't steal her from Tobey Jones entirely because he fell in love with her. Now that their love was rocky, though, relying solely on Ruth's accountancy skills wasn't working out very well. He had called her again on his way to the Goldfish to tell her what was happening and ask her to meet him there, not to eat lunch with this crazy menagerie but so they could go somewhere afterward. So when Fred arrived, haloed in the doorway like an emissary, Lars at first thought Ruth had grown large.

"How do you do? Fred Kelso," Fred said, sticking his hand out to Lars.

"Fred Kelso and Red Kelso," said Cindy. "The Brothers Grimm of my life."

"They do look pretty grim," said LaVeronica as Fred sat down beside her. Lars had been right about the goldfish. There was only empty space below the thick glass tabletops. If he owned the place, he would put in goldfish cutouts.

"Red called and told me what happened when he was driving over here," said Fred. "Maybe you should have stayed behind that log, Lars. It's embarrassing having our dirty laundry aired in public. Where do you get off sticking your nose into other people's business?"

It was a very short distance from "How do you do?" to belligerence.

Lars tried to stare Fred down while LaVeronica asked him if Red had told him what he'd actually said to Cindy. "Tried to make her go out into the water up to her . . . Heck, I can't even say the word," she said.

When Fred looked at Red, it was like watching a made-up actor see his un-made-up reflection in a mirror.

"In the end, we have to look out for each other, Fred," said Lars.

This was contrary to what he'd been thinking, but he chalked it up to the difference between speech and thought.

"Bullshit, Lars," said Fred. "I have to look out for Red, Red has to look out for me, and Cindy's in the mix with us, but it doesn't have a thing to do with you."

The Buddha at the end of his earring did a little dance, like it was trying to shake nonviolent beliefs out of its head.

"It doesn't have a thing to do with you," echoed Red.

"I guess I shouldn't be surprised to find two dipshits in one family," LaVeronica said, "but what's up between you and these doofuses, Cindy? They each get to suck one tit?"

That shocked Lars, but Cindy only said, "Unfortunately, I was engaged to one of them. Back when they were both clean-shaven."

"She was engaged to me," said Red. "Till she started meeting Fred, too, the wicked bitch."

"You know I thought he was you!" cried Cindy. "How many times do I have to tell you? He had all the same moves, even made the same noises. . . ."

"Hold on! Don't go violatin' no one's trust," said LaVeronica. "If I learned one thing since I last saw you, Cindy, it's the horrible cost of trust violatin'."

"You slept with Johnny's brother, too, I suppose," said Red.

"Nope, he was a drummer I used to know before I knew Johnny, that's all."

"See?" said Cindy. "Anyone can make a mistake. Ask yourself who you really can't forgive, Red, me or a man who knew he was hurting you by pretending to be you?"

"Yes, Red, ask yourself that," said Lars. "You pushed her into Puget Sound, threatened her with a rock, but it's Buddha Boy here you should be mad at."

Cindy smiled at Lars, while Fred gave him the look of a Buddhist martial arts expert.

"Lars Larson's right," said LaVeronica. "Think of it this way, Red. A guy who looks exactly like you takes the woman you love and not only messes with her body but completely undoes her head. That's an unfair advantage over all of human life that ain't twins. Fred's not your alter ego. He's the pus in a boil on your heart, and you got to squeeze the sucker out."

Everyone looked at her but Fred, who kept his eyes on Lars. "Lars Larson from the TV ads?" he asked.

"That's Lars's dad," said Cindy.

"Your whole family is a bunch of cheating used-car dealers and you have the nerve to call me pus?" Fred said. "You better worry how you're gonna look on TV if I catch you outside."

Lars despised himself for it, but he gulped, like the same lame coward he'd been when he was fourteen years old. He sipped his beer so his second gulp had liquid in it instead of fear.

For the last little while, Cindy had been trying to hold Red's hand. "Don't you see how wrong you were?" she asked. "LaVeronica sees it, Lars was able to see it from the other side of a log he was hiding behind, and I've been telling you and telling you . . . Fred is just a pus-head, Red, the boil on the ass of our relationship."

"I wasn't exactly hiding," said Lars. "I just didn't want to talk."

"Fred 'Pus-head' Kelso," said Red. "Ladies and gents, here sits a man who doesn't care about anyone but himself."

"Fred 'Pus-head' Kelso," said Cindy, like it was a testament in church.

"All right, Lars, I want you out in the parking lot right now," said Fred. "Call me a pus-head, will you? Well, I'm gonna turn you into a real one!"

He stood so quickly that his chair fell over. The bikers and the bartender turned to stare, and when the bartender said,

"No fighting inside, boys," Fred looked over at the bar and asked, "Who wants to be next?"

Lars believed in clarity of speech. In the car business, you had to be clear or you wouldn't sell any cars. You couldn't throw words around, or numbers, either, since customers always remembered what was most favorable to themselves. So he said, quite correctly, "I didn't call you a pus-head, Fred; that was someone else. I was just sitting here, same as I was behind that log."

He hoped one of the bikers would raise his hand when Fred asked who wanted to be next, but no tattoo twitched. Until, that is, Red stood up and said, "Hey, Pus-head. I don't want to be next; I want to be first."

Fred spun around so quickly that his Buddha earring rode out from its earlobe like a kid on the swing ride at the Puyallup Fair.

"You're better than this, Red," said Cindy. "This just brings you down to his level," but LaVeronica shook her head. "No, honey, that ain't true. This is a required course for Red, like biology was for us back in high school. He got to beat the bad out of himself while he's beatin' the shit out of Fred. Otherwise, things will never change. Ain't that right, Red?"

"Yes it is," Red said. "He needs to be gone from our lives, Cindy. If Fred goes, so does the guy you saw me turn into down at the beach. If Fred goes, then I can be myself again."

"He's got a devil on one shoulder, angel on the other, and it's them doin' battle, Cindy, not Red himself."

Red and Fred stared at each other like LaVeronica's words had turned them into Old Testament warriors on a mountaintop. And then, on a signal no one else could read, they turned and walked outside, with everyone following along.

Fred had a T-bird, too, also with oversize tires. The twin T-birds faced each other while each man stood in front of his, and the bikers stood beside their bikes. Lars looked at his VW for a second but decided not to stand in front of it.

"This will go on forever if we fight like we used to," said Fred. "So no holds barred this time, Red. Might be only one twin survives."

Once, back in the day, the kid who'd bullied Lars had said, "Last time I got into a fight, the other guy went to the hospital," so Lars knew as well as Red did that this was a tactic. Still, had *he* been fighting Fred, it would have worked like a charm.

Fred took off his Buddha earring, looked for someone to hand it to, then set it on the hood of his T-bird. Red reminded Lars of Gary Cooper in *High Noon,* a movie he sometimes watched with his grandfather, while Fred reminded him of Gary Cooper, too.

Fred and Red came away from their cars to circle each other. Red kept his hands down, fists not balled yet, and Fred did also. When Fred feigned left, so did Red, and when Red missed with a quick left hook, Fred countered with a left of his own, also off the mark. When Fred kicked, Red kicked, and when Red went straight at his brother, the two men bumped chests hard, bouncing back. Fred threw dirt in Red's left eye, while Red threw dirt in Fred's right, and when Red tried a karate kick, his own thigh got whacked by Fred, who had the same idea at the same time. It was like watching two thumbs doing battle over a pair of folded hands.

"This ain't solvin' much," said LaVeronica.

Red slapped Fred when Fred glanced at LaVeronica, and when Fred slapped him back, both men's heads flew sideways, their opposite cheeks aflame. They both rubbed the thighs that had been kicked, then limped backward. Red was sweating and Fred was sweating and when one looked up into the descending rain, the other did also. They were like two huge turkeys in a barnyard.

There was so little traffic on the road in front of the tavern that Lars could easily see the Jag Ruth liked to drive, an old MK VII, coasting down toward them. Most days, he kept the MK VII in his showroom, though he knew it was a risk to the sale of newer models, since it highlighted what cars had been like when style was really style. Red and Fred were car lovers, too, and when Red saw the Jag roll in next to Lars's VW, he dropped his guard. "Look, Fred," he said. "What I wouldn't give for one of those in my Christmas stocking!"

Fred hit him on the right side of his jaw with a powerful roundhouse uppercut that knocked Red's teeth loose and cracked so loudly through the rain that the others heard it even before Ruth turned the Jaguar's engine off. Red slammed onto the hood of his T-bird.

"Tell you what, Lars," said Fred. "Sell me that car and I might let you live. I'll even throw in my T-bird. It's a hundred percent original, never mind the tires."

Fred was the evil twin but knew his T-bird was diminished by those tires, which was more than Red seemed to know about anything. If the T-bird had been from an earlier year, Lars might have considered the deal.

Fred looked at Lars as if waiting for an answer, thus allowing Red time to get off his car and execute an uppercut of his own, sending Fred across the parking lot to crash into the T-bird he had just offered to trade. His Buddha earring leapt up off the hood like a jumping bean, sailed over the T-bird's left front fender, and disappeared into a mud puddle. Ruth, meanwhile, saw what was happening and restarted the Jag. She'd had enough of fighting in Eritrea and just about enough in her current life. She rolled down the MK VII's window and said, *"Lars,"* but a delivery scooter cut through her line of vision at just that instant.

"Here are your pizzas," said the bartender. "Maybe you could take a break, call this round one."

Red looked at Fred, who had stood up off the hood of his T-bird, rubbing his jaw. And when he muttered, "I've lost my goddamn Buddha," LaVeronica said, "You shouldn't wear it anyway, Fred, not till you get closer to what Mr. Gandhi and Dr. King and all of them other Buddhist motherfuckers was tryin' to tell us. You want another earring in the meantime, I'll give you a fine ruby elephant minus his trunk."

She pointed to her bag as if the ruby elephant were hiding in it.

At first Red seemed to want to continue the fight, but Fred was unable to take his eyes off LaVeronica's bag, as if thinking maybe a ruby elephant minus its trunk would be a very cool thing to wear around. When Ruth put the MK VII back in gear, creeping out of the parking lot again and driving back up the road, Lars noticed the raindrops on his face for the first time since coming outside. They felt like someone else's tears, like another person's heartache. When he looked at Cindy, she said, "You can share my pizza if you want to, Lars. You were great down at the beach, popping up like some kind of strange detective."

"No thanks, Cindy," said Lars. "I'm late for work as it is and I want to make sure that Jag gets cleaned up properly."

He nodded up the road, as if the car were all that had really left him.

When Cindy hugged him, he patted her back, then shook hands with Red before Red and Cindy followed the bartender and the three silent bikers back inside.

Fred and LaVeronica were still over by Fred's T-bird, with Fred kneeling down in front of her while LaVeronica affixed the ruby red elephant to his ear. It didn't look trunkless, the elephant, but half-trunked, a truncated trunk, thought Lars, and that made him laugh, causing Fred to cast him another mean look.

"No, no," said Lars, "the time for fighting is over, Fred. I'm just laughing at my own sorry life."

It surprised him to hear himself say those words, and it also made him think of his grandfather, up at Tobey Jones.

When Fred and LaVeronica went back into the tavern, clearly expecting him to follow, Lars knelt down where Fred had been, in order to try to see up the hill to where his grandfather maybe still sat looking out his window. Lars felt like praying, so he bent his head to his knees, his hands out in front of him, prostrate before everything that had brought him here, his childhood, his marriages, cars and money and Ruth. The rain had increased to the point where he could feel it needling his hands and the back of his head. He liked rain, always felt secure in it. "A truncated trunk," he said, and knew right away that this was his prayer.

He sat up again, fearful that someone might have heard him, but when he looked around, he quickly knew that he was alone but for the smiling face of Fred's Buddha, which had popped back up and was floating on the surface of the mud puddle with its hands behind its head. He remembered that the Buddha's hands had been laced across its belly when Fred came into the bar, but now they were behind its head. Lars scooped his own hands into the mud puddle and, careful not to disturb the Buddha, lifted it out, stood, and hurried over to his VW. Worlds within worlds within worlds. Could this Buddha possibly know that his meditations were now taking place in the two cupped hands of a man like Lars in Tacoma, Washington? And, in turn, could Lars possibly know whose hands he was cupped in?

He managed to open the VW's door with the extended pinkie of his left hand. A half-empty Lars Larson Motors bottom-heavy travel mug sat on the console, so he tipped his hands quickly, letting what water they still contained, plus the Buddha, flow into the mug. The Lars Larson Motors bottom-heavy travel mug had a small mouth, giving the Buddha, when he popped up yet again, an even smaller pool than that made by Lars's hands.

"The secret to happiness is in not wanting," Lars said. It was advice he'd received from someone once. It hadn't kept him from wanting, but it was something to think about, and something to say once in a while.

The Buddha's hands were still behind its head as it looked up out of the coffee mug, making Lars doubt that they had ever been laced across its stomach.

"Ah doubt," he said, and when the Buddha didn't answer, he pulled out into the empty street and headed back across town.

Sarco-gophus

[2007]

I

WIZENED, GRIZZLED, INTO HIS SIXTIES, and back in Tacoma for the first time since joining the Merchant Marines after high school, Perry White sat in the docket at the County-City Building, listening to his arraignment on murder charges. His hands were in his lap and he stared at them.

"He grew up here, Your Honor, he's got roots," said his attorney, Susan Blake. "He's not going anywhere."

His attorney had been appointed by the court.

"Mr. White?" asked the judge. "Could you assure me of that directly?"

"Not goin' anywhere. Got roots. Got my brother. He's right back there."

"Half brother, Your Honor, just to be clear," said his attorney.

She turned toward the back of the room, where Perry White's half brother sat with his hands in his lap, too. He raised one of them in order to salute the judge. "Nice to see you again, Your Honor."

"Likewise, Mr. Lilly," said the judge.

Both men smiled at the formalities. They'd known each other since college, when Judge Follett used to write wills for people in a tavern where Richard Lilly tended bar.

Judge Follett turned his attention to the prosecutor's table. "Ms. Packer, I'm about to set bail if there are no objections from your office," he said.

"Bail, Your Honor?" said Ms. Packer. "Are you kidding me?"

Though the courtroom was nearly empty, she looked back into it anyway, not at Richard Lilly but at the rows of vacant benches, as if they should also be shocked by the idea of bail for a transient charged with second-degree murder. She faced the judge again. She knew he wasn't happy with "Are you kidding me?"

"My office *vigorously* objects," she said. "Mr. White's been gone for forty years. If he has roots, they're planted somewhere else."

Thank God the room was empty. She'd had a hellish fight with her mother last night and hadn't slept.

"I don't have roots nowhere else," said Perry White.

"And Mr. Lilly has agreed to provide domicile as well as bail, Your Honor," his attorney said.

"Anyone can see he's a flight risk," said Ms. Packer, but the judge set bail at $300,000. "That'll put a dent in your wallet if he does fly the coop, Mr. Lilly," he said.

"I know, Your Honor, but family is family," said Richard Lilly. "And Perry has promised me he'll stick around."

"Family is family," Ms. Packer muttered. "Can't beat that as a tenet of the law."

HERE ARE THE DETAILS OF THE CASE as we know them thus far. Perry White found a teenage girl wandering around in a cemetery, killed her, and placed her body on top of someone's grave. The dead girl, Katie Smothers, had lived near the cemetery, and Perry had been seen during his time back in Tacoma visiting the grave Katie's body was found on, that of a certain Winifred Wilcox. When questioned by the police, he said he'd simply been paying his respects. Before his arrest he'd lived at the Salvation Army apartments on Sixth Avenue, without contacting anyone from his past. But when the story hit the papers, Richard Lilly came forward, thus getting us to the point of his release on bail.

And here are the details concerning Ms. Packer's fight with her mother and her poor performance in court. She'd made it clear to her mother *and* her mother's longtime boyfriend that she wouldn't recuse herself from the case. Her mother had asked her to do so because, in precisely the sort of coincidence that happens in towns like Tacoma, her longtime boyfriend was Richard Lilly, the defendant's half brother.

Outside the courtroom, Perry White's attorney was chatting with Richard Lilly when Beverly Packer came out. Though the judge had granted bail, it would take a while to complete the paperwork, and Richard hoped to lunch with Beverly in order to smooth things over from the night before. He'd been her mother's boyfriend since Beverly was in high school and loved her quite as if she were his daughter. And she, though she'd have been hard-pressed to admit it at the moment, felt the same way.

When Susan Blake saw Beverly approaching them, she shook Richard's hand and strode away while Beverly muttered, "How can you stand her, Richie? She's more famous for her bleeding heart shenanigans than those Humane Society ads you hate so much on TV."

Richard Lilly shrugged. "She champions the underdog," he said, "but what's gotten into you, Bev? You weren't very good in there, you know."

"My fight with Mom's what's gotten into me. I don't mind fighting in court, but fighting with her makes me hate myself."

"Why don't we have lunch?" asked Richard. "Everyone said too much last night." But Beverly said she had to meet her paralegal, prepare for possible jury selection, and develop a strategy. She hugged him and got out of there fast, before last night's tears demanded a return engagement.

When she got to her office a half an hour later, her boss was there, sitting on the edge of her desk.

"Got a minute?" he asked.

Her boss was not the prosecuting attorney but his chief assistant, with eyes too close together and shoots of unruly hair that gave him the look of having just gotten up. Beverly put her briefcase down. She was in no mood to hear what she feared she'd hear, and hoped her look let him know it.

"Okay, Clement, who called you?" she asked. "Or is this coming from the horse's mouth?"

"I'm afraid it's coming from the horse's mouth. He's reassigning the case."

"The hell he is," said Beverly. "It's my turn, dammit. Don't we do things in rotation around here? What ever happened to our storied office backbone?"

"The man's your father's brother, Bev. You should've known that wouldn't fly."

"He's *not* my father's brother; he's the *half* brother of my mother's boyfriend. That's it. Who's in line to take the case if I do recuse myself?"

She picked up her briefcase again, pressing it against her breasts.

"You know as well as I do that it's me," he said. "That way, you won't miss your turn."

"Too bad I'm not recusing myself then," she said. "Tell the horse's mouth he can kiss my horse's ass."

But he only told her to have her notes in his office by the end of the day.

"Look, Mr. White," said Susan Blake when they got to *her* office a few minutes later. "My job is to counter what the prosecution throws at you; your visits to the cemetery, your talk with Katie Smothers over the fence to her backyard, and most of all your first words to the cops, which they thought were a confession. But *I* don't want a confession from you; I hope that's clear."

"Weren't no confession anyway," said Perry, "'cept on how her body got over to Winnie's grave."

Susan fingered a message she'd found taped to her door. Clement Page had called. "I think they have an offer for us," she said. "How about I see what's up before we talk?"

She picked up her phone to call Clement Page at about the same time that, back across town, Beverly Packer picked up *hers* to call her husband, Bill.

"Hey," she said when Bill answered, "did Richie call you?"

"Yep," said Bill, "and so did your mom. Richie told me

what happened in court just now, and your mom told me what happened last night."

Bill had been asleep when Beverly got home the night before, and he'd left for work before she woke up. Bill owned a garage.

"Mom wants me off the case and now so does Clement. Should I fight it, Bill, or cave like a wuss?"

"How are you gonna fight it? Doesn't what Clement says go?"

Bill had grease on his thumb and little finger, so he held them away from the phone. It made him look like he was pantomiming a phone call.

"Usually it does, but I've got an ace up my sleeve, which I'm thinking of pulling out," Beverly said.

Bill didn't ask what her ace was since he knew she didn't have one.

Meanwhile, Clement Page hadn't called Susan Blake with a plea offer but with word that Beverly was off the case and he would be opposing Susan now. He said it was a courtesy call, but Susan knew a come-on when she heard one. Clement was famous for hitting on women who opposed him.

"Thanks for the warning, but how about we talk about his innocence?" she said.

That made Clement laugh. "I'll recommend the minimum sentence if he pleas out," he told her. "That means he might not die in jail."

"Come on, Clem, give me something I can work with here."

She knew that saying "Clem" would appeal to him.

"I don't know the case yet. Let me catch myself up on it, and then we can talk about it over drinks," he said.

"Works for me," said Susan.

When she got off the phone, she and Perry went over again what he remembered from the night of the murder, what he'd told the police, and why he had been at the Wilcox grave in the first place.

"You knew her when you were kids, but the last time you saw her was years ago? That's your story?"

"It's my story 'cause it's true. Winnie was kind to me when others wasn't, kind to her family's pets after they died, digging 'em proper graves and such."

"Do you have a thing for graves, Perry? Did you wander around when you were up there, look at other people's names and dates?"

"Yeah, but only so I could let Winnie know who her neighbors was. I suppose you think that's nuts."

"I think a lot of us would like to talk to those we once loved. But tell me the 'when' and 'where' of it one last time, and why you dragged Katie over to Winnie's grave."

"First off, I didn't drag her; I carried her. I seen her lyin' across the way 'bout eight o'clock but left her alone 'cause I thought she was asleep. Kids was always fooling around up there, so I figured maybe Katie was tired."

"You recognized her as Katie, as the girl you talked to over the fence to her backyard?"

"Not till I went over to her."

"I don't know, Perry, if I spied a sleeping girl in a cemetery, I think I'd worry I might scare her if I woke her up."

"Which is why I didn't go earlier. Not till I thought she'd get in trouble for stayin' out late."

"But you just said you didn't know it was Katie."

"Any kid might get in trouble for a thing like that."

"Okay, what happened when you did go over there?"

"I knew the grave she was lyin' on belonged to a man named Jonathan Fleming, whose wife come up there sometimes. I even thought it might be her sleepin' there. Grief makes a person do funny things."

"First you say you were worried about Katie and now you say it might've been Jonathan Fleming's wife?"

"That thought only fluttered by; I knew it was a kid all right. I weren't wearin' shoes, so I went over quiet and nudged her with my toe. That's when I saw she was dead and I shoulda called the cops."

"Why didn't you? It would have saved us all a lot of trouble."

"You ever been to Egypt, Ms. Blake, or seen King Tut at one of his traveling shows?"

"Haven't been to Egypt, but I saw King Tut when he came to Seattle that time."

"So you know what a sarco-gophus is? Them carved-out depictions of folks?"

"Sarcophagus, yes . . ."

"I ain't sayin' Katie looked like Winnie. I don't know what Winnie looked like as a grown-up person, but I knew her kid face, and that night Katie looked like Winnie would have if she'd died young. So I carried Katie over so Winnie could have a sarco-gophus. Maybe it was crazy, but I wanted Winnie's goodness to show itself aboveground one more time."

That stopped Susan Blake. He'd answered her questions, but how could she take that into court? He was watching for signs of ridicule, so she asked him casually, "How come you weren't wearing shoes?"

"'Cause you don't wear shoes when you go into one a them Egyptian mosques. It's how you show respect."

"So if you did what you said you did, who killed Katie Smothers and left her on Jonathan Fleming's grave?"

Perry said he didn't know and asked her to take him to Richard's house.

Beverly was standing in Richard's kitchen with her mother when Susan Blake dropped Perry off. That alone should have told her that fighting her removal from the case was a bad idea. She *should* be removed; she *was* too close to it.

She hadn't meant to stay at Richard's this late, so she hid in the pantry while Richard greeted Perry and showed him to his room. And when he came back downstairs, Beverly was gone.

"Are you surprised by how hard she's taking this?" he asked Donna, Beverly's mom. "All these years, who has been the levelheaded one among us if not that daughter of yours?"

"I'm not at all surprised," said Donna. "This case has caught the public eye like nothing since the Frugal Gourmet. And you know it's more complicated than simply having Perry in the family. There are too many weird connections. . . . We both knew Winnie as kids, for crying out loud."

"Winnie, my god," said Richard. "They quoted her sister in the paper, calling Perry a pervert and a lowlife. Only the good die young, I guess."

When his phone rang, he answered to hear Bill ask for Beverly, then say that he'd found a letter she had written, resigning from the prosecutor's office. He said if she didn't get home soon, he would go out looking for her.

"That Bill always was a snoop," said Donna when Richard hung up.

"Maybe *I* should go look for her," said Richard. "It's odd she's isn't home yet. It isn't that long a drive."

"If she doesn't get there soon, *I'll* go," said Donna. "She's probably watching the Canada geese down on Ruston Way. And speaking of geese, Perry will be up with the chickens, so you should get some sleep."

That was Donna's way of saying Richard wasn't Beverly's father. She didn't say it often, but each time she did so, it stung.

When he went upstairs again and saw Perry asleep *on* his bed instead of in it, he found an old family afghan, covered him with it, then sat in a rocking chair by the window. Perry had simply been a kid in the neighborhood before they found out about the affair between Richard's father and Perry's mother, and though they'd tried to act like brothers after they found out, it hadn't lasted long. And now here he was, dead to the world in Richard's house. When Donna asked him why he'd come forward not only with bail but with the offer of a place for Perry to stay, Richard had said he was doing it for his father, though that was probably a lie. His father had never embraced the fact that Perry was his son. When his father died, in fact, Richard hadn't looked for Perry, nor had he looked for him when Perry's mother died the next year, alone and decrepit in Perry's old house. So whatever had been between them had long ago run its course. . . . Still, there was no question he'd felt compelled to offer Perry a place to stay.

When Richard stood up from the rocking chair, the chair kept rocking, as if it were nodding to itself.

THE BAR CLEMENT PAGE ASKED SUSAN BLAKE to meet him in had a "lounge-around" feeling to it, with windows that looked out onto the street. And it wasn't a sports bar, so you could hear yourself think.

Susan didn't see him when she walked in, so she ordered a beer and paid for it. She wouldn't let him buy her anything. Indeed, after her talk with Perry, she wished she hadn't agreed to meet him, for it now seemed a cheap sort of move, another round in the game she sometimes liked to play when she ought to be fighting for her client. She decided that if Clement didn't show up by the time she finished her beer, she'd go home. She drank down a quarter of it and looked at her phone. Seven minutes after nine. She finished the beer and ordered another one.

Beverly, meanwhile, wasn't watching Canada geese down on Ruston Way but was at a market up on Proctor Street. She began eating the ice cream she'd been craving right there in the store while scanning the numbers in her phone for those of Susan Blake and Detective Triplet, the lead cop on Perry's case. She wouldn't call either of them tonight, of course, and surely not Susan until she'd officially resigned. But she didn't have Susan's number anyway, only Detective Triplet's. She punched it in, knowing he wouldn't be there, not this late. But he answered right away, saying, "Hi, Ms. Packer, what's up with you tonight?"

"Do you think we could talk?" she asked. "It's about the Katie Smothers case."

If he knew she'd recused herself, he might turn her down she realized, but he said quite cheerfully, "Frisco Freeze in half an hour? I don't have long."

She held her phone away from her in order to see the time. Nine-seventeen. "I haven't had dinner yet," she said.

After she ended the call, she went home to put her ice cream in the freezer and pick up her resignation letter, which she would mail before meeting Detective Triplet. She hardly noticed that Bill wasn't there.

Meanwhile, back at the bar, when Clement Page finally did arrive, Susan was sitting in an easy chair near the bar's front door.

"So sorry!" he said. "I was talking with my boss about your erstwhile opposing counsel. Please now, what are you drinking? My treat."

"Only the bartender knows," Susan said, "but how come she's 'erstwhile'? Did something happen to Ms. Packer?"

He said only what he'd said on the phone, that she'd recused herself, then went to get their beer. While he was gone, Susan tried to sit properly, but the chairs were meant for sprawling, which was what, she often feared, her body was also meant for. She sometimes looked up *sloth*, expecting to see a photo of herself, but only got that three-toed animal.

"Look," she said when he got back, "I'm sorry about Ms. Packer, but why are we here? What do you have to offer?"

"I just gave you what I have to offer," he said, pointing at her beer.

Good, he was pissing her off. He saw it and said, "Thing is, I read the case notes and think your client confessed. We'll still lighten the sentence for a guilty plea, but otherwise it's you and me, babe, facing off in court."

"If he confessed, I'll eat my hat," said Susan. "You all at your office . . . don't you ever get tired of thinking everything anyone says is just the tip of the iceberg?"

She was pleased with "eat my hat," but he only pushed his beer mug across the gap between them, clicking it against hers.

She wrapped her legs around each other when he sat down.

WHERE WAS BILL AND WHY HADN'T BEVERLY NOTICED that he wasn't home when she stopped to put away the ice cream and get her resignation letter?

The answer was that for the past few weeks Bill had either stayed late at his garage or gone back to it in order to avoid confronting what he feared might be happening between himself and his wife. There was plenty for him to do at the garage. A '54 MG roadster that Richard had given him sat under tarps. He meant to make it cherry again, but all he'd managed so far was to sit beside it drinking beer. And on this night, too, while Beverly met Detective Triplet, he took the tarp off the MG and picked up his notebook. There were drawings in the notebook, not of the repairs he had to make, but of the MG with Beverly in the driver's seat, her scarf stretched out behind her in the wind. He got a can of Miller High Life, stepped over the MG's sidewall, and sat down. Richard had done that years ago, making Bill like him right away. If not for Richard, in fact, he and Beverly wouldn't have made it through Beverly's college and law school. There were other men back then, but Beverly always returned to Bill; he was sure this was because she saw in him something like what her mother saw in Richard. Now, though, as he sat in Richard's car, the old fear came back: that Beverly would leave him as soon as she discovered who he was.

"It's a double meat, double cheese burger," said Detective Triplet. "I can't go a week without one. I got fries and coffee, too. If you want, we can eat in my car."

Beverly'd bought a regular burger and a strawberry milk shake she didn't want. They walked across the parking lot to a police-issued Chevy, its seat pushed back to accommodate Detective Triplet's height and bulk. They sat their drinks on the console and ate for a while in silence until he said, "Okay, shoot, Ms. Packer. What's up?"

"I've got two questions: Do you think Perry White is guilty, and did you think, when you interviewed him, that he confessed?"

"He didn't confess to the murder, but he did confess to moving Katie's body," Detective Triplet said. He reached around to grab a file. "'Suspect insisted that he *carried* Katie to the Wilcox grave. Then he talked about King Tut.' I'd say that adds up to some pretty substantial sanity questions."

Beverly sat there thinking about that for a while, then asked what his opinion was of Susan Blake. The expression on Detective Triplet's face didn't change, but his voice grew flat.

"Whatever fishing's going on here, I suggest you do it in the light of day," he said. "I agreed to talk to you about the case."

"I don't understand," said Beverly. "Do you have some kind of beef with Susan Blake?"

Both of them looked at their burgers, but she was the only one who smiled. "I don't have a beef with her; I have a *history* with her," he said.

He picked up his coffee and sipped from it. When he put it back down, Beverly took it and sipped from it, too, making the warmth of the coffee invade them both.

"I quit the case," she said, "and since I called you, I have also resigned from the prosecutor's office."

Detective Triplet took his coffee back, though he loved the fact that she'd sipped from it.

"I only asked about Ms. Blake because . . . well, because I'm tired of putting people away, wouldn't mind helping defend them for a while."

Was that the truth? If so, it hadn't occurred to her until she said it.

"Susan Blake has two gears," Detective Triplet told her. "One is aimed at the acquittal of her clients and the other at the destruction of whoever gets too close."

He pulled out one of his business cards, found a pen, and wrote Susan's cell phone number on the back of it.

And then he reached across her to open her door.

THE BAR WAS OTHERWISE EMPTY when the bartender said, "Last call."

"I'm done," said Clement Page. "You, Ms. Blake?"

"Three's my limit," said Susan, though by then she'd had four.

The bartender gave them the bill.

"A nightcap at my house?" Clement asked. "Not to be forward, but I do have a terrific Bordeaux."

Susan waved him away and stood. She was about to step out into the rain but then looked back down at him.

"How terrific is it?" she asked.

2

ON THE MORNING AFTER ALL THE BUSYNESS with Bill and Beverly, Detective Triplet, Susan Blake, and Clement Page, at Perry White's request, Richard drove him out to visit some of their old haunts at Brown's Point.

"Do you remember that boulder that sat on the beach in front of yer house?" Perry asked. "More'n half buried and underwater when the tide come in?"

"Remember it well," said Richard. "We used to dive off of it."

They had already driven past where Perry's house once stood and were parked near their old school bus stop. Rain was dotting Richard's windshield and he didn't want to get out of his car, hoped that he could get away with simply driving around a bit and going home. Brown's Point hadn't changed much, but he didn't live there anymore.

"Let's go find it," Perry said. "What's with the tide? Is it in or out?"

Richard had a tide app on his phone.

"It's more than halfway in," he said. "And there's a wind coming up."

The part about the wind was not on his tide app.

"In Egypt, they revere old things, but here we tear 'em

down," said Perry. He cast a thumb back to where his house had been. Donna's old house, across from it, was also gone. "Come on, man, let's go," he said. "This is what we come for."

They got out of Richard's car and walked to the beach. Richard's childhood home was off toward Dash Point and high up on a bank. The boulder Perry wanted to visit wouldn't be visible until they got to it. Richard knew that something was up. He didn't fear—yet—that Perry might get violent with him, but it was a fear he'd had often during their childhood.

"Do you want to talk about the case?" he asked. "It won't go further than us, no further than right here and now, Perry. I promise."

"Okay, then," said Perry. "No one knows this, but over there in Egypt I had me a girlfriend who looked a lot like Winnie. When she died, too, there weren't no sarco-gophus for her, so when I carried Katie over to Winnie's grave, I was pretty much thinkin', Two birds with one stone. I may not be good at much—no one thinks I am—but I know how to mourn those I loved. And I loved 'em both, Richie, one for all my life and the other for a while."

Years ago there'd been a piling sticking out of the water some fifty yards offshore in front of Richard's house. It was long gone now, but Richard couldn't help thinking of it as a sarcophagus for his poorly spent youth. He looked toward where it had been.

"Your girlfriend died, too?" he asked. He could hear the caution in his voice.

"She was darker'n Winnie, didn't care 'bout pets, and half the time she didn't like me, but other'n that she was Winnie's whatever you call it . . . like a twin you never met. That's how I first come to notice her."

"Winnie's doppelgänger?" said Richard. "What was her name?"

"Name was Hetshepsit, but I called her 'Hetty.'"

They had walked down to just below Richard's old house. During the month or so that Perry'd lived with them, when Perry's mother and Richard's father were trying to work things out, Richard had tried, too, to make an actual brother out of him. But as soon as it grew clear that living together wasn't working, Perry'd picked a fight with him. They'd been right here, and the tide had been more than halfway in.

The boulder seemed smaller and more ancient than it had at the time of their fight. It extended only a foot out of the rocky beach.

"Winnie lived next door to you," Perry said. "I used to sneak into her basement. Snuck into yours a couple a times, too."

He stepped up onto the boulder, looking down at Richard.

"Let's get back to Hetshepsit," said Richard. "How did she die, and does her death have anything to do with Katie's?"

"Died of bein' a whore. Her mother was a whore before her 'cause whorin' was the family business. If you wanted, you could find 'em in the Egyptian whores' registry, but I pretended I didn't know about it."

A burst of cold wind came in off the bay. The rain had not let up. Perry got down off the boulder again and bent to pick up a couple of rocks, this time looking at Richard out of weasely eyes. "Okay, since yer askin', she died of gettin' a pillow in her mouth," he said. "Come home late and laughin'. Late's okay and laughin's okay, but a man don't cotton to both. . . ."

He threw a rock up toward Richard's house, where it disappeared into an ivy bank. "You coulda let us keep on livin' here. . . . You coulda told yer dad that drinkin' weren't the worst thing in the world, but you wanted me outta yer life."

"The way I remember it, it wasn't just drinking. Your mom was a little like Hetshepsit," said Richard.

He braced himself for Perry's fury, but Perry was concentrating on his remaining rock.

"It weren't just you. Seems like 'Get out of my life's' been people's slogan for me my whole life long, so I figured I'd oblige 'em. That's why I wanted us to come out here today, Richie. Figured I'd get myself gone where yer daddy and my mother got me started. You remember how I always used to hate to swim?"

"I do," said Richard, "but I think we came out here so you could say you smothered Hetshepsit and admit to killing Katie. So go ahead and say it. I'll keep my promise."

He braced himself again, but Perry only said, "Well, I guess you're gonna think what you're gonna think. What's the word the newspaper used for how Katie died? Was it ass fixation? They think the man who killed her had lewd thoughts, but even if he did, Katie weren't messed with. I made sure of that before I picked her up. Any fool knows that Winnie couldn't have no messed-with sarco-gophus. I hope you'll tell her parents that if you ever run across 'em."

Now Richard stepped up onto the boulder, to look for exit routes, he supposed. But all he saw was empty beach.

"The word the paper used was *asphyxiation*," he said. "I guess that's how Hetshepsit died, too."

"When we was livin' here, my mother told me lots of times she'd change, but she never did. I guess yer dad was right about that much. . . . You can't teach an old dog new tricks. I also guess my mom and me is just about the same."

He swung his arm around, kicked his leg back, and flung the rock he still held down toward a seagull standing in the nearby shallows. In the old days, he'd have brained the seagull first try, but the rock landed in front of it. He picked up another, bigger rock, turned to smile at Richard again, then smashed it mightily into his own forehead. It knocked him back a couple of feet, but he managed to stay upright.

"Perry!" screamed Richard. But Perry's eyes shone merrily below a starburst of blood. He hit himself twice more, until he fell to his knees and the seagull he'd tried to brain flew off.

BACK AT RICHARD'S HOUSE, Donna and Beverly grew worried after Richard and Perry had been gone for a little over six hours. Donna'd called Richard's cell a few times, but he didn't answer, so at her urging, Beverly called Detective Triplet, who agreed to come over before his night shift started. At Detective Triplet's urging, she also called Clement Page, who drove over, too, with Susan Blake beside him in his car. He hadn't received Beverly's letter yet, so he believed the call to be from his subordinate.

Why these five would so readily gather at Richard's house, which probably wouldn't happen normally, can be credited to the goings-on of the day before. These five, plus Bill, who worried about Richard, too, but was glad to see Clement Page's interest in someone other than his wife.

"I'm sure it seems so to you, but six hours isn't that long," Detective Triplet said. "After twenty-four hours maybe we can act."

His reaction at seeing Susan Blake was the opposite of

Bill's when seeing Clement Page. It made him fall back on his rule book. When Beverly asked if he wanted coffee, Donna's frustration boiled over.

"We've got soda, too, or how about a beer?" she said. "Good Christ, under these conditions six hours is plenty long!"

"Why not try calling again," said Susan Blake. "Sometimes persistence pays off."

"Harrumph," said Donna, but she pulled out her phone.

She could see by its clock that the number of hours Richard and Perry had been gone was now a lot closer to seven.

NEAR THE ROAD THAT RICHARD AND PERRY used to get to the beach stood an ancient cement boat ramp, crusted with barnacles and stacked with driftwood and seaweed and kelp. Richard meant to carry Perry all the way back to his car, then hurry off to the hospital, but by the time they got to the ramp he'd grown too heavy and Richard had to put him down. The tide had come in sufficiently to lift the driftwood slightly, but Perry's weight plus Richard's settled it back down. Perry's blood was all over Richard's arms and face and chest, so he dipped his hands in the water to wash himself off. He'd been aware of his vibrating phone when standing on the boulder, and when he felt it again now, he pulled it from his pocket, nearly dropping it in the bay when he tried to answer it.

"Listen, Donna," he said, "you have to call nine one one."

"Richie, thank God! Are you hurt, Richie? What's going on?"

"Remember the old boat ramp? Used to belong to the

Irwins? Tell them that's where we are. Please, Donna, hurry up and call them. I don't think we have much time."

"Richie?" said Donna, but Richard disconnected. He chanced a look at Perry, who lay beside him with his head smashed in and his eyes half open. Did that mean he was alive or dead?

"You know them sarco-gophuses, Richie?" Perry asked.

Richard leaned down close to him. "Yes," he said, "I know them."

When Perry said "Be mine," those heart-shaped candies that children used to pass around on Valentine's Day came into Richie's head. He looked at his phone again. What if Donna didn't remember the boat ramp? What if her sense of their youth was different from his? He'd just decided to call 911 himself when Donna called back.

"The firemen are on their way and so are we," she said. "Now what happened, Richie? I've got you on speakerphone."

"He wants me to be his sarcophagus," said Richard.

He heard "What?" from Beverly, Bill, Detective Triplet, Clement Page, and Susan Blake, all of whom were in Donna's car with her.

"We're on a stack of driftwood and the tide's coming in," he said.

"Are you stuck there, Richie? Come on, honey, answer me. Are you hurt?"

Richard knew he wasn't making sense, that seeing Perry beat his head in had scrambled his brain, too. He couldn't think and also couldn't see very well. When he looked at Perry now, Perry seemed to rise above him.

"Richie?" said some of those in Donna's car, but he heard

only murmurs. When the tide came farther in, never mind their weight, the driftwood groaned up off the boat ramp.

"We're on our way now, Perry," he said. "Set sail for Egypt, maybe, or for wherever Winnie is."

"Richie? Richie?" said the phone murmurs.

Perry wore a threadbare jacket zipped to his neck. Beneath it Richard imagined the same striped T-shirt he had worn as a kid. As the driftwood lifted, a wind rose, too, to tack them out toward the shipping lanes.

"I can't be your sarcophagus, Perry," said Richard, "I haven't lived well enough," but Perry only said, "Be mine" again.

The rain and the wind increased as the emergency medical crew showed up. Men got out of their truck and ran down to the shoreline to raise their arms and shout. Donna's van skidded on the gravel, turned sideways, righted itself, and stopped only inches from the fire truck. Donna got out and ran to the end of the boat ramp. She took off her shoes and was about to dive into the bay when Beverly caught her and held her in her arms.

Clement Page and Susan Blake stopped midway between the top of the beach and the waterline while Detective Triplet hurried down to show the firemen his badge. Bill had run onto the boat ramp, too, chasing Beverly, but when he saw how Donna's love for Richie made her want to swim to him, he took off his shoes and pants and shirt. No one noticed it save Susan Blake, who left Clement Page's side to gather Bill's clothes. "Go and get them, Bill," she said. "Bring them back to shore."

Bill didn't look at her, but his eyes met Beverly's when she turned and saw him standing in his underwear. He went to the end of the boat ramp, slipped into the water, and began swimming out.

"Hey! Come back here!" yelled a fireman, but Bill wasn't taking orders from anyone.

When Richard noticed his phone again, he saw by its timer that he'd been connected to Donna for twenty-five minutes. He sat up to look at those who'd gathered on the shore. And then he saw Bill.

"Someone's coming to rescue us, Perry," he said.

"Ain't no rescuin', Richie," said Perry. "The time for rescuin's over."

As commanded by his words, a swell from a passing freighter reached them just then, causing the part of the raft holding Perry to break away from the part that Richie was on. When Perry's side began to sink, he moved his hands from his sides to link them on the top of his chest. Richard watched him disappear from the surface of the water, his face still visible beneath it. When the strands of kelp that connected them broke and also went down, however, Richard lay back, linking his fingers, too.

He stayed that way until Bill got there and pulled him back to shore.

MUCH LIKE THE KELP HAD KEPT PERRY ATTACHED to Richard for a while, Perry's disappearance kept the rest of them together for most of the next week while police boats dredged the shoals of the bay. By week's end, however, a deluge caused the postponement of the search.

Clement Page was the first to break the bond they'd formed

when he finally got Beverly's resignation letter and told them without looking Beverly's way that his workload was such that he had to get back to it.

The second to break away was Detective Triplet. He, too, spoke without looking at Beverly, but she thought she understood something in it and walked him to the door, with Bill not far behind her.

"Thanks for everything," she said.

"Good-night and good luck," said Bill, making Susan Blake laugh.

Each night after Perry's disappearance, Bill went to his garage to work on Richard's car, and twice Richard joined him. To work on a car with one's son-in-law seemed just the thing after all they'd been through. That Bill was not his son-in-law was entirely beside the point.

The next to leave, two days later, was Susan Blake. On the night of Clement's departure, he'd called her to say he had another terrific Bordeaux, causing her to say she'd grown partial to cabernet sauvignon. The next night, when he called to mention a good cabernet, she said that Malbec was more to her taste. He didn't call again, and Susan went home alone.

That left the nuclear family: father, mother, daughter, and son-in-law. Bill and Beverly had their own house, of course, but when one of them went there, the other stayed at Richard and Donna's. Donna didn't like that. She was tired of having people around, so on the evening of Susan Blake's departure, she asked Richard to go with Bill to his garage, then told Beverly that she needed time alone. She thought Beverly might argue, but Beverly said she could use some time, too, and left after giving her mother a kiss.

Donna found some bourbon in Richard's cupboard,

poured a couple of fingers of it into a glass, got some ice, and went into his living room to sit. She hadn't been back to *her* house since Perry's arraignment, and now she played with the idea of selling it. Richard had asked her to a couple of times before, but she'd put him off. It had been a good move for her financially—the house was worth twice what she'd paid for it—but she sometimes feared that Richard thought it meant she didn't love him. And she did love him, if not with all her heart, at least with the part of it that told her whatever she waited for wouldn't come. Or wouldn't come again. She rarely thought of Beverly's father, unless she was drinking alone.

Beverly never thought of her father. She didn't think of Richard much, either, and though she often thought of Bill, it wasn't in the way he wanted her to. On the night she left her mother, in fact, she drove past Bill's garage, not because she was thinking of him, exactly, but to make sure he was there. He was and so was Richard. She could see them through the window, looking into Richard's old car. She parked and took out her phone. Since Detective Triplet wasn't working nights that week, she tried his home number. It rang seven times before he answered. He said he'd been asleep, that he'd needed an early night after all they'd been through. He didn't say more until she told him she was thinking of buying a couple of double meat, double cheese burgers at the Frisco Freeze and asked if he'd like to share them with her. She thought he might say he'd meet her there, but he said they could eat at his house if she liked. She didn't pause before saying she'd be right over.

When she got off the phone, she texted Bill to say they needed to talk. When Bill got the text, he sighed before he read it. Not because of some premonition but because it was the second text he'd received that night, the other one from Susan Blake, and he thought she was texting him again.

Two weeks later, when their lives were once again in disarray, Perry's body washed up among the detritus that the tide brought in at Point Defiance. When Richard heard about it, he cried like he hadn't since he was a child. When Clement and Susan and Donna and Beverly heard about it, they went about their business, only nodding to themselves.

Bill was the last to hear about it but the first to offer to go to the morgue and identify the body. It was there he met the parents of Katie Smothers. They might not have spoken had Bill not seen their photos in the paper and stopped to offer his condolences.

"It's all just the damnedest shame," said Mr. Smothers.

That struck Bill as odd. Why would they come view the body of the man who'd killed their daughter, and what was the damnedest shame?

It wasn't until the following morning, when he went out onto his porch to get his paper, that he understood. An autopsy had come back saying Katie had died of asphyxiation, yes, but caused by a heroin overdose.

Bill would have shown the paper to Beverly, had Beverly been home. Since she wasn't, he called Richard and shared it with him. Richard shared it with Donna, and Donna shared it with Beverly, who'd been sleeping in the house she grew up in.

News of Perry's innocence was picked up by the wire services and printed in one of the English-language dailies in

Egypt. Hetshepsit read it while working in her mother's stall at the local bazaar. She hadn't died of getting a pillow in her mouth, nor was whoring the family business, nor had she lived with Perry White. When she shared the article with her mother, her mother remembered that Perry had often come to their stall. She remembered that they'd put up with him for a while but had finally told him that if he wasn't going to buy anything, he had to make room for those who were. After that, he didn't come again, and now they were reading the article. When the news broke in Tacoma, Judge Follett dismissed the charges against Perry, posthumously. It hadn't been necessary, but when Richard called to thank him for it, he said it was only just, and that justice was his business.

Richard quoted him at dinner that night before asking Donna to sell her house again. Donna said she couldn't sell it while Beverly was staying there, though both of them knew that Beverly spent most of her time at Detective Triplet's.

Their dinner was a particularly delicious salmon that Donna had bought down on Ruston Way after sitting and watching the Canada geese for a while.

Perry was buried in the same cemetery as Winnie, but several sections away, in a plot next to his mother.

For the next half year, someone brought him flowers every Saturday.

Out for a Drink

(2016)

Two old friends, Lars and Mary, meet for drinks at a bar they frequented fifty years earlier, up on Twenty-first Street in Tacoma, Washington. Mary lives in Berkeley now, but for a decade before moving there, she worked for Lars, selling Jaguars at his automobile agency. Strange to say— from Lars's point of view—these days Mary is a respected Bay Area artist, known for cutting up earlier paintings and hanging strips of them on clean blue canvases. Lars has one in his den at home. He doesn't like it much but loves the fact that Mary made it, and that her work often sells for upward of ten thousand dollars. He paid nine for his and thinks of it as a sound investment.

"I'm surprised you'd want such a thing," says Mary when he tells her about his purchase. "I think I remember you had an actual Edward Hopper in your office at work."

"Hopper knockoff," Lars says. "I used to tell people it was real, but it was only worth a couple thousand bucks."

Mary leans closer in order to gaze into his eyes. He thinks she's remembering their friendship, but she is looking for dollar signs. She lightly slaps the side of her face. "It never occurred to me that the Hopper wasn't real," she says.

Lars thinks the face slap is cute. He tells her that his grand-father bought the painting.

"The man who started your company? I met him a couple of times."

When Lars asks her what she'd like to drink, she tells him pinot gris, but he comes back from the bar with pinot noir.

"Sorry to hear about your mom," he says.

The reason for Mary's return to Tacoma is the death of her mother at ninety-six. "I'm sorry, too, though she was a very tough nut to crack."

"Like my grandpa," says Lars. "Right up to the day he died he kept telling me how to run my company."

Mary remembers Lars's ability for turning every conver-sation into one about himself. He was a decent boss, but now she has to wonder why she let him know she was in town. She'd called Richie, too, another old friend, but Richie hasn't called her back.

"Do you ever see Richie?" she asks. "Since I started paint-ing, I often remember how crazy he was to become a writer. Do you know if he ever became one?"

"He did," says Lars, "but you didn't hear? Richie's in hos-pice now."

Mary wraps her hands around her wineglass, the muscles in her jaw contracting. For a moment, she feels she might be sick. Back in college, she and Richie worked together at this very bar. Often they would close the place and stay into the wee hours of the morning, drinking and talking. He was her absolute pal and her only platonic male friend. She says, "I can't believe I didn't know this. I've got to go see him. What's wrong with Richie, Lars?"

"Oh, I don't know. Leprosy? Syphilis? I've lost touch."

Syphilis? What?

A smirk sneaks across Lars's face, red and spreading out. Mary nearly throws her wine at him. "Lars," she says, "you made that up?"

She stands and picks up her coat, thinking, good fucking Christ!

"He might as well be in hospice, dead as he is to me," says Lars. "But come on, Mary, don't you want to know why I'd say such a thing? And maybe why Richie hasn't called you back?"

She does want to know those things, but she's beyond furious. Who says such a thing about an old friend? She shoves the wineglass across the table at him. "Get me a beer, then," she barks.

When he heads to the bar, she sits back down, her back as rigid as a two-by-four. She forgot about Tacoma's tangled web, forgot how lucky she's been to escape it. Her husband sometimes tells her that Tacoma is a bruise she plucks at, caused by the unfinished business of her childhood. But she often misses the place. Richie in hospice, though . . . goddamn!

"I got us a couple of IPAs," Lars says when he returns. When he sees her anger's not diminished, he adds, "I only said it because I figured after what Richie did, you'd get the joke. I'm sorry to have scared you like that."

"Nothing Richie could do would make me want him dead, you shit."

"Yeah? Well, say that again after you've read his book. Three of his stories are about me, full of lies and half-truths, and you're in two. You bask in the glory of your own beauty, then go off to marry a chemist."

"I did marry a chemist," Mary says. "Richie has been keeping tabs."

"Keeping tabs and taking notes. But he also thought he had the right to make stuff up. He says you slept with customers to get them to buy Jaguars, back when you worked for me."

He looks at her slyly. "You never did that, did you?"

"No!" says Mary. "Who, me?"

She takes out her phone, shows Lars the number she's got for Richie, and when he confirms it, she calls him again. "Richie, my dear, Lars and I are out for a drink in the bar that used to be Pat's," she tells his machine. "You'd better come defend yourself. It's Mary, by the way, and Lars is steaming mad at you. Says you gave him a life he didn't lead."

When she hangs up, she asks, "What did I do in the story besides sleep with customers? And what do you think? Did he capture my personality?"

"He put you in bed with Earl," Lars says. "And for both of us he uses our real names!"

"What Earl? You don't mean Earl Earl?"

"Of course I mean Earl Earl—what other Earl do I know? And if you want to know more, read his fucking book." He pauses, then says, "Okay, I wasn't going to tell you, but I brought a copy of it with me."

He pulls Richie's book from the back of his pants and throws it across the table to her. Mary looks at Richie's jacket photo, then flips through the pages. And when she sees her name she stops to read aloud. "'Who is the me that I want Earl to see if the me he sees isn't me?'"

She glances suspiciously at Lars. "How did he know that? Did you tell him that? By the time I worked for you, I wasn't still hanging out with Richie, was I?"

"None of us were. It's plagiarism, Mary, pure and simple. Remember Jonathan? Remember Andy, the will guy? They're both talking about taking him to court, and Andy could do it, too, 'cause he's a judge."

"It isn't plagiarism, you nit, but it sure as hell is license taking. Me in bed with Earl, good Lord!"

She finds the beginning of the story and reads for a long few minutes in silence. When she stops, her expression is sober. "Was there really such vanity in me back then? Was I as shallow as that, Lars?"

"All you do in the story is worry about vanity and shallowness," Lars says. "How can you be vain and shallow while warding those things off?"

That earns him a smile, and when Lars smiles back, she quite suddenly sees how old he is. Richie looks every bit his age in his author photo, too. She fights the urge to retrieve a compact and check herself out.

"Those things . . . those strips you hung from the painting I bought look like dangling socks," Lars says. "Every time I see them, I think they ought to be matched and folded and put away in drawers."

"They do not look like socks. They look like what they're supposed to look like: everyone's past failures. It's just that we usually hang them on the inside, Lars, and I've put them out for everyone to see. It's liberating, don't you think?"

She thinks it's liberating, but Lars is hunched around his beer like a walrus protecting its young. He's clearly never been liberated by anything in his life, never mind art. Mary wishes she hadn't asked for the beer. She wants to go to her mother's house, get started with sorting her mother's things. Despite herself, she imagines drawers full of mismatched socks.

"*I* don't wear my failures on the inside. I wear them right here on my face," says Lars. "Do you know what I want on my tombstone, Mary? It's 'Here Lies Lars Larson, Three Ex-wives and No Kids.'"

Mary touches his arm. Was Lars this maudlin when they were barely past being kids themselves?

"I need to get back to Mom's," she says. "I've got a month's worth of work to do and I'm heading back to Berkeley in a week."

She looks at her phone, and when she turns it to show him how late it is, it rings out the theme to *The Bridge on the River Kwai*. One of her husband's tricks is to change her ringtone to reflect whatever old movie they have recently seen. It's hokey, but she loves him for it.

"That'll be Bert," she says, but she sees that it's Richie. She stands away from Lars. "Hey," she says. "You've got a lot of chutzpah, buddy, putting me in bed with Earl like that. And how come it took you fifty years to write a book?"

"I'm standing across the street," Richie says. "I can see you through the window."

Mary looks at the window but sees only her reflection looking back.

"You're not coming in?"

"It would be better if you came out. I don't want to fight with Lars."

"Why not? I remember you as one who faced his fears."

"Nah," he says. "You've got me confused with someone else."

Mary looks at Lars, who is leaning back in his chair with his hands behind his head. "Lars told me you were in hospice, Richie; that's how upset he is by whatever you wrote about him. Why not come in and make things right? We can all get drunk."

She looks around the bar. It's twice the size it used to be and empty of other customers. Quite suddenly she does see Richie out the window, his body growing larger as he darts across the street. When he opens the door, Lars is looking directly at him.

"He came when you called, Mary," he says, "just like someone's dog."

"Howdy, Lars," says Richie.

When the door swings shut behind him, the stillness of the place banks down. Richie is carrying two copies of his book, one in each of the pockets of his jacket. Mary swears it's the same jacket that he wore when they worked together fifty years earlier. He comes across the room to give a book to her, then takes the other over to Lars. At first, it seems that Lars won't move, but then he brings his hands down, takes the book, and opens it to see if there's an inscription. There is. It says, "To Lars K Larson, the dearest friend of my youth."

Opposite the inscription is a drawing of the bar as seen from outside, its windows smoky and with a lot of people standing around inside. Musical notes linger around the words "Pat's Tavern, Saint Patrick's Day, 1968." The drawing takes up most of the page. When Mary comes over to look at it, Lars takes her copy of Richie's book to see if it also has a drawing. It does not. He has written only "Mary, my dear, you have always been my inspiration."

"He stole that one from the Beatles," Lars says.

"If my name were Martha, it really *would* be plagiarism," Mary tells him.

Richie goes to the bar to get more beer. While he's gone,

Lars and Mary stare at the drawing in Lars's book, which, though only pen and ink, is really quite exquisite. Mary thinks it looks like a Hogarth, with herself behind the bar under great thicknesses of hair, and with Richie carrying pitchers of beer in the foreground, *his* hair somehow made to look green. Between them, Lars is dancing with Immy, the woman who became his first wife. Every bar stool is taken by some man or woman.

"That's Jonathan," says Lars, pointing, "and there's your old pal Earl."

"Earl," Mary says, "good Lord."

"Next to Earl is Ralph, the old gay English teacher, and next to Ralph is the girl with the famous parents."

Richie comes back with the beer. "Becky Welles," he says. "After that night, we all pretty much lost touch. She died a few years back."

"So you wrote these stories to talk about how things might have been?" asks Lars. "You imagined peoples lives for them?"

His expression is hopeful, like that might be something he could understand, though it sounds fairly creepy to Mary. People ought to be allowed to imagine their own lives, at least, she thinks.

Richie holds his glass up, as if to toast Lars's acuity, but when the name of the girl with the famous parents finally registers with Mary, words flow out of her unbidden. "Do you think a town can act as a hedge against the unabated loneliness of the human heart?"

That stumps Lars, but Richie puts his glass to his lips and sips from it, looking into Mary's eyes over its rim. "We take the roads we take," he says. "I was only providing alternate routes."

In the drawing, there is movement now, with people standing out of booths and getting down off bar stools. They walk over to the bar's front window, raising their own glasses up. Perhaps they are toasting Mary and Lars and Richie, reflected in the window from fifty years later, or perhaps they are simply getting drunk. But the words one of them utters—"May your life have meaning on the day you die"— express a sentiment each of them would like to embrace but hasn't yet—would like to embrace but hasn't because, for the most part, they are entirely too young.

"So much water under the bridge," says Richie.

"So much water under the bridge," say Mary and Lars.

When the tavern door opens and a group walks in, Mary decides that she can clear her mother's house tomorrow, Lars decides to let go of his irritation, and Richie decides that he will try to write another book, maybe a novel. This time, though, he'll change everyone's name and not set it in Tacoma. He looks at Lars. "Sorry, Lars," he says.

He looks at Mary, but before he can speak, she puts a finger to his lips. "Let me read the other story first," she says.

"You're happy in the next one," Lars tells her.

When Mary opens *her* copy of Richie's book, Richie says, "You're going to read it now? Have the decency to wait until I'm gone, at least."

But Mary reads the story, one hand up to guard against Richie's intrusion. He intruded enough in writing the stories, alternative routes or not.

Lars and Richie watch her. It was that way years ago, too, everyone watching Mary while pretending to do something else. Richie thinks she's kept her beauty and believes he got her right in his stories. He's less sure about Lars. Later he'll have to deal with Jonathan, though he did get a nice note from Andy. A note and a dinner invitation.

Those who came into the bar a moment earlier are as young as the old friends were when they frequented the place. There are only four of them, three young women and a man, but they order two pitchers of beer and are soon sitting back, drinking and laughing. It makes Lars and Richie smile to see how they once were, but Mary is busy reading and barely looks up.

Until blaring music comes on.

It's entirely too loud for them, so they decide to finish their own night of drinking somewhere else.

ACKNOWLEDGMENTS

THANKS, as always, to my wife, Virginia Wiley, my first and most trusted reader, for putting up with draft after draft of these stories. Also, thanks to Erika Goldman, my editor and publisher at Bellevue Literary Press, for understanding that the specific order of these stories is of significant importance, and for reading my collection's most troublesome story many times. Thanks to Elana Rosenthal, also of Bellevue Literary Press, for her openness and her attention to detail.

In Tacoma, thanks to my old friend, Denny Hall, for helping me remember the band name Blueport News, as well as many other details of a now distant past; to all of those who grew up with me at Brown's Point and who might think they find their childhood homes, youthful shenanigans, and even some of their names represented in these stories; and to those who haunted Pat's Tavern in the winter and spring of 1967.

Thanks to *Arches Magazine* for publishing "Your Life Should Have Meaning on the Day You Die," the story that gave me the idea for this collection, and also for publishing the obituary of Becky Welles, thus reminding me of her calm goodness in the face of all the ravages of fame.

Lastly, thanks to my friends, colleagues, and wonderful graduate students at the University of Nevada, Las Vegas, both in the English department and at Black Mountain Institute, for supporting my work over the course of many years.

BELLEVUE LITERARY PRESS is devoted to publishing literary fiction and nonfiction at the intersection of the arts and sciences because we believe that science and the humanities are natural companions for understanding the human experience. With each book we publish, our goal is to foster a rich, interdisciplinary dialogue that will forge new tools for thinking and engaging with the world.

To support our press and its mission, and for our full catalogue of published titles, please visit us at blpress.org.

BELLEVUE LITERARY PRESS
New York